THE
LUCIFER
CHILD

by

Shelley Katz

A DELL BOOK

To Beth

Published by
Dell Publishing Co., Inc.
1 Dag Hammarskjold Plaza
New York, New York 10017

ISBN: 0-440-15076-0

Printed in the United States of America

First printing—March 1980

**IN A WORLD
RULED BY SCIENCE,
THEY WERE LIKE GODS—
ALL-POWERFUL. . . .**

Nobel prize-winning scientist Irwin Schaftner did the groundwork . . . a genetic manipulation that eliminated every chance of all-too-human error. Where others failed, he succeeded. Before he died in agony, he created perfect life.

Now brilliant Richard Cassidy and Adonis-like Mark Foreman take up Schaftner's daring experiment. They will create Adam, the perfect child. Driven by dreams of fame and glory, they will ignore every warning.

**BUT IN A WORLD RULED BY
THE DARK FORCES OF EVIL
THEY ARE ALL AT THE
MERCY OF . . .**

THE LUCIFER CHILD

Book One

THE EXPERIMENT

Chapter 1

It was early morning. Light was just beginning to stream through the dirty laboratory windows. Glass test tubes and beakers were gleaming, reflecting prismatic arcs in air dancing with dust.

A shaft of light reached toward the dark corner of the laboratory where 3476 floated in its incubating chamber. As the sun spilled near the little cluster of cells, staining it a golden rose, did it feel a thrill of brilliant warmth? Did it feel it and want more than ever to live?

3476 was no larger than a period at the end of a sentence, a speck of dust. Under the microscope it appeared as merely a translucent blister, a cluster of less than three dozen cells swimming in a sea of tissue culture medium.

It looked so ordinary, so simple. But there was nothing simple about it. It was the most highly developed, awesomely complicated organism known to man. It was man himself, gene-manipulated, scientifically engineered man. It was perfect man, three days old.

In that group of cells was the potential of an Einstein, a Beethoven, Dostoevski, Plato, or all of them wrapped up in one. 3476 wasn't just embryonic man, it was an embryonic superman, and it was deadly.

As light glanced off the chamber, the cluster shifted, then once again began its gentle spinning dance. And somewhere on Hollywood Boulevard, an old man felt the stir of life rushing through him.

Professor Irwin Schaftner stood totally still in the middle of the sidewalk, a tall, stooped man with a clay-white face and hair the color of steel. He was wearing a loose, rumpled raincoat, and his thin, bony shoulders looked like a coat hanger under the soft folds of material. Motionless, he gave the impression of a figure constructed of wire and papier-maché. He seemed not so much a man who was close to death as a man who had already passed over to the other side.

All around him the boulevard was just beginning to come to life. A whore with bootblacked hair and stiletto heels trundled by. A young policeman with a Dick Tracy jaw and still innocent eyes watched a gay couple as they strolled arm in arm.

Schaftner shivered, shoved his fists deep into his pockets, and hunched his shoulders against an internal chill. The feeling was still with him. It hadn't been a voice or a vision. It had been something far less tangible than that. He couldn't even begin to put what he felt into words. It was as if a will, separate from his own, but strong and clear, was calling out to him, as if that tiny cluster of cells he had secretly created only three days before had read the computer printout over his shoulder and knew the truth, that it would have to be destroyed.

A cold premonition swept over Schaftner and he shivered again. Of course it was impossible. It had been nothing of the sort. His own regrets, his own dread, his own almost suicidal disappointment maybe, but it wasn't telepathic communication with a tiny speck of matter that was no more than thirty cells.

Schaftner laughed at himself and started to walk to the luncheonette where he had eaten breakfast for the past thirty years. He had originally chosen the place not because it was very good but because it was near his two-room walk-up and because there was nothing about it that interfered with what was really important to him, his thinking.

Professor Schaftner was known by his colleagues at UCLA as "the machine." As far as anyone knew he had no friends, no family, no home. He was a shadowy presence, a man who never drank coffee with the fellows or gossiped or got sick. He never even received a phone call.

He worked amongst a clutter of beakers and test tubes and a great mountain of paper, covered with illegible chicken scratches. His staff was limited to one assistant, Cassidy, a scraggly young man with the manners of a barnyard animal.

But while there was no denying Professor Schaftner was something of a weirdo, there was also no denying he was a brilliant one. Every few years he would emerge from his laboratory, blinking like a mole, and publish an insanely written, outrageously misspelled treatise. It would stand the world of science on its ear, knock the foundations of biology clear out of this galaxy. Then he'd shuffle back to his laboratory, not to be heard from for another seven years.

Schaftner had won various prizes, including the Nobel. He always accepted them with a sarcastically worded return telegram. He never appeared.

There were those who said Schaftner was a robot,

plugged into a socket at 7:30 in the morning and not shut off until well into the night. Since Schaftner was rarely seen outside the laboratory this was difficult to disprove.

Schaftner checked his watch as he entered the Golden Spoon Luncheonette. It was ten minutes past seven. He was running late for the first time in thirty years and he took it as a sign. He sat down in his accustomed place at the counter, jerked off his raincoat, and looked around for his newspaper. He'd forgotten to buy it. He had never forgotten to buy his newspaper before. Another sign.

He looked around. On either side of him, ten blank faces were hunched over the counter like cows in their stalls, attacking their quivering fried eggs and slurping coffee. Somewhere in the back, a radio blasted a jingle reminding anyone who was listening that Coke was the real thing.

Schaftner started to laugh at the irony. His laugh was a little too loud, a tinge of hysteria just under the surface. He quickly swallowed it, worried that everyone would think he was crazy. But the ten bovine faces didn't even turn around.

Maybe he truly was going crazy. There was some relief in that thought, but it vanished as the feeling came over him again. Somewhere inside he felt 3476 tumble and shift. He could feel the tiny cluster pinch at the poles, then flatten out and pull apart, until where there was one, there were now two. And he knew that in that mother-of-pearl bit of matter, a cell had divided.

Schaftner sat transfixed, an electric charge running through every part of his body.

The experiment would have to be destroyed. He knew that now. Thirty years of work, a whole lifetime of thinking, had gone into that tiny cluster of cells, and he'd have to destroy it, flush it down the toilet and send it rushing with the rest of the debris under the greater Los Angeles area and out to the blue Pacific.

He had risked his entire career by keeping 3476 a secret, by tampering with lab reports, by doing the forbidden experiment at all. He had known the risks. Ever since those bright boys had outlined nuclear fission and found themselves with more than a figurative bombshell on their hands, every scientist knew that whatever he touched could be explosive. Schaftner had struggled with that thought but eventually he'd decided to disregard it. If he didn't do the experiment, someone else would. And in the end, there was no answer. There was just the necessity to go on, give up everything, everyone, even conscience, and go on.

Now it was over. Schaftner tried to view the situation with detachment, but he couldn't. Everything had centered around that experiment. He had ignored the rest of his life. Love, comfort, joy, even pain didn't exist for him. All that was left was his two-room walkup, dinner at the same Italian restaurant every night, then a review of technical journals until sleep overtook him. There was a once-a-month liaison with a plain but lonely widow down the street, but that was it. Day after day, week after week, and almost without noticing it, year after year, his life had slipped through his fingers.

The truth was, it was worth it. Schaftner had seen enough brilliant men waste their lives on split-levels, pudgy wives, and barbecues on mosquito-infested patios. Long ago he'd made the choice to live with his mind rather than indulge in the "smelly little orthodoxies," as Orwell had so aptly described them, and he had never for one day regretted it.

In that laboratory he was Joe Namath on a Sunday afternoon, a general conducting global warfare, a handsome young lover rolling in silk sheets. From 7:30 in the morning until eight o'clock at night, every cell in his body was alive and vital, tingling with life, pulsing and eternal. In his own way, he lived more dangerously, more intensely than anyone else on earth.

Again the feeling came over him. The tumbling, weightless microscopic particle in the laboratory pulsated inside of him. Perhaps he was wrong. Perhaps there was nothing wrong with the experiment after all. He could run the program again. While computers didn't make mistakes, he could have made an error. Human error. That would do it.

But he'd already checked the program long into the night. There was no mistake. The thing that was so hard to reconcile was that the computer hadn't concluded that 3476 would be a freak *physically*—no fourteen toes, no extra heads lolling on soft shoulders. If 3476 were brought to full term, it would probably be physically perfect, even beautiful. It wouldn't be a freak mentally either. The baby would be the most brilliant ever born. Schaftner had carefully selected his genes, manipulated them, culled them. The child would be more than a genius; he would be the beginning of a new race of men.

But he'd be a freak, a moral freak. Was that possible? Several hundred tons of IBM equipment said it was.

Schaftner tried to push what had happened last night out of his mind, but he met with little success. Yesterday he'd seated himself at the console of

Sylvia, the giant IBM 3033 Processor, 3850 Mass Storage, and typed out the usual coordinates, trying to get an estimate of just how successful his experiment would be if everything continued as planned. He asked random questions and received fairly specific and optimistic answers, a bit of mechanical backpatting. Then he hit the snag. Basically he'd been asking the computer to extrapolate personality, in other words, to try to determine just what kind of guy 3476 would turn out to be. It was one of the more complex questions one could ask, considering just what goes into making a personality. Genetics had a lot to do with it. How much, no one knew, but there was no question that genes were important.

He remembered staring at the answer for some time, then typing back, "Repeat procedure. Answer incorrect."

The click of the typewriter was almost immediate. "No mistake in previous answer. 3476 will be evil."

"Why?" Schaftner typed.

"He will never make a mistake."

Schaftner laughed. There was no logic to the answer and the vague uneasiness he'd been feeling disappeared.

"If he will never make a mistake," Schaftner returned, "then he will be good."

"No."

Schaftner wondered why he'd ever begun this line of questioning. Still, he was not the type of man who knew when to leave bad enough alone. He typed back to the computer, "Explain."

"3476 will have no humanity."

"Bullshit," Schaftner muttered under his breath. The whole thing made no sense to him. "I still do not understand. Expand." Schaftner angrily punched the keys.

The answer he received was remarkable. He had to read it several times before he understood what the machine was trying to say. "As a child, 3476 will never stumble or fall or skin its knees. There will be no boundaries, no limits. Mistakes and stumbling give a man inhibitions, compassion, morality. 3476 will be evil."

"You are telling me that the entire legal and moral code of mankind is a result of skinned knees?"

"Yes."

Schaftner laughed. This was getting more preposterous by the second. He quickly typed back, "Why should 3476 necessarily choose evil? Why not choose good?"

"He will be a man, mentally superior, but emotionally still a man. Not above anger and cruelty. Just above the law."

Truly a remarkable, specious bit of logic, thought Schaftner. How the hell could a computer comment on the moral rectitude of a man? Good Lord, the greatest minds throughout civilization couldn't agree. And yet the gnawing at his stomach.

Schaftner looked around the computer room. It was getting late and most of the other people had gone home. Only a few desperate graduate students bustled around, with that frenzied look he remembered from his own school days. Schaftner decided to go home. He would come back tomorrow and rerun the program. There was obviously an error that would be easy for him to find after a good night's sleep.

But Schaftner didn't leave. He reran the program many times, varying the questions, challenging the computer on various fronts. The answers ranged from poetic to philosophical, but always the answer was the same. Evil. 3476 would be evil.

Schaftner sat totally still at the luncheonette counter, staring straight ahead. Inside he could feel those strange messages surging through his body like rising sap, green and full and alive.

"You okay, honey?" The waitress, a large woman with a platinum wig and eyebrows like two caret signs, loomed over Schaftner with his accustomed breakfast.

Schaftner's brain screeched into drive. He was even able to come up with something resembling a smile. Then he looked down at his plate. The two eggs, golden orbs floating in a sea of white, made his stomach turn. The intense meaty smell of bacon closed in on him.

Schaftner pulled on his raincoat and threw several dollars on the counter. He ran to the door and out onto the street like a man pursued.

Schaftner rushed through the growing crowd on Hollywood Boulevard back to his aged Chevy. He had to get to the lab; 3476 had to be destroyed. He climbed in, fired up the ancient green and white clunker, and pulled out into the street.

The traffic was monumental. Schaftner crawled along the streets like an insect. Even today he refused to take the freeways. They frightened and confused him. Schaftner knew he was not a man of his time. Good Lord, he was more like a dinosaur. The vision of himself as some great lumbering reptile soon to be a lump of coal or a drop of oil soothed him. That was more like the old Schaftner.

Then once again the urging pulsed through him.

Suddenly he felt sick. His heart was wriggling in his chest like a small rodent; he was having trouble breathing. It occurred to him he might never reach the laboratory alive. 3476 was trying to stop him. But he knew that was impossible. He was trying to stop himself, the last desperate attempt of a desperate man.

Schaftner urged himself forward, no longer trying to hold it together. He stepped hard on the gas. He had to get to the laboratory and do it before he changed his mind, do it before his assistant Cassidy came in and persuaded him not to. The experiment meant a lot to Cassidy; he would try to stop him. He'd probably succeed, too.

Schaftner felt the rodent in his chest shiver and shake. But he pressed down harder on the gas.

Half an hour later, Schaftner pulled into his parking stall outside the Quonset hut that served as his laboratory. He turned off the motor and fell back against the seat with a sigh of relief. He had made it.

It was several minutes before Schaftner left his car and walked to the door. Everything seemed to be slowing down. His muscles felt weak and unsteady. His body didn't want to move and fought him for every step.

Schaftner unlocked the door, then stopped just inside, looking around. He'd never really looked at his laboratory before. He'd spent thirteen hours a day, seven days a week in that room for thirty years, and yet he'd never really seen it. The gleaming metal, the sparkling glass looked beautiful with the sun playing over it. Even the dirty windows, subject of many a

screaming fight between him and the university jan-
itorial service, looked like patterns of clouds.

Across the laboratory, he could see the incubating
chamber. Sunlight shone through liquid and broke
into a thousand planes around it. There was nothing
evil about it. It was just a bit of organic material,
the building blocks of a man.

Schaftner walked toward it slowly, a man sentenced
by himself with no chance of reprieve. What would
he do once the experiment was gone? He didn't
want to think about that; he'd spent too much of his
life working up to 3476.

He stopped in front of the incubating chamber,
staring down at his life's work. Schaftner's eyes caught
sight of the safe next to the chamber where his logs
were locked up. He would have to destroy those too;
otherwise he couldn't trust himself not to try again.
He couldn't trust himself beyond this one moment.

Still he didn't move. He listened to the dull throb-
bing in his ears as his blood, thick and viscous, pulsed
through his veins. Half-formed thoughts, flashes of
memory, objects in the room were all jumbled together. For a moment there was only one thought,
clear, pure, and sharp. He couldn't do it.

Suddenly a flash seared his brain. Pain exploded in
his head, burning out everything, even the knowledge
that he was human. His body froze. It no longer belonged to him. Nothing belonged to him but the pain.
It was like an intense light, exploding outward into
the black universe. He was having a stroke.

Schaftner's body went limp. There was no body, no
Schaftner, only the light and the pain. He fell against
the laboratory bench, sweeping glass and bottles across

it, sending them crashing to the floor. His arm caught on one of the tubes connecting the incubating chamber, pulling it with him as he slipped slowly to the ground.

Then there was quiet. Schaftner lay motionless in a pool of chemicals and broken glass. Next to his hand was the speck of matter that was his life's work, exposed and naked, flattened on the laboratory floor. He had done it after all. 3476 was dead.

Chapter 2

Richard Cassidy's morning routine rarely included a shower. Nor, usually, did it include combing his hair. For the most part it didn't include any contact with water at all. He would step into pants, sometimes shoes, and wolf down something or other from a refrigerator that would have been condemned by the board of health if they could have gotten through the unholy mess that was piled, stacked, and scattered almost waist high in his living room.

Had anyone taken the trouble or been interested in doing so, a cataloging of Cassidy's room would have included books ranging from the general to the specific on all aspects of biology; enough scientific journals to fill three library shelves; close to a hundred sleazy pocket books, dog-eared; a week's supply of dirty underwear; three clean black socks and one white one; wrappings from several Big Macs, Taco Bell, In and Out Burger, Pink's Kosher Hotdogs, and a box of Colonel Sanders' Kentucky Fried Chicken with several shattered, marrow-sucked bones; broken pencils; inkless pens; a telephone hidden under a pile of T-shirts in varying stages of decay; bills, advertisements, Jesus pamphlets, and liquor store fliers, all mixed together in no apparent order, like an inorganic stew. There

was barely a space where the floor showed through,
so covered was it with his scattered, piled, and stacked
junk: clothes, food, papers, notes to himself. The secret
life of Richard Cassidy.

Cassidy crawled out of bed, grabbed a pair of torn
jeans from a moldering pile of clothes, threw on a
shirt, and staggered to the refrigerator. He held onto
the door and stared into the almost empty box for
close to a minute. Finally he pulled out one wilted
stalk of celery, a petrified slice of American cheese,
and a carton of half-and-half that dated from the
previous month.

He started to eat, then took a large gulp of the
cream. Cassidy leaped into the air, sour milk gushing
out of his mouth, and ran to the water faucet. He
hung over the spigot, gulping like a madman. He swore
silently; any movement in his mouth might churn up
the taste of sour milk.

After several minutes of alternately gulping water
and spitting out, he remembered he hadn't taken a
shower. In fact he couldn't exactly remember the last
time he had. He dipped his head toward his armpit
and recoiled. There was a general clamoring for soap
from that area.

Cassidy walked to the bathroom, peeling off clothes
and letting them fall to the floor, creating a new pile.
He emerged five minutes later.

Cleaned up, Cassidy had definite possibilities.
Though his was not what one would call a handsome
face, there was an inner excitement, a profound sense
of being alive in every feature. Cassidy was short and
wiry, with a sharp, hawklike nose, a jutting forehead,
and curly black hair that he often let grow until he
was haloed by it like a crucified Jesus. In fact, despite

the scruffy old jeans and torn, wrinkled shirts he always wore, there was a great deal of the Renaissance martyr about the way he looked. The lean, angular body, the thin intense face. But Cassidy's strange, haunting divinity was nowhere more evident than in his eyes. They were dark, intelligent eyes, indicative of a brain so quick and comprehensive that his IQ had been impossible to calculate. They were the kind of eyes that peer out from time-darkened frescoes of saints and villains, the kind of eyes around which history turns. For with all their smoldering passion, they were always fixed toward the horizon and out into infinity.

Cassidy leaped over the couch and into his pile of clothes. He began pulling them on haphazardly, his back pockets turned inside out, scattering bits of fluff; only one of the buttons on his shirt was done up, and that one was in the wrong hole.

He paused for a moment, looking around at the mess. He felt more alone than he had in years. Except for Schaftner, his boss, mentor, surrogate father, and friend, there was not another person in the world who had a clue to who the real Richard Cassidy was. Cassidy had loved and respected the tragic old man with a profound devotion he'd never felt before.

Schaftner had cared. No one had ever cared about him like Schaftner.

Certainly his foster parents, large-boned, small-minded factory workers whose future could be read between the covers of next week's *TV Guide*, hadn't cared. Cassidy had always confused and angered them. There was something almost obscene about his extraordinary brain, like having an institutionalized uncle. The only legacy he got from them was their

name. He liked the name Cassidy. Visions of black-
suited, pistol-packing, fast-drawing outlaws went with
a name like that. As to his real parents, they were
just two blank spaces on his birth certificate. Cassidy
preferred not to deal with that one.

Putting the larger questions of fear and loneliness
aside for a while, Cassidy opened the door and went
out once again to face an even bigger question. The
question of living death, in the form of a pitiful lump
of flesh and tubes that lay comatose on a hospital bed,
the lump that was once Schaftner.

Selma Bass was a tall, brutal-looking woman whose
level of testosterone must have been a good bit above
average even for a man. She stood six feet two in her
stocking feet and weighed over 250 pounds of pure
muscle. Her thick, flushed face was crowned by gray,
frizzy hair cut combat short, and her large body was
clothed in oversized coveralls and a man's shirt.

As a child, Bass had always believed she was a boy,
and that she'd wake up one morning to find the missing piece of equipment magically restored. But Mother
Nature had other ideas. At the age of thirteen, Bass's
brain started sending out breast-making signals which
her body obeyed in spades.

At first this had confused and alarmed little Bass.
But at the age of fourteen, having met a large group
of boys from the next block in what might laughingly
be called a gang bang, since who was ganged and who
was banged was not entirely clear, she had to admit
she enjoyed being a girl.

Even now, despite Bass's gray hair, sagging breasts,
and one sightless wall-eye, she always had her men.

Today's was named Julio, and he was in the kitchen making breakfast.

If Bass had only one good eye, she at least had two good ears, and they were telling her that the pounding noise she was hearing on the stairs belonged to that deadbeat tenant of hers from upstairs.

Bass raced for the door, threw it open, and caught a last glimpse of Cassidy's shirt-tails as he made for the front door.

"Just one minute," Bass bellowed.

She didn't wait for a reply but bolted down the stairs, taking them two at a time. She threw open the front door, stood on the stoop, and gazed menacingly up and down the length of Fairfax Avenue.

"I said stop!" Bass repeated.

Cassidy obeyed. He had gotten only ten feet from the door, just far enough for the line of old people who were spending their golden years sitting on folding chairs outside the Palace Arms Retirement Home to watch what was about to happen from ringside.

"Come back here, young man!" Bass demanded. If there had been an echo on the street, Bass's would have been a fine one.

"The name's Cassidy," he reminded her as he ambled back, showing a nonchalance he didn't exactly feel.

Bass, however, did not seem all that interested in Cassidy's name. What interested her more, what in fact totally consumed her, was last month's rent, the sum of $96.50, which Cassidy had neglected to pay her.

Cassidy didn't know what to say. He could hardly claim an oversight, since Bass had been stuffing reminders into his mailbox at a rate of two a day for

several weeks. On the other hand, the truth, which
was that when they canceled Schaftner's grant they
also effectively canceled Cassidy, left something to be
desired.

"I'll give it to you tonight, ma'am." Cassidy turned
to go.

"Not good enough!" Bass rumbled loudly.

A chuckle spread up and down Fairfax Avenue.
Several old men in bathing suits sat up in their folding chairs and smiled with toothless glee. A group of
nine-year-old girls playing Chinese jump rope ran out
of a vacant lot and stood in the middle of the street
watching.

"I'll give you one hour, Mr. Hopalong Cassidy. No
more."

"An hour and a half," he answered, though why he
said this he couldn't imagine. A half hour one way or
the other would make absolutely no difference, as
Cassidy was a shade under flat broke.

"Don't Jew me!" Bass shrieked. "I said one hour
and I meant it. Otherwise I get the marshal and
you'll find all that trash of yours out on the street.
That is unless I find something in that bordello you
have upstairs that's worth anything. In which case,
I'll pawn it."

A grizzled old man in a pair of ripped suit pants
and a straw hat with Disneyland embroidered on it
chortled. "You tell him, Bass," he yelled.

"Shut up, you creep. I lent you five bucks last
week." Bass threw a threatening glance at the old
man. A woman like Bass didn't need allies.

Everyone laughed except the old man, who turned a
withering look on Cassidy as the one who had started
the whole thing.

Bass stood at the top of the stoop and glowered down at Cassidy. "Now, personally," she continued, "I hope you don't have the money, because as far as tenants go, you're worse than any of them. You're as filthy as a cockroach and a lot less good-looking. And I don't like your friends either. Most of them have got enough hair to stuff a queen-sized mattress. If you ask me they're just a bunch of unsavory rapists and dope fiends."

"They're intellectuals. They can look like rapists if they want to." Cassidy's voice was growing loud and belligerent.

"What's that?" an enormous old man with a hearing aid stuck inside an ear the size of an elephant's asked a shriveled old man sitting next to him.

"I think she said his friends raped her."

"Horrible," shuddered the fat man, though it wasn't clear whether it was the thought that Bass had been raped or the thought of raping her that unnerved him.

Cassidy's stomach sank. He could see the handwriting on the wall as clearly as if a hundred Mexicans with spray cans had been working all night. Bass was going to evict him and all the polite bows and "yes, ma'ams" in the world weren't going to change her mind. He had two choices. Either he could slink away, sniveling like a coward, crawling down Fairfax Avenue on his bony knees, or he could stand up for himself like a man. Either way he came up a loser. Still, even losing should have its compensations.

"Look here, Bass," he yelled. "To tell you the truth, I don't go for your looks either. In fact, you're just about the biggest load I ever saw dumped on this street."

Bass's eyes became two tiny points of fury, her broad muscular jaws began to work.

"And let me tell you something else," Cassidy was only beginning to get warmed up.

"Julio!" Bass yelled. Her voice carried up and down the street like a sonic boom.

"You're the reason we don't need pest control in this flea trap. One look at you would start a stampede unequaled since Noah's Ark took off and left the rest of the world to drown."

"You tell her, bro," a fat old black woman stood up from her segregated chair at the Palace and raised a beefy arm in salute.

"Julio!" Bass screamed again.

This week's Mexican cucaracha stuck his head out the window and looked down at Bass with sleepy eyes. "Yeth, honey," he lisped.

Bass softened as she looked up at her latest flame. "I want this deadass's belongings dumped."

"Ho yeah?" Julio smiled, displaying more teeth than any human ought to be allowed.

"That's right, sweetie pie, throw 'em out the window."

Julio's head disappeared back into the house. The pounding of his feet as he raced up the staircase could be heard outside.

"You can't do that," shrieked Cassidy. "You have to evict me. I have my rights."

Bass laughed. "Go tell a cop. You got enough weed up there to send you up the river on a twenty-year excursion."

Cassidy glared at Bass and started marching up the stairs toward her. Bass threw her enormous frame in front of the door, so effectively blocking it that even a mosquito could not find egress.

Cassidy looked around. The entire ambulatory section of the Palace Arms had gotten out of their chairs and were moving in for a closer look. Even those confined to wheelchairs were making a valiant effort to get in on the action, though many of them were stopped at the steep curb, and like Moses had to content themselves with viewing the Promised Land from afar. If Cassidy had ever believed in the perfectibility of man, here was a whole street full of arguments against it.

Suddenly Cassidy's belongings began to rain down onto the street. Bills, journals, dirty socks, his best jeans flew out the window. Occasionally Julio's youthful head would appear, flashing his toothy smile that was going to make some dentist a very happy man. Then another load would rain down. Julio chuckled loudly. He seemed to be enjoying himself.

Cassidy saw red. He leaped at Bass, grabbing her around her middle and tackling her. Through sheer surprise Cassidy was able to floor her. The two of them lay across the entrance, panting like two mismatched lovers.

Almost immediately the crowd tightened into a knot around them, yelling like Mexicans at a cockfight. The man in the Disneyland hat began taking bets, but he had to give up quickly, since despite the fact that she was floored, the odds were all with Bass.

Bass lay motionless on the ground like a beached whale. She looked up and saw Cassidy grunting above her, his face beet red, his mouth open and gasping for air. Bass threw a right to his nose, landed it, and

followed through with a stunning left. She could feel
Cassidy's skin give under her hard knuckles and smiled
with pleasure.

Cassidy's grip loosened. Suddenly he felt the earth
moving underneath him. Bass was rolling and Cassidy
was crunched to the ground. Bass put her enormous
foot on Cassidy's chest and stood up. Cassidy was
pinned like a butterfly.

A loud cheer went up from the crowd. Bass waved
her mammoth arms in the air in a victory sign. Cassidy was wriggling beneath her like an overturned
beetle. He looked up at Bass's leg rising above him like
a giant fir tree. He bared his teeth, took a big chunk
of Bass's muscular leg between his teeth, and bit down
hard.

Bass howled in agony. In one gesture she grabbed
Cassidy by the shirt front and lifted him up. Again
Cassidy was wriggling, this time in midair. Cassidy
gathered all his strength, and with a power born of
necessity, kneed Bass in the stomach.

Bass released him, whimpering like a baby. Cassidy
dropped to the ground and tried to muster the energy
to scoot away from Bass, but he had none left. His
chest felt like a two-ton truck had been playing
chicken on him. He looked up at Bass with terror in
his eyes, but Bass was no longer looking at him.

"Julio, help!" she cried out plaintively. "Please
help me!" Julio was nowhere to be seen.

Just as Cassidy was pulling himself into a standing position, he felt something tapping on his back.
He turned to find the old man in the Disneyland
hat raining weak punches on him with gnarled fists.
"Hit a woman, will ya?"

The fat old man with the elephant ears joined him.

He put up his fat little fists like a boxer and danced around Cassidy with infuriated bloodshot eyes. Cassidy waited for the inevitable racial insults or genealogical references.

"You Jew bastard," the fat man yelled.

Cassidy had to hand it to him. With unparalleled economy of style, the man had done both in one short phrase. Bass was still yelling for Julio, who was hiding upstairs, the door blocked by Cassidy's bed.

All at once, a nine-year-old with long braids and her first layer of acne pushed her way up to the fat man. "What the hell's the matter with being a Jew?" She grabbed the old man's hearing aid and pulled it out of his large hairy ear. The fat man bellowed with rage and grabbed her by the pigtail.

It was like a signal. Suddenly fights broke out all up and down the street. Ash cans went flying, spilling orange peels and fishbones. Old men battered each other with folded newspapers. The man in the Disneyland hat found himself surrounded by a group of angry pubescent girls and started backpedaling down the street as fast as his reedy legs would carry him. Even those confined to wheelchairs revved their motors and crashed into one another, locking wheels.

Cassidy stared in amazement as an old grandmother picked up a folding chair and crashed it down on the back of an old lady who was busily ripping the dress off a woman she had hated for fifty years.

Bass too was watching from the sidelines, whimpering in the arms of Julio, who, seeing the turn of events, had come back to the arms of his meal ticket.

As Cassidy was watching the fight, a feeling of great relief swept over him. It was as if by losing his home he had cast off a rope. But the relief only lasted a moment before reality interceded. When ships pulled out to sea, they generally had a new port waiting for them. He had nothing.

Cassidy heard a distant police siren, offering the prospect of a place to spend the night but nothing else. He turned and hotfooted it away, never to return.

Schaftner lay, thin and blue-white on the bed, rolling from side to side rhythmically, attached to the juices of life by tubes and wires, every function of his body being monitored and controlled by a roomful of machinery. As he rolled, his wild, scared eyes scanned the room like an animal. Sometimes they would fix on Cassidy, and for a moment he would feel that Schaftner knew who he was looking at.

Cassidy walked over to Schaftner and took his thin matchstick of an arm. He pressed it three times and said, "If you understand me, squeeze my hand." Quickly he grabbed Schaftner's bony hand and waited. Nothing happened. Again he squeezed Schaftner's arm, then held his hand, waiting for a return message that never came.

Cassidy sighed sadly. It had been six weeks, time he admitted the experiment was over. Cassidy had taken the laboratory logs, but without Schaftner's grant they were no good to him. It had been Schaftner's grant, not his. It would cost millions to resume the experiment. Even if Cassidy could manage the science part, and he believed he could, he didn't see how he could swing saving that kind of money before A.D. 3080.

It was time to start considering alternatives. But what alternatives were there? Even if he could get someone else to hire him, which, since his best work was secret, seemed highly unlikely, he had spent the last four years working on genetic engineering. He doubted he could get it up for the digestive system of a paramecium or the liver of a rat.

Cassidy grabbed Schaftner's arm and pressed on it three times, but again there was no response. He threw Schaftner's hand back on the bed angrily. For a second a look of lucidity crossed Schaftner's face.

Cassidy jumped forward. "Schaftner, do you hear me?"

Schaftner's wide-open animal eyes held his for a moment. Cassidy's voice grew more desperate. "Schaftner, do you understand what I'm saying?"

Once again Schaftner's eyes swept over the room. Cassidy watched for close to a minute before he fell back into his chair and his own thoughts.

He remembered the first time he had heard about Schaftner. He was fresh out of Columbia University, just twenty years old, and standing on the corner of Twenty-third and Ninth eating a hot dog and reading a scientific journal. He never finished either the hot dog or the treatise. He just stuck out his thumb and five days later was standing on the star dedicated to Lassie.

The next morning he found Schaftner. He cornered him outside his laboratory and began railing at him like a deranged wino. Schaftner said nothing. He simply walked to his laboratory and called the university police.

The following morning, Cassidy was back, howling like a bitch in heat, screaming his credentials, telling Schaftner he'd received A's from the moment he sat wetting his pants in kindergarten to the day he received his degree. This was something of an exaggeration, but he figured he could mend fences later when he'd won the Nobel Prize. The police cut him off in midsentence.

But the next morning he was back again. He'd scrub floors, clean test tubes, wipe Schaftner's very ass if he would only give Cassidy a chance. Schaftner didn't even bother to call the police. He just let him whine in front of the door.

After that Cassidy dogged Schaftner's footsteps. Every time the professor turned around, there was that disreputable blob of hair, loping after him.

One day Schaftner turned around and for the sake of peace offered him a job washing test tubes. A week later Cassidy was his assistant.

It didn't take long for Schaftner to see that as far as native intelligence was concerned, Cassidy had it all over him. Schaftner never knew which he felt more strongly, resentment or a kind of paternal pride. He was strung out between the two of them like a taut laundry line. Nevertheless it added a certain spirit to their relationship that resembled the love-hate most people said went with marriage.

No one had ever touched Schaftner before, not the once-a-month widow, nor his shadowy Episcopalian parents, nor even his brief college romance. Cassidy had touched him. He was the only person in the world who understood not only what he was talking about but that unspeakable obsession that had driven him for thirty years. There was no need to discuss the dream—it was always there before them. They had both found something more important than either of them. They didn't just love their work; they *were* their work.

And now it was over. Cassidy looked at Schaftner rolling from side to side on his sweat-soaked bed. Schaftner's eyes swept past Cassidy. They stopped, then backed up. What were his eyes saying? "Kill me." Or "Keep me alive. I'll be back." Then in the next moment they went back to their scanning, like an electric eye, and Cassidy was deserted and alone.

A terrible rage came over Cassidy. He wanted to take the clear plastic respirator tube and wind it around Schaftner's throat, or take the bottle dripping life into his arm and throw it out the window.

He got up from his chair and stood over Schaftner, his heart pounding furiously, his hands clenched into tight fists. He could hear nothing but the airy pumping of the breathing machine. All he could see was the open wound with the plastic tube leading from Schaftner's neck. He hated Schaftner at that moment more than he had hated anyone in his life. Schaftner, who he loved, who had given him the most important thing in the world, had taken it away.

The rage lasted less than a minute, then sanity returned. Cassidy turned from Schaftner and walked to the door. Things had gotten out of hand. If he didn't do something soon he'd go crazy. He felt himself throwing off another rope, casting himself adrift toward a destination he couldn't even begin to imagine, let alone see. A thrill of expectation and fear went through him. It was as if his life were no longer his own, as if he were spinning out into the black starry universe toward an uncharted world.

Afternoon sunlight spilled over the windowsill and dappled the two intertwined bodies.

Cassidy didn't move. He could feel Lenny trembling

beneath him, her thighs pressed tightly to him, her head tilted back, her eyes closed. Traces of the pain-pleasure of lovemaking were still on her face. It was a small, childlike face, with a thick mop of curly black hair encircling it. Lenny was thirty-five, a good ten years older than Cassidy, but one would never know it to look at her.

Cassidy's eyes moved down her body, from her face over her slim neck, past her arms which held tightly to him and the gentle swelling of her small breasts pressed tightly to his chest. His eyes continued down to the curve of her hips, making a slow deliberate survey, as if trying to record a memory for the future. Suddenly Cassidy knew he was casting off the last rope. He was saying good-bye to Lenny. A terrible stab of regret went through him as he looked down at her tousled head.

The tension of lovemaking began to leave Lenny's body. It was always the saddest part of lovemaking, the pulling away and becoming oneself again.

Lenny opened her eyes and watched Cassidy as he watched her. He could feel her large black eyes nailing him, reading thoughts she wouldn't want to know.

Finally Lenny spoke. Her voice was soft and tentative. "You're making a decision, aren't you?"

Cassidy turned sadly and looked down at the floor. "I guess I already made it," he answered.

Lenny waited for a moment, hoping that he'd say more and she wouldn't have to be the one to ask, but knowing in the end she would be.

"Well," she said lightly, "are you going to let me in on it or is it a surprise?"

Cassidy was still staring at the floor as if he found the old peeling wood immensely interesting. He felt sick. He would have loved to have been anywhere but lying on the warm bed with Lenny beside him, staring down at the floorboards. At last he answered, "I'm leaving."

Lenny moved and Cassidy rolled from her. She reached for a cigarette on the night table, lit it, then scrambled out of bed. She was trying to be nonchalant, but Cassidy knew her too well. He reached out and held her arm, stopping her.

"You son of a bitch," she said softly and pulled away from him.

She walked to the closet, feeling exposed, ashamed of her body. In the year she and Cassidy had been together, he had taught her not to feel shame at being naked. At first she'd refused to sit and talk with him undressed, and when she did, she'd sit curled in on herself. Finally the shame had gone, but it had reappeared at the first sign of desertion.

She pulled out a terry cloth robe and slipped it on quickly, then put on her ripped bedroom slippers. Still she didn't leave the closet.

"A woman?" Lenny's voice was small, and it killed Cassidy to hear the tears in it.

He got up and walked to her. "No, no woman." He touched her shoulders, hoping she would turn back to him. She didn't.

"Where are you going?" She turned, flashed a false smile, and walked to the kitchen.

Cassidy followed. He stood in the doorway and watched as Lenny put water in the kettle. "I don't know where I'm going," he said.

"Don't know or won't tell?" Again the false smile. Lenny could feel the falseness and hated herself.

"Look, it's hard to explain. I didn't make the decision to go anywhere. I made the decision to do something and that means I may have to go."

"Do what? A new job?"

"Maybe. I don't know. It's just that I feel like I'm being pushed toward something, like maybe there is a fate and she's whipping up something special for me."

Cassidy started to pace, his eyes burning with an intensity Lenny had never seen before. For a moment she wondered if what she was seeing was madness. But she knew that wasn't it. What she was seeing was genius and she hated and loved him for it.

He stopped. "I know you don't understand. I don't understand it myself. But I won't be able to see you for . . ." He paused. He didn't know how long. He suspected forever.

Lenny read the forever in his eyes. She turned back to the stove and began measuring the coffee. She spilled the grounds all over the stove and laughed, trying to seem casual, but she knew she was doing one hell of a bad job of it.

Cassidy sat down at the table and looked at the kitchen he'd grown to know so well. It was a cheerful room with blue and white tiles, white café curtains, huge copper pots hanging from the walls, and a bush of bright red flowers almost growing into the window. It was full of memories. Good memories. He'd been happy in this kitchen. He was crazy to leave it on a harebrained mission to nowhere.

Next to him on the table was a typewriter. Papers were scattered all around the table and in a large pool on the floor. Lenny was a nurse trying to be a writer. Five days a week, eight hours a day, she'd work maternity, then she'd drag herself home and sit at the typewriter, a cigarette sending up swirls of smoke, coffee going, and she'd write. How she did it, and why, had always been a mystery to Cassidy.

When they were just becoming lovers, Cassidy had sneaked into the kitchen and read several pages. He read about himself and became scared, but now it no longer scared him. Lenny had her own way of teaching nakedness to him.

Lenny poured the coffee. Again she laughed, but it was a mirthless laugh. "Funny, I always thought I'd be the one to leave you." She kept her face turned from him; there were tears in her eyes.

"I'm hurting you, aren't I?" he asked sadly.

Lenny shrugged. She was holding onto the coffeepot as if for support. Suddenly everything collapsed inside her.

"Oh God, you're fucking killing me!" She threw the coffeepot against the wall. Steaming grounds and coffee splashed down the wall to the floor.

The tears started to come. Cassidy walked over and put his arms around her. She was too weak to fight and clung to him tightly. He was hating this and yet he couldn't leave. For a moment he was tempted to say he'd chuck everything and stay, but he knew that was only a passing need. The other need was greater and stronger and would not leave him alone.

"You're giving up a good thing. Do you know that?"

"Yes."

"I'll make you dinner."

Cassidy felt like laughing. Either that or crying, he wasn't sure which. Lenny was always cooking for him. He wondered if that was because she was older and had been married.

"I don't want dinner."

"There's some eggplant and rice from last night. I'll just reheat it." She went to the refrigerator and took out a couple of plastic containers. She knew she was stalling for time. Suddenly she understood why. She was going to ask him to take her with him. She knew she was going to ask and he'd refuse and that would ruin their last few minutes together. She tried to stop herself, emptying the coagulated eggplant and rice into a saucepan, turning on the fire. "Can you at least stay awhile?"

"If you want me to," he answered and walked up behind her, putting his arms around her waist.

"Oh, Cassidy, please don't touch me. Look, I'm crying into the goddamned eggplant." She smiled at him, tears streaming down her face.

Cassidy smiled back at her. He could see her sitting at her kitchen table, typing, curls of smoke all around her. She'd be okay.

Then Lenny broke down. "Take me with you."

Cassidy shook his head. "I can't."

Lenny's body became rigid. "Then go! Just get the hell out of here!"

Cassidy hesitated for a moment, then walked to the bedroom and threw on his clothes. As he passed the kitchen, he saw Lenny standing exactly where she was. He left.

It took almost a minute for Lenny to move. She just stood in the kitchen, stirring the eggplant, tears rolling down her face. "Fucking masochistic idiot," she said to herself.

She called Cassidy's name and rushed to the door. But when she looked out at the darkening street, Cassidy's beat-up old car was already halfway down the block in hot pursuit of his future.

Chapter 3

Basketball having been one of his better sports, it was quite natural that Mark Foreman would pick the basketball court on his father's estate to mourn his father's death. Except for the remnants of an Indian headdress and hastily applied, if somewhat smeared, war paint, he was nude, a factor that greatly inhibited his running and jumping with anything resembling vigor. In fact, it hurt like a bastard when he went up for a lay-up. But Mark considered it was better than crying, which, since he hated his father, he didn't want to do, and besides, the additional factor of his swinging, aching dong added a kind of piquancy to what Mark was now calling his "last stand" and, in general, fit his pattern nicely.

Mark missed a hook shot. The ball rebounded off a statue of a little black boy with a ring and flew into the bushes. Mark got down on his hands and knees and scurried through the bushes after it like a rabbit.

Mark was about as drunk as he had ever been. He had the sensation of a swollen tongue lolling in his mouth. His face felt bloated and distorted, his body numb. It seemed to Mark that if someone happened by, which was highly unlikely since the court was in the driveway of his father's thirty-room mansion that took up several acres of prime Bel-Air land and was completely surrounded by an electrified fence, they would run screaming from the nude, dropsy-laden freak.

That was how he felt. How he looked was an entirely different matter. Mark Foreman wasn't just handsome, he was a god, an Adonis, a young girl's dream and a mother's blessing. Mark was tall and slim with the smoothly muscular body of a born athlete. His suntanned face and silver blond hair were as close to perfect as nature could manage. His teeth were straight and white. The only flaw on his entire body was a thin appendix scar the doctors had taken great pains to make almost invisible. Most women thought it was a turn on.

The icing on the cake was that Mark Foreman was rich. And now he was even richer. Only a week ago his father had died, leaving him heir to a fortune that reached from the plains of Africa to the tundra of the poles, both of them; millions and millions of dollars suddenly spilled into Mark's lap, and he'd never have to do anything the rest of his life but kick back and marvel at his bank statements.

On top of that, Mark didn't even really need his father's money. He was making it on his own. Mark was a junior executive at one of the networks, and while he hadn't come up with the concept of *Charlie's Angels,* he hadn't made any major blunders either, which in Hollywood was the same as success. His life-style was Beverly Hills chic. He went to the best restaurants; he was the handsome presence at all the industry screenings, the man on the arm of this week's hot television sex symbol.

And yet Mark was plagued by the specter of his own

failure. It visited him everywhere, at his large mahogany desk, between the sheets, even in the can, and he lived in a very tenuous truce with it, a truce that could be broken at any moment. Mark supposed that was exactly what was happening now.

He found the ball, made a flying leap, and tried to sink another hook shot. He missed the backboard and let the ball bounce off the court, then walked over to the bottle of Wild Turkey nestled several feet away on the manicured lawn.

The bottle was only a third full. He was going to have to ration it from now on, one sip an hour. If he was careful, he could make it last another day. As to food, he'd run out of that two days ago. His "last stand" was drawing to a close. It wouldn't be long now before they battered down the electrified fence and swarmed all over the grounds looking for him. They'd find his wasted skeleton, bones picked dry, in the middle of the basketball court, and all the craziness he'd been torturing himself with for the past week would be over.

Mark lifted the bottle and said, "It'll be a grand death. Worthy of a hero in a Fitzgerald novel. In fact, worthy of Fitzgerald himself." He laughed and downed a huge gulp, then put the bottle back on the grass and joined it on the ground.

It had all started a week ago. Mark had come over to his father's house for one of those little chats he detested even more than the disapproving silence his father usually had for him.

The fake Tudor house had seemed even quieter than usual. There was no Japanese gardener sweating his guts out on the massive front lawn, no chauffeur polishing the twin Rolls-Royces, no maid shaking out quilted silk bed covers. When Mark walked in the door, he was greeted not by the old rogue but by Smithly Jones, his father's lawyer and hatchet man.

Smithly seemed even more lugubrious than usual. He gritted his huge horse teeth as if he were suffering from acute gas. Actually he was suffering a much more acute pain, the pain of losing his cushy job, his heavily mortgaged house, his pleasure trips to Vegas, and his young, blonde, voluptuous wife. Smithly was in a hell of a pickle, that was for sure. His boss had just kicked the bucket, and try as he might, he wasn't going to be able to plug up the leaks he'd made.

Smithly put his pin-striped arm on Mark's back. "It grieves me to be the bearer of tragic news." Smithly sighed deeply. It took several moments before he felt able to continue. "Sandford Delano Foreman has just passed away." Smithly bit his lip and rolled his eyes heavenward in grief.

Mark was shocked. Somehow in the back of his mind he'd thought his father was immune even to the Angel of Death.

"Passed away?" he repeated, staring at the same portion of ceiling Smithly had been looking at, as if his father's shade were hanging from the rafters.

"Last night. It was mercifully swift and painless."

"Of what?"

"Massive coronary."

Mark laughed sadly. "It would be massive, wouldn't it? Old Sol wouldn't have anything but the biggest and the best."

Smithly ignored Mark's remark and gently prodded him into the mammoth sunken living room and toward a large leather couch. He waited until they were both seated before he spoke.

"As you are well aware, your father had considerable holdings."

"You mean he was filthy rich?"

"Yes. I suppose you could say he was filthy rich." It was clear from the way Smithly daintily pronounced every word, holding each one out like a dirty rag, that this was not quite the way he would have said it. "Now I know you never took an interest in your father's business. Nor was it necessary at the time. But your father's interests cover a broad range of spheres. Very few people are aware of the extent of Foreman Industries. There is Foreman Can Co., of course, Foreman Oil, ForClair Soap. . . ."

As Smithly continued his recitation of the boundaries of the Foreman empire, Mark's eyes cruised the sunken living room. The walls were cluttered with pictures of his father standing with everyone who was anyone short of the Pope, and Mark's thoughts drifted to the late great founder of Foreman Industries.

Sandford Delano Foreman, a.k.a. Sol Formanowitz, was something of a mystery not only to the world business community but to his own son. His broad, blood-red face had appeared on the covers of all the leading financial magazines, and his name was well known to the masses as well as several Senate investigating committees and one or two judges.

But, in truth, practically nothing was known about Sol's origins. His early history was as shrouded in mystery as if he had killed his brother or committed incest. Sol's history began after World War II. In a manner of speaking, he rose like Venus, fully formed. Mark had heard rumors that the Foreman empire began in a small rowboat off the coast of Cuba, where some rusty military hardware, still bearing the U.S.

serial numbers, fell out of his boat and a bag of white powder mysteriously appeared in its place. It helped Foreman to say, as he often did, "I never took a penny for anything illegal." Whether he had instead taken drugs was something Mark never knew. Recently the newspapers had begun dredging up some pretty unsavory facts about Sol, but by this time, Mark no longer cared. And, in fact, he already knew all he needed to know about his father.

Mark turned and saw Smithly staring at him. "Perhaps this isn't the time," Smithly said. "We can set up a meeting at my office and go over all the various companies."

"Why?" asked Mark. "What difference does it make what he owned? He cut me out of his will four years ago."

Smithly looked at Mark. If tears had been a possibility for that man, he would have been bawling like a baby. "Mr. F. died intestate."

"He what?" Mark almost jumped out of his seat.

"Terribly inadvisable. I can't tell you how many times I tried to convince him . . ."

"That he'd die?" Mark said acidly. "The old bastard wouldn't have believed that, though, would he? Or at least he wouldn't have considered the possibility that after he died anyone would dare walk the streets or screw their wives or eat dinner, let alone do business."

Smithly looked shocked, but he remained where he was. "Intestate" suddenly made Mark rather important to his future.

"I'm aware that the two of you were not on the best of terms," he said quietly.

"You can say that again."

"After the cigar incident Mr. F. was most angry at you."

"It was the high point of my life."

"Yes. Of course." Smithly began nervously working on his lower lip with his teeth. If he did it just right, it hurt quite nicely.

"How much do you know about the cigar incident?" asked Mark.

"Mr. F. was most discreet."

"Good. Then I'm going to tell you a little story." Smithly clapped his hands to his knees and started to get up. "Really. I think not now. Perhaps in a few days in my office."

Mark grabbed Smithly's arm and prevented him from moving. "Now!" he said through clenched teeth.

Smithly began working on his lip again. He could taste the barest hint of blood, which was part of the enjoyment. Mr. F. had been right. His son was disturbed. Considering the fact that he was the only living heir, however, Smithly felt compelled not to argue and settled back into the couch.

Mark smiled. "Okay, Smithly, now you can take this story home and mull over it if you like, or, as I suspect you'll do without my telling you, forget it entirely. I don't care. But all those years I saw you following old Sol around, your nose up his asshole so high all you could see was his rosy pink intestines, I wanted to tell you how much I hated that big-mouthed, unprincipled cannibal's guts."

Smithly threw a mildly disapproving look at Mark. Inwardly, though, he had to admit that was a fairly apt description of the big-boned, bald-headed, cigar smoker

who had pulled himself up from the slums of New
Jersey to the pinnacle of high finance by his fingernails.

"Unfortunately," said Smithly, "the feeling was
mutual."

"Don't I remember. You know what he used to call
me?"

"I have no idea."

"I'll bet. Go on, say it."

Mark waited but Smithly remained mute. Mark
grabbed Smithly's arm. "Say it!"

Smithly cleared his throat uncomfortably. "He
called you that faggot, I believe."

"And."

"Jive turkey."

"And."

"Ass licker, sometimes."

"Not to mention wimp, yellow belly, and my personal favorite, the spineless, gutless wonder."

Smithly nodded gravely and shot Mark a concerned,
understanding look. He could see his only chance of
surviving the massive back stabbing and conniving
that would now be going on in Foreman Industries
was to desert the memory of its late great boss and
join with the new ruler. Men like Smithly were good
adjusters, like the cockroach.

"Do you remember my mother?"

"Ah, yes, your mother."

"Ah, yes, my mother." But Mark fell silent. Even
in his fury he couldn't subject her to this verbal
massacre. She had long ago passed away, and anyway,
it hadn't really been her fault. She'd been as much
of a victim as Mark.

Mark remembered Clarissa only as the smell of

perfume leaning toward him, the rustle of chiffon. Later, when Mark was ten, she was the hustle and hush of doctors as they wended their way up the staircase. An occasional kiss to her blue-veined cheek.

Mark did not learn what was wrong with her until later. One day his tutor was talking with a new maid. He had pointed upstairs and circled his finger around his ear. This Mark understood.

Clarissa's mental illness may never have been discussed but it hung over the household like a heavy fog. Mark was often said to take after his mother. He was slim like she was; he had her coloring, her delicate beauty, but that wasn't all they were referring to. It was the other thing.

"It bugged the hell out of old Sol that I looked like her," said Mark finally. "Oh boy, none of the hearty Formanowitz genes over here. Poor old Sol, there he was, spilling out that robust strain all over the world, and what did he end up with for a son? A pale wimp."

Smithly could feel sweat trickling down from his armpits. He looked over at Mark, whose face was beet-red from anger, and became frightened. Once again he clapped his hands to his knees. "I really must be shuffling along."

"You leave this room and it's your job."

Smithly sank back into the couch quickly. "To tell you the truth," he said, "your father was faithful to his wife. He had other fish to fry. Business and bargaining kept him pretty tired most of the time."

"Bullshit!"

Smithly shrugged. What he had just said was the truth. Most of the famous Formanowitz strain had been dissipated in the boardrooms of various companies and over Scotch and sodas poolside while consummating the next big deal. The fact of it was, if organs atrophied from disuse, Sol's member would have been smaller than his baby finger. But Smithly didn't say any more. He could read in Mark's face that it was something he didn't want to hear.

"Remember that time I ran away?" asked Mark, a look of nostalgia crossing his face.

Smithly relaxed. "It took us three months to find you."

"Not bad for a fifteen-year-old, huh? Shacked up in Texas in a cozy R.V."

"There was a waitress to keep you warm, as I remember." Smithly winked at Mark.

Mark shook his head, his eyes dancing with the memory. "Just how much did it cost you?"

"Not much, really," said Smithly, casting his steel trap mind back and catching the exact figure in its viselike grip. "One hundred and fifty dollars, plus the R.V."

"Yes, sir," said Mark, "we go way back."

Smithly nodded. "Many years."

"A real trip down memory lane." Mark's face was tight and angry. Smithly noted it and began once again to feel the trickling sweat.

"After you brought me back to Los Angeles, literally kicking and screaming, I rarely saw my father. Just those once-a-year ceremonies where I'd be dressed up like a sacrifice and paraded in for an hour of backslapping and cigar smoke blown in my face. Which brings us back to the cigar incident. That was a real funny one, wasn't it? Come on, Smithly, admit it."

Smithly tried to get the right degree of smile on his

lips, but the crack he had made with his teeth was stinging, and anyway, he was scared.

"There I was, just twenty-one," said Mark, "and summoned to the good old twin tower office buildings. You ever notice that Sol always did things in two's? Nothing done singly was ever enough. I can see him now, his face all red, his cigar belching smoke. He made a nice little speech, then offered me a cigar, a job, and called me son. I choked on all three." Mark laughed. "I'll never forget his face as I shoved that big black cigar right down his throat till it almost came out of his asshole. I did some damage too, didn't I?"

"Third-degree burns and a broken jaw."

"Not to mention shattered pride. He threatened to have my balls on the family silver platter, have me arrested, disinherit me, the works. But you know what he did instead?"

"He left the next day to consummate a deal he was making with the Russians."

"Good old Sol, he couldn't even get it up enough to hate me." For a moment, Mark was overwhelmed not with anger but a great sense of loss. It made absolutely no sense to him. He had hated that man more than any other creature on earth, and here he was feeling a profound sadness and loss.

Suddenly he turned on Smithly like a rabid dog. "Get the hell out of my house!"

Smithly hesitated only for a second, then leaped from the couch, flew out the door and down the driveway at breakneck speed.

Slowly Mark began to remove his clothes. First his beautifully hand-tailored suit jacket, then his tie, then his shirt, until he was stark naked. He called for the servants and, standing nude in front of his father's portrait, he told them all to pack their bags and get their asses out within the hour. That night he made himself an Indian headdress, pulled the fire ax out of the glass box, and went on a rampage, not stopping until there wasn't a piece of furniture or TV in his father's house that he hadn't scalped. The next morning he had an electrified fence installed. The king was dead.

Unfortunately it wasn't until later that Mark checked his father's larder and discovered that Sol had not stocked up for such an eventuality as Mark's takeover. An even greater disappointment came when he realized that the electrified fence, installed to keep out the world at large, had the same effect on the liquor and grocery store delivery boys. In effect, Mark was under seige. After a while, he came to realize that was exactly what he'd wanted in the first place.

The news, not only of the king's death but the new king's lunacy, didn't take long to reach the world. By noon the next morning, lawyers, executives from his father's multitude of companies, possible legatees, and the press were milling around in huge numbers outside the gate. Mark's "last stand" had even been on the evening news. A tall, foxy-looking blonde with Eastern clench jaw stood in front of his house and fried an egg on his fence. Various helicopter shots had been taken with NBC's minicam. Mark had run out into the yard and mooned, but the helicopter had been too high, and he'd looked like an oversized rabbit scampering through a field.

Mark reached over for the bottle and took a big swig. He remembered he was going to look for his basketball. He stood up shakily and started across the lawn. After a few minutes, he spotted the ball lying near the front gate.

Mark ducked behind some bougainvillea and looked out at it. Even if he moved from bush to bush, the ball was still a good twenty yards out in the open, not far from the electrified fence and the crowds. He could see them all out there. There were more of them now than ever before. The gentlemen of the Fourth Estate and the hounds of business had been joined by spectators hoping to catch a glimpse of the dipso who lived inside. One young entrepreneur had set up a makeshift ice cream stand and was selling Foreman Specials, which turned out to be no more than two scoops of vanilla ice cream with an imitation rum topping and a sprinkling of nuts.

Mark approached cautiously, slipping from hedge to hedge, his bare brown ass bobbing up and down like that of a young deer. He stopped at the last clump of bushes and peeked out.

A snot-nosed kid in a ripped T-shirt caught sight of him immediately. "Hey, man, there he is!" yelled the kid.

A hundred heads swiveled, many of them with Foreman Specials streaking their mouths. Mark was furious. It was his house and his last stand, and he wasn't going to let a few lawyers and tourists ruin it. He gathered his courage, then stepped out from behind the bush.

A maid from one of the neighboring houses shrieked, "Hey, will ya look at that! That jive turkey's naked as a jaybird!"

Suddenly everyone began pushing toward the fence to get a better look. Smithly Jones, who'd been among the interested onlookers, found himself lifted into the air and carried toward the fence. His briefcase fell to the ground, spilling writs and petitions to the winds. Smithly screamed but no one seemed to notice it over the din. Finally Smithly caught sight of one of the executives from the Foreman Can Company.

He yelled, "Mr. Black! Remember me? Foreman International? We met at the San Diego convention!"

But Black smiled vaguely as if he'd never seen him before.

Smithly couldn't believe it. He knew Black had to remember him. They'd spent a whole evening together. Then a certain disagreement over some proxies came back to him. Surely Black couldn't still be angry about that, he thought.

It seemed Black was indeed still angry about the little matter of the proxies, however, and as Smithly was swept forward, Black gave a karate chop and a little shove of assistance to the crowd.

As Smithly was carried parallel to the fence, his pleading hands found something solid to hold onto. It was a tall, athletic-looking black maid from a nearby house. The woman felt the eager hands exploring her and whirled around. No one remains a maid in Beverly Hills for long without knowing how to take care of herself. She lifted poor Smithly from the other people's hands and tossed him into the fence.

Smithly screamed as the back of his trousers sizzled and turned black like a marshmallow at a Boy Scout picnic. Finally a Japanese tourist took pity on him, removed him from the fence, and laid him down, still smoking, to recover.

Mark was standing perfectly still, staring out at the

huge crowd. Flashbulbs were popping and people were yelling all around him. He was confused and frightened, like a hunted deer. Why had he done this? Up until now he'd been reacting to vague urges, fragments of thought, undefined desires. Now, standing naked in front of a jeering crowd, Mark began to ask himself why. Of course the obvious reason was that he'd gone crazy. That was the answer everyone else would have given and what Mark himself wanted to believe. But deep down he suspected that wasn't the whole story, and while this wasn't the act of a sane man, it wasn't the act of a madman either. Mark tried to ignore that thought. He wanted to be crazy. That way he'd never again have to do anything, say anything, be anything. He wanted to go out in a lunatic blaze of glory and then fizzle into a bit of fine, black ash.

Mark opened his mouth to speak. He felt the need to issue a final statement, maybe to enlist support and sympathy. But before the first booze-soaked word had issued from his mouth, a shiver passed over his body and he slowly collapsed into a neatly clipped clump of jasmine.

When Mark woke up the next morning, he found himself in bed with a cool towel on his forehead and a spoon being shoved into his mouth. He opened his swollen, aching eyes and saw the cloudlike burr head of Cassidy. Then he fell back into a deep and profound stupor.

"Good morning!"
Mark opened his eyes and tried to focus them. Sunlight was streaming through a window, the light so

blinding that for a moment he thought he'd been
sent to Mars on a rocket and was closer to the sun
than any human had ever been.

After a while, the light seemed to soften and Mark
was able to recognize a window. It was a familiar
window, one he was sure he'd seen before. His memory
was a little slow to catch up, but eventually he figured
out it was a window in his father's house. He looked
around the room. It was indeed his father's room,
but every inch of the floor was covered with TV wires,
tubes, underwear, shoes, ties, in fact, the entire con-
tents of his father's double closet, as well as everything from his rolltop desk and the bathroom medicine
cabinet.

He could have sworn he heard someone say, "Good
morning," to him. He searched among the junk and
finally focused on Cassidy, who was sitting directly
across from him in what had once been a $1700 leather
easy chair.

Mark's swollen, red-rimmed eyes narrowed with
suspicion. "Why did you do this to my house?" He
indicated the wreckage that lay all around them.

"I didn't. You did."

Mark searched Cassidy's eyes, but Cassidy didn't
flinch and Mark began to wonder if it was possible
that it was he who had done it.

Cassidy was smoking one of Sol's Havanas and
drinking cognac with a pedigree good enough to put
it in the running for the throne of England.

Mark's eyes were wide and confused. "The last
thing I remember was taking a hook shot. I missed."

"When was that?" Cassidy sent up a billow of smoke.

Mark hesitated. He couldn't remember. He felt like
the back of his head had been blown off by heavy

artillery. He touched it and was surprised to feel everything intact. Finally he said, "I think Saturday. No, wait a minute. I'm not sure." His confusion made him feel even more weak and vulnerable than his gigantic hangover. "What day is it today?" he asked resentfully.

"Wednesday."

"You're lying!" Mark threw back the covers angrily, sending the entire frontal lobe of his brain on what felt like a journey to China. He fell back on the bed and waited for it to make the return trip. He felt like crying.

"It's not really Wednesday, is it?"

"I'm afraid it is."

"Oh, God!" Mark said, the words resounding through his head with a deep rumbling echo. "And when did I do this?"

"Sunday."

"I don't remember Sunday. In fact, I don't remember Monday or Tuesday either. What did I do then?"

"I don't know about Monday. But you spent most of Tuesday over a toilet."

Mark shuddered. A vague memory of cold porcelain and strong biological urges came back to him.

"I feel horrible," he moaned.

"You deserve to."

"Don't lecture me. Okay? If there's one thing I can't stand it's virtuous lectures on taking responsibilities and other est-isms. I'm in great distress and close to physical, mental, and moral collapse. In essence, what you see before you is a man on the brink."

"On the brink of what?"

Mark looked at Cassidy with faraway eyes. His voice softened and became wispy, drifting to the ceiling like a butterfly. "Haven't you heard? It's in all the papers. Eccentric millionaire goes flip city. Even Cronkite gave it a minute. I'm famous."

"Infamous."

"Let's not quibble over words, Cassidy."

"All right, we won't quibble," Cassidy said sharply. "But we won't pretend you're nuts either. Because you aren't nuts. You know it. I know it."

"I am too nuts," Mark said with the morose defiance of a five-year-old.

"Wanting to be and being are two different things."

"It's a sign of deep disturbance, Cassidy. I took psych. I know what I'm talking about."

Cassidy allowed a great cloud of smoke to issue from his mouth. He watched as it swirled into the air, dissipated, then reformed as a cloud on the ceiling. He was getting tired of Mark's whining. It was also becoming hard to hold in his excitement. Everything was falling into place now. First his decision, then, as if by a miracle, seeing his old college roommate on the news. He was beginning to feel it was meant to happen. But he had to approach Mark carefully; he could mess everything up if he steamrolled.

"How the hell did you get in here anyway?" Mark asked supsiciously.

"I rerouted the circuits of your fence. They did a lousy job installing it."

Mark shrugged. "It was something of a rush job."

"How much they charge you?"

"Jesus Christ, Cassidy, I don't know. A couple of thousand, I guess."

"I could have done it for under a hundred."

"That's the way it is when you're rich. They figure it won't make any difference to you."

"Does it?"

"Not a bit."

Cassidy smiled. It really didn't make any difference to Mark. It never had. Cassidy had just about lived off of him all four years of college, and he'd never seemed to mind. It wasn't just that he had a lot of money; there were plenty of skinflints even in their teens. And he certainly didn't have to buy friends. Everyone liked Mark. Cassidy had often wondered why Mark was friendly with him. For Cassidy it had been a matter of dire necessity, but Mark hadn't needed him for anything.

"Why did you come here?" Mark looked very small and tired in his father's big bed.

Cassidy blew out a thick cloud of smoke and sat forward in his chair, his face transformed. This was the moment he'd been waiting for, the money shot.

"I've come to make you one of the two most famous men in the world. The other being me."

"Cassidy, I have a headache, okay? And my guts feel like whipped shit. So let's just keep this a nice, down-to-earth, simple chat."

But Cassidy could hold it in no longer. "I've never been more serious in my whole life, Mark. I've got the key to life. Right here in this journal." He held up Schaftner's log and waved it in the air. "I can do what scientists have been struggling toward since that goddamned obscure Austrian monk Mendel wrote the ultimate *Roots* for the sweet pea. I can make life, and not just ordinary life, but perfect human life. A superman."

It was Mark's turn to eye Cassidy as if he were crazy.

"I'm not bullshitting you. I did it once before. And I can do it again."

Mark sat up in bed. "So what in the hell do you want me to do about it?" It was clear from his eyes, which held Cassidy's with shrewd clarity, he knew exactly what Cassidy wanted him to do about it. Never had the Formanowitz strain been so evident.

"I need money."

"In other words, you want to use me?" Again the money-changer eyes held Cassidy's.

Cassidy nodded. One thing Mark could always depend on was Cassidy's honesty. He remembered similar dealings with him in college in one agonizing swoop.

"And in exchange?"

"Immortality."

"Personally I find one life painful enough." He stared out of the window in silence for a while, then pointed to a fat robin that was terrorizing the worm population. "The weed killer they put on grass kills the birds too. Did you know that?"

"I'm offering you the chance of a lifetime."

"Look, don't you see? I'm a wreck of a human being, and the effort it would take to make myself any more than I am is exhausting even to think about."

"Proud of it?"

"Well, it is something, isn't it? I didn't just become a lawyer and marry some wire-jawed heiress. I'm ruining my life in a grand way."

Cassidy applauded. Mark watched him, a self-pitying smile on his thin worn face.

"Cassidy, I'm tired, so be a good boy and get the hell out of here. Go play with some of Sol's toys downstairs."

"I'm not leaving until you promise to listen to me."

"You must need that money bad."

"Almost as bad as you need me."

Mark didn't turn from the window. He just stared out at the robin, pecking on the ground. Finally he laughed. "Remember that blonde? The one who always wore her cheerleading costume on campus and used to wave her pussy in time to 'Rah, Rah, Columbia'?"

Cassidy laughed and nodded. Mark turned from the window and looked at Cassidy. "I don't know. I just don't know."

"All I'm asking you to do is listen."

Mark nodded, then slowly sank back into the bed. His eyes drifted closed, his feet left the earth, and he floated in the blackness of space. He fell asleep.

Cassidy walked over to the bed and readjusted the covers. It was a tender gesture, and Cassidy recognized it as such with surprise. He felt linked to the young, wasted man who lay sleeping, linked not by their past but by their future. He turned out the light and quietly left the room.

"A DNA molecule looks like this." Cassidy took a grease pencil and drew a large double helix across one of the fabric-covered walls of Sol's palatial living room. He stood back and looked at it. "Crick and Watson's double helix. You know what one of the original researchers said about it? 'A structure this pretty just has to exist.'" Cassidy pointed to the lines between the two winding staircases of the double helix. "Now this molecule is made up of four different organic bases linked by rungs of sugar and phosphates."

"I don't remember what DNA is. How the hell am I supposed to help you if I can't even remember what DNA is?"

"I'll explain it to you."

"I probably won't understand."

"Then I'll explain it to you again." Cassidy smiled at Mark. "Now let's start at the beginning. Do you remember what a chromosome is?"

"One of those dark, rodlike things in the nucleus of a cell?"

"Right. In the nucleus of all cells, everything from a sweet pea to a human being. Do you remember what they're there for?"

"I think they have something to do with heredity."

"They have everything to do with heredity," said Cassidy, his voice full of excitement. "Okay, now, like I said, all living things have these chromosomes. Some have two, some have eight, human beings have forty-six, except in the sex cells, where they have only half that number. During reproduction, the Mommy and Daddy chromosomes meet and sort of dance around each other, trading genetic information. We call this crossing-over. That way some poor unsuspecting zygote of a kid can end up with his father's bulbous nose and his mother's ass. Are you with me so far?"

Mark nodded. He was sitting up and listening intently.

"Good. Now these chromosomes are made up almost exclusively of deoxyribonucleic acid. That's the DNA stuff I was just showing you. It's the agent that carries genetic information."

"Almost exclusively?"

"Well, DNA transcribes into RNA for export to the cells. But that's another story."

Mark's face was screwed up tight in concentration. "Where do the genes come in?"

"That is the genes. That's what they are." Cassidy stabbed the picture of the DNA molecule with his finger. "That sugar-phosphate ladder is us. Everything that goes into making us human beings and not onions or frogs is written on the tiny twisting double strands that make up the chromosomes. Just this molecule here contains enough information to fill over a thousand books. Everything about us, everything we do, from digesting a meal to taking a leak, is written on a chain like this. You see, genes order up enzymes which order up our lives."

Mark shook his head. "I don't understand."

"Don't worry. Nobody does. Just take my word for it."

Mark smiled. He was enjoying this despite himself.

"Okay, now I told you about crossing-over, the way we become the sum of our parents. Well, up till now, we pretty much had to leave things to chance. That's why that poor turkey got his dad's schnoz and his mother's ass and probably grew up looking like hell and spending about a million dollars on a shrink's couch. But things are changing. You see, Schaftner broke the DNA code. Well, at least a lot of it. Now we know which genes control fingernails and which control intestinal development and the brain and the heart. We can look at this chain here and read it like a book."

"So?"

"Jesus, Mark, do you have any idea how many man-hours it took to break the DNA code? You're taking scientific history from Mendel and his goddamn peas, Morgan and his fruit flies, Crick and Watson and their double helix, Schaftner and his gene sequencing, and what do you say? 'So?' "

"Okay, okay," said Mark, laughing at Cassidy's serious face. "Wow, so they finally broke the DNA code, eh? My God!"

"What if I told you they also found a way to do this?" He took out a penknife and sliced off the top half of his drawing, taking a good bit of the fabric wallpaper with it.

"Hey, Cassidy, watch it."

"You can afford it. Do you realize what I just did? We can actually clip off part of the molecule. We can do it once, twice, dozens of times, and with complete accuracy. We use a restriction enzyme called EcoRl. It's like a biochemical scalpel. We can lop off a bit of molecule easy as pie. And remember we can read it now, so we know what we're lopping off. But here's an even better part. When we use this EcoRl, it leaves behind sticky ends. Beginning to get the picture?"

"No."

"Remember that poor kid with the big nose and the fat ass? Let's call the family the Murphys. All right now, Mrs. Murphy has passed her fat ass on to her son. Let's call him Evan, that's a nice Irish name."

"Scottish."

"Well, never mind. Mr. and Mrs. Murphy have got nine months to figure that out. Okay, now, we use our EcoRl to lop off Mrs. Murphy's ass genes. Isolate Mr. Murphy's ass gene and throw it in with the rest of Evan, along with some plasmids, tissue culture medium, nothing big. Then we go off and take a leak or have dinner or something and when we come back, just like a miracle, there are Mr. Murphy's buns, safe and snug, where Mrs. M's used to be. And we can do the same with Mr. M's nose. I tell you it's simple. Any high school student could do the rest."

Cassidy whirled around and waited for Mark to stand up and cheer, burst into tears, thank him for giving new meaning to his life. Instead he was greeted by a blank stare.

"Well," said Cassidy, "don't you see the implications?"

"For Evan, certainly. For me, no."

Cassidy fell into a torn-up Eames chair and shook his head. "Mark, you're looking at the most important discovery the world has ever known. Try and see it. Look, if we can fuck around with asses and noses, we can fuck around with anything. We can genetically engineer a whole new species. We can mate a cow with a horse, a petunia with a goldfish, an ape with a cobra. It's all possible. It's all being done right now, as we sit here. Scientists are changing the course of evolution."

Cassidy hesitated. When he spoke again, his voice was hushed and awed. "But no one is working on a human being. No one but us."

Mark sat up abruptly. "Unh, unh, I don't like it."

Cassidy flared. "You don't even know what 'it' is. How can you say you don't like it?"

"I read the papers. You're talking about cloning."

Cassidy laughed. "Cloning is rinky-dink compared to what I want to do." Cassidy paused. Understatement had never been one of his faults. "Okay, well maybe not rinky-dink. But cloning is just the reproduction of a cell that already exists. Imperfect, flawed man constructing mausoleums to himself."

"So cloning does exist, then?"

Cassidy smiled. "The only documented cloning was done on *Xenopus laevis,* what you might call a toad, by a guy named Gurdon in England. But let's put it this way, the technique is there and in countries like England and Switzerland so are the facilities. What do you think?"

Cassidy stood up and began pacing. His face was tight with intensity and need. "But what I'm talking about is something far greater than just cloning. I'm talking about making a perfect baby. A superman."

Mark started to laugh. "How about Batman? I always liked Batman better than Superman. All that changing in a phone booth was pretty dumb for a guy who was supposed to be smart."

"I'm not kidding, Mark."

"I can see that, my friend. That's why I am."

Cassidy began to pace even faster. His eyes were hot and the pupils were like two little pinpricks, as if he were on a drug. It was Cassidy's eyes that unsettled Mark even more than what he was saying. They were hungry eyes, blind to today or even tomorrow. They were the eyes of a visionary or a fanatic. They were magnificently riveting and yet terrifying.

"Just listen to me for a moment," Cassidy said. "We have the science today to create perfect, beautiful human beings. We can make Einsteins, millions of them. Great writers, great scientists, great philosophers. And they wouldn't have to be puny saps either. They could be beautiful, handsome human beings. Within a few generations, this world could be another Eden. And we can start it all. You and me."

Cassidy was no longer aware of Mark, so obsessed was he with the idea he was communicating.

"You and me, Mark. We can conduct the experiment. But more than that." Cassidy's voice became calm and reasonable, as if he were proposing a game of tennis. "Have you noticed that you and I would make one hell of a human being if we were put together? Well, I noticed it long ago. My brain, your body, a combination of the two of us. Created in the laboratory, in a test tube, then fed gland extracts, nurtured in the perfect fetal environment, super-oxygenated, watched carefully from the moment the first cell divided till we took him from his carrier. You notice I said carrier? But I'll tell you all about that later."

Mark's voice was full of fear. "You're crazy."

"If we don't do it, someone else will."

"Like the Nazis?"

Cassidy recoiled. He stood motionless for a long while. "You really believe that of me?"

"I don't know," answered Mark. "But in the least you're talking about creating a Frankenstein monster."

"I'm talking about creating perfection, not a monster."

Cassidy sounded reasonable, grounded. Mark wondered if what he had seen before wasn't just excitement. "How can we be sure?" he asked at last.

"Mark, we're not just throwing some things in a test tube, then taking a walk for nine months. We'll be watching its development at every turn. Believe me, no ordinary baby would get the kind of monitoring I'm talking about. If something goes wrong, we'll be the first to know."

"And if something goes wrong? Then what do we do?"

Cassidy didn't answer for a while. That was the

only part of the experiment he didn't like. "I guess we'll have to destroy it."

"Cassidy, go home. Take two aspirin, get laid, do anything, but don't do that experiment. It's wrong."

"What's wrong about it?"

"It's tampering with nature, for starters."

"Every step civilization takes is tampering with nature. The fact that the strongest and smartest are using birth control has changed evolution and done irreparable harm. Every time we give a guy a pair of glasses or a woman a fertility drug we're tampering with nature. In the jungle, half the people living today wouldn't survive past the first month."

Cassidy caught his voice becoming sarcastic and hard-edged. He was blowing it and he knew it. He slumped into a chair. "I'm not talking about horror story experiments, like crossing an ape with a man to make a nice hard worker, or any of the other garbage you hear about in the science underground. All I'm talking about is making one child, one perfect child. And with a little luck and a lot of pushing from us, maybe this one will be smart enough not to make war or screw up the environment or any of the other dumb things we seem to be doing."

"The Messiah, huh?"

"Yeah, that's right. Like he was the Messiah."

Mark leaned back and sighed. "No," he said finally. "I won't do it."

"Why?"

"I told you why. It's wrong."

"It's wrong. Or you're wrong."

Mark felt Cassidy's eyes burning into him. He got up and walked to the window. He pulled the heavy damask curtain aside and stared out into the garden.

"A little of both, my friend. A little of both. If you must know the truth, I really don't give a damn if this experiment is the Second Coming. As far as I'm concerned, the world is at liberty to blow itself to smithereens. I just don't give a damn."

"Then do it yourself."

Mark laughed bitterly. "As much as I don't give a damn about the world, I care a whole lot less about myself."

Cassidy watched Mark standing by the window, a pale and fragile victim of a world that was too hungry and frightened to notice he was dropping behind. "What's happened to you? Don't you remember how we used to talk about doing something great with our lives?"

"You talked. I listened."

"Okay. But you wanted it too. I know you did."

"As you said, wanting to be and being are two different things."

"No. Not in this case. We could do it."

"You mean you could do it. I don't know anything about science."

"You don't have to."

"That's just the point, though, isn't it?"

Mark stared out the window. There was another robin, or maybe it was the same one, working over the lawn.

Mark sighed. "Why did you have to come here? Why did you goddamn have to come here," He turned back from the window. "Find someone else with money. There are a great many of us around."

"We're friends."

Mark laughed but it was empty and flat. "I always hated you."

This surprised Cassidy.

"I can't believe you're surprised," Mark said. "I hated you from the moment we moved in as freshmen. You smelled of greatness, and I knew I'd never do anything." Mark threw a shrewd glance at Cassidy. "And you want to know something else? I think you always hated me too. Hated and envied me."

"I never envied you, Mark. Not in the end."

Cassidy felt as if the floor were lurching out from underneath him. He could see defeat smiling complacently from just around the corner, and he was beginning to realize there was nothing he'd be able to do about it.

Cassidy's stomach was a tight knot of pain. "I'll do it, you know. I'll do it with or without you."

Mark's voice was flat and expressionless. "Good luck."

Cassidy stood up. Everything was whirling in front of him, all his plans, hopes, dreams were spinning madly through the air, then breaking apart, shattering like glass, falling to earth in a million pieces. He couldn't even look at Mark. Mark made him want to puke. Cassidy walked to the door and stopped, clinging desperately to a faint glimmer of hope that couldn't have lit a closet.

"The chances were a thousand to one we wouldn't succeed. But let me tell you something, I'd sacrifice everything, my whole life if I had to, for that one chance. I don't care if there is a God and he condemns me to burn in everlasting hell, I'm not going to end up like the rest of you. I'm going to try."

Mark didn't even turn around. "Like I said, good luck."

"If I were you I wouldn't be giving any away. Be-

cause you are headed to the four-star loony bin with
fricassee of pink pill and designer straitjackets."

Mark didn't answer; he just kept to his window,
staring out at the lawn.

The buttery sun streaked across the grass and fell
on the gate, making it sparkle like a million jewels.
For the first time Mark realized there was no one
waiting there. "How did you get rid of all the people?"

"Didn't have to. They got bored. More fighting in
the Middle East, another Patty Hearst."

Mark nodded but didn't turn from the window. He
just stared out at the lawn and the blood-red lights
of approaching evening.

Cassidy slammed out and Mark felt the quiet closing in, hooded and endless, muffling out everything,
even the sound of his own heart. "I tried," Mark whispered. "Can't you see, Cassidy? I tried to make it."
But there was no answer. And his voice quickly faded
into the chilling deathlike silence.

Mark soft-shoed across the floor singing, "When
I'm sixty-four." But he'd forgotten most of the words,
and those he knew were quickly eaten up by the quiet.
He thought of checking into the Honolulu Hilton. He
thought of taking the *Concorde* to London and fucking every five foot six blonde from Edinburgh to
Portsmouth. Then he ran out the door, down the
long winding driveway, out the palatial front gates,
howling Cassidy's name.

Chapter 4

Cassidy was driving Mark's Porsche at top speed, his arm out of the window, his bushy hair rustling like wheat. Mark sat next to him. His window was also open. They were following an intestine of roads that wound and undulated over and under one another, futuristic roads, swinging around in broad, smooth arcs of glistening concrete. The tape deck up high, blasting Steely Dan's unexpected harmonies.

Mark stuck his head out the window and let the rushing wind pour over him. He could feel the tension that he had come to take as natural beginning to leave his shoulders and neck. His mind started to drift into the half-asleep, half-awake world of riding in a car. Snatches of daydreams and bits of remembrances became all jumbled up with the view. The usual regrets came rushing back, but they never got a chance to get their licks in because of a house or tree or a field of bright purple flowers. The warm wind blew through the car, lifting all thoughts and all anxiety with it, tossing them off to the side of the road as they whizzed past. It was perfect happiness.

Outside the window, the boxy, one-family, two-car houses that make up the greater Los Angeles area, the used car lots with their flapping banners, the industrial complexes with their packed parking lots, even the drive-in restaurants began to disappear. They were entering the country.

The soft, sweet perfume of grass and flowers filled the car. Even the air seemed warmer, calmer. Up ahead, the San Bernardino mountains rose like great, hulking black giants, and the road began to curve and wind as the countryside turned into foothills.

Mark knew that what he was about to do was crazy. Locking himself into his father's house had been minor league crazy compared to this. But he didn't care anymore. Maybe one day he'd come to regret his decision to go along with Cassidy. But that was in the future. For one perfect moment, he felt sane and happy. Anything that happened after this didn't matter.

Ahead Mark could see a thick rolling ceiling of storm clouds hanging over the San Bernardino mountains in folds, black and dense with rain. They followed the highway as it wound into the heavy hanging clouds. Cool damp air rushed into the car. A chill went through Mark, but he didn't close the window. It was a perfect day for a fire.

"Does the house have a fireplace?" Mark asked as he breathed in the heavy damp air with its scent of flowers.

It took a long time for Cassidy to answer. He too was wrapped up in his own thoughts and words seemed an intrusion.

"I didn't notice."

Mark waited for Cassidy to say more, but he didn't. For some reason Cassidy had been reluctant to talk about the house. Whenever Mark asked a question, even something as simple as how many bedrooms,

Cassidy would say he hadn't noticed. Mark figured the house had to be a pretty large one because so far he'd shelled out close to half a million for it and at least as much for a whole crew of workmen brought over from Mexico. He knew it was in the desert, about sixty miles from Las Vegas, though when he'd looked on the map, he couldn't find a decent-sized town near there. Beyond that, he knew nothing more.

It had been six months since he ran naked across the lawn and through the gates calling Cassidy's name. Six months of signing away his businesses and liquidating the assets of the Foreman empire. Six months and close to $3 million, but still he knew little more about what they planned to do than the day Cassidy explained it.

At first he'd been hurt and angry not to be included, but now, winding through the mountains with their heavy, hanging clouds, it only heightened the adventure. Besides, Cassidy had been more than willing to let Mark tag along as he purchased the laboratory equipment. They had spent days poring over catalogs, phoning manufacturers, walking through warehouses. Besides the heavy equipment they had needed like lab benches, a microsurgery chamber, a biological safety cabinet, a centrifuge, an incubation chamber, and a good-sized computer, there had been boxes of test tubes, tissue culture dishes, miles of Teflon tubing, notebooks, pencils, lab coats, chemicals that looked like Jell-O, chemicals whose smell made you nauseous, chemicals you couldn't smell at all, until cash registers all over the country were jingling.

Mark loved the sound of all those cash registers. He loved spending all that money. In particular he loved imagining what his father would have said about spending his fortune on some half-baked scheme. Suddenly it occurred to Mark that in fact Sol might not have disapproved. There was an egotism in this that might have appealed to him. He would have loved the idea of his beloved Formanowitz genes growing a superman. He would have wanted to preserve a bit of himself in evolution's hall of fame.

Mark shrugged off the momentary disappointment that his father would have approved of something he did and got down to the meat of the matter. Sol's genes were not being perpetuated; they were rotting under a grotesque stone monument at Forest Lawn. It was Mark's genes that were going to be blasted into the future. This was something that had absolutely nothing to do with the old man.

As the long shadow of Mount Baldy fell over the car, Mark's eyes began to close and he fell asleep.

An hour later, he woke with a start, just as Cassidy turned down a bumpy dirt road. Joshua trees rose all around them, twisted, gnarled silhouettes against the night sky. The moon was out and the scrub of the desert made dark blurry holes in the lighter rock and soil. There were no houses on either side of the road, and the desert stretched out eerie and empty into the wide, flat horizon.

They passed a broken-down barbed wire fence which seemed to be separating nothing from more nothing. Cassidy pointed to the land around them. "All this is ours," he said.

Mark looked out at the vast emptiness in stunned silence. Cassidy noticed his reaction and smiled. "One thousand acres," he added.

Still Mark didn't say a word. He just shook his head in disbelief.

Cassidy laughed. "See, I knew you'd love it."

"Not funny, Cassidy," Mark said angrily.

"Wait'll you see the house."

"I can just imagine."

"Oh, no, you can't," Cassidy's voice was full of malicious glee.

Mark looked back out at the moonlit desert. Except for the Joshua trees and dried scrub there seemed to be no life here. Even the insects that had stained the windscreen with their life's blood, so that they had to stop and wash their windows every few miles, weren't there. There was nothing to attract life. No water to quench thirst, no food to quell hunger, only dry dust and rocks, a few weeds sucking desperately for the tiny bit of moisture that remained, and vast emptiness.

Ahead was the hunched shadow of an enormous building. Cassidy turned off the road and onto an overgrown path toward it. The road was deeply rutted by what must have been the workmen's trucks, and the Porsche bounced in and out of the grooves, sending rocks and bits of weeds flying.

They drove through another barbed wire fence and pulled up in front of the building. Even the flat, empty land they'd been driving through hadn't prepared Mark for what he saw.

The building was large and square, like an old factory or warehouse. There wasn't a window that hadn't been broken; there wasn't a door that wasn't boarded up. The building was made from wood, and loose boards stuck out everywhere, curling from the intense heat, leaving gaping holes big enough for a coyote to walk through. At one time the building had been painted green. Through the years it had also been painted yellow, red, blue, and white. Remnants of all its past lives still stuck to some of the boards, flaking like dandruff.

Next to the large building were several dilapidated shacks. The only thing that predated World War I was the barbed wire fence that surrounded the whole complex. It looked new.

Cassidy was watching Mark, a devilish smile on his face. Mark swallowed hard, trying to remain a good sport to the end, but having a hell of a time of it. "Have you thought of going into real estate?"

"Don't worry, it's better inside." Cassidy laughed.

It was the laugh that got Mark. "For Christ's sake, you fucking moron, do you realize you spent $1 million of my money on this dung heap?"

"We need privacy."

"Privacy? Don't worry about that. No living thing is going to venture within a mile of this turd's nest."

Cassidy got out of the car and walked to the building. Mark didn't follow. He just sat in the car moaning.

Cassidy stopped when he got to the door and yelled back to Mark, "You coming?"

"Are there any snakes out there?" Mark yelled back.

"Mostly lizards."

Mark shuddered. "That's worse. I'm not coming."

"What do you expect? Godzilla? They're little things that scurry—"

Mark interrupted. "I hate scurrying. I hate it even more than slithering, and I'm not getting out of this car until you have the entire place exterminated. No, scratch that. I'm not getting out of the car, period. I'd rather sign myself into the booby hatch or, worse, go into my father's business."

Cassidy walked back to the car and leaned against Mark's side of it. "I never bought your crazy routine. And I'm not buying it now. Get out of the car and follow me."

Cassidy turned from Mark and walked back to the building. Mark watched him go, furious and yet somehow relieved. Finally he got out of the car and walked to the house.

Cassidy was standing at what must have passed for a front door when the building was occupied. The door was heavy, and Cassidy had to use his shoulder to push it open. Paint showered down on him and several loose boards fell to the hard desert floor before he got it open enough to allow them to pass through. In the distance, the crazy cry of a coyote cut the intense quiet, as they passed through the door into the black hole of the building.

Mark stood still, waiting for his eyes to adjust. He could hear Cassidy scrambling around in the dark somewhere nearby. After a while he heard the striking of a match, and in the flare of light, Mark saw Cassidy was lighting a kerosene lamp. He didn't even bother to mention that for the amount of money he'd shelled out, they should be able to bring the midnight sun to a city the size of Detroit. He was beyond seeing any humor in the situation.

With the coming of light, Mark saw that they were indeed inside an abandoned factory. Heavy machinery, draped with cobwebs as thick as damask, loomed all around them. It looked as if no human being had been there in decades. There were no cigarette butts, beer cans, nylon stockings, used condoms, none of the debris that told of man's having crossed this territory.

Cassidy walked across the rickety floor, holding the lamp up, a pale yellow beacon fighting the darkness. A loose hanging board from one of the walls fell down, and Cassidy replaced it in its precarious position almost as if he wanted it to look that way, then continued to a ladderlike staircase, winding down to what must have been the basement. He paused, looking back at Mark, then started down.

Mark took a deep breath and followed. The loose rungs creaked under his feet. One of them loosened and for a second Mark expected to fall through to the floor below, but miraculously it held.

Cassidy disappeared down the stairs with the light. Mark steeled himself and followed quickly. As frightening as the stairs were, the dark seemed even worse.

As Mark climbed down, he clung to the wall. It took him awhile to realize that under his hand, a soft, wispy film completely covered the paint. In the dim light he was able to discern that the film was spider webs. Still he continued; keeping up with the disappearing light was all that mattered.

As Mark reached the basement, he saw Cassidy working on the lock of a huge steel door. There was a click and suddenly everything was intensely lit. After the darkness, the light was so blinding that Mark couldn't see for some time. There seemed to be glass everywhere, reflecting itself in sparkling points of light. It took close to a minute for his eyes to get used to it and even when they did, he wasn't sure of what he was seeing for a while.

In front of him was a laboratory, staggeringly

futuristic, as complicated and foreign as those glimpses of a space capsule one got on television.

Mark gasped, "My God!"

"Wait. Just wait." Cassidy led Mark into the brightly lit laboratory.

As Mark entered he could see it wasn't just one laboratory but a series of them, divided by a lead glass partition, making a lab within a lab within a lab.

"What you're looking at is three laboratories," said Cassidy. "Each one is at a different air pressure. The outer room that we're in is at zero air pressure. This is the room where we'll keep our supplies and do our housework. The next lab is at negative one air pressure. It will be our working lab for the most part. The last lab is at negative two. If there's anything we suspect might be a problem as far as biohazard, that's where we go. Because of the different air pressures all the air travels toward the last lab and out a filtered ventilating system."

Cassidy walked around the first room, pointing to shelves of supplies. He opened a door and showed Mark a room with two large steel sinks and a huge machine that looked like a giant washing machine. "This is an autoclave. It cleans by steam under pressure. You'll soon become real familiar with it, believe me. Scientists use more glasses than a good-sized bar on Saturday night."

He opened a steel door and revealed what looked like a meat freezer. To Mark's surprise that was what it was. "We gotta keep a lot of things cold," said Cassidy. He let go of the door and it slammed tight and locked.

Cassidy opened the first lead glass door and led

Mark into the main lab. Two laboratory benches cut
across the room, each with its own intercom, Geiger
counter, microscope, bath shaker, fractionator, and
small centrifuge. Along the walls were rows of
chemicals, tea trolleys, an X-ray machine, a Haynes
decompression chamber, two hoods, and a large centrifuge. Above their heads a Ping-Pong ball in a glass
tube was showing the air pressure to be negative
one.

"Watch," said Cassidy as he walked to the light
switch. For a second they were plunged into darkness,
then Cassidy threw another switch and the whole
room was bathed in blue light. "Ultraviolet to kill
germs." He pointed to several chains hanging from
the ceiling. "Those are showers. You'll find them all
over. If you spill anything on yourself that you're
worried about, pull the chain. But only if you're
worried. They make one hell of a mess. Anyway,
most of the time you'll work under one of these."

Cassidy walked to one of the hoods and lifted its
glass front. "Once again, negative air pressure, so air
circulates in and up. But don't worry. We won't be
working with anything too dangerous. And if there's
any risk at all, we'll be in the next lab."

Cassidy walked toward the third laboratory. Instead
of a lead glass door, he walked to a black floor-to-
ceiling cylinder, the width of outstretched arms.
There was a red triple-ring symbol on the black drum
and a red light over it. Mark had seen the same em-
blem on containers of chemicals they had bought. It
was the warning mark of biohazard.

Cassidy opened a small closet and pulled out two
laboratory gowns and paper booties. He put his on
and waited until Mark had done the same. Then he

walked to the black cylinder and slid it open. The red light began to flash. Cassidy walked into the cylinder and motioned for Mark to follow him.

Cassidy slid the door shut and for a moment they were plunged into darkness, then Cassidy slid the opposite panel open and they were in the last laboratory. Once again it was brightly lit, but thick black shades hung above the glass for the times they would need darkness.

Running the length of one wall was a biological safety chamber, which looked like a lab bench enclosed on all sides by glass. The only opening into the chamber was two small holes covered with a soft plastic—just enough room for a man's forearms. On the back wall was a microsurgery cabinet. Once again, this was enclosed in glass, but instead of armholes, there were remote controls that seemed no less complicated than the cockpit of a 747. Inside the theater, instruments were attached to mechanical arms that would deamplify the movements of the man doing the surgery.

Cassidy shook his head. "Christ, I wanted to buy an electron microscope, but at a cool one hundred and fifty thou, I couldn't justify it. Besides, you can only use dead samples and you have to slice them so thin it's almost an art. But I did get a nifty microscope you don't need to use slides with." He was talking out of a strange urge not to feel what was happening. And his voice drifted off into silence.

The room became totally still except for a soft humming which seemed to come from underneath their feet. Mark decided it came from a generator. It would take a complex power system to run the air filtration, heating, and cooling of the labs. Mark remembered he'd even seen a telephone in the front room. There was no question this was one awesome lab.

Mark looked around, stunned by the complex machinery. The sparkling glass and plastic, the intricate machines, the colored liquids seemed mystical and unreal, more improbable even than the revolving surgical table and retractable roof of Doctor Frankenstein. Yet it was real. And it was his. Mark felt a rush unlike any he'd ever experienced.

Cassidy and Mark entered the black cylinder and walked out, throwing lab coats and booties into a special hamper outside the door. Mark watched Cassidy's back as he walked toward the outer lab. If Mark was awed by what he saw, he couldn't even begin to imagine what Cassidy must be feeling.

But Cassidy was a man blinded by the light of his dream, and in fact he was numb, beyond any feeling at all. While he'd been planning the laboratory, even while he was supervising the workmen, he'd been so involved with the minutiae of it, so oriented toward problem solving, that he hadn't stopped to think what he was doing. But now, after taking Mark through the completed laboratory, Cassidy began to grasp that the dazzling, overpowering future he'd been running toward was in front of him. All along he'd been able to contemplate the end, but the beginning was too magnificent, too overwhelming, too real, and he couldn't even think anymore.

As Cassidy and Mark passed into a long dark hallway, a low grunting came from farther down. Mark turned to Cassidy in question, but his only answer was a small knowing smile.

Cassidy walked toward the loud noise and opened a

door. The room was large and, except for a thin corridor that ran the perimeter of it, completely surrounded by iron bars. Grasping the bars, jumping up and down with a loud series of squeals and grunts, was a gorilla.

As Cassidy entered, the gorilla shook the bars and chattered loudly in greeting. Mark watched in amazement as Cassidy opened the cage and made a whole sequence of hand signals to the animal. The gorilla turned, looked at Mark, and made several gestures back. Then Cassidy walked out, leaving Mark alone. The cage was unlocked, yet the animal stayed where it was and Mark could have sworn it was staring at him. Mark quickly turned and left, unsure why he found the sight so disturbing.

Cassidy had opened the door of the next room and was standing in a small bedroom, with two beds, dressers already filled with clothes for both of them, and a small bathroom.

Cassidy stood in the middle of the room, his lips stretched into a huge grin. From the next room they could hear the gorilla, and Mark thought he could even feel the room shake as it jumped up and down.

Mark started to laugh. At first it was only a giggle, but it built rapidly until he was staggering around the room, holding onto the dresser, the walls, anything for support.

"Jesus Christ, Cassidy." Mark could barely get the words out. "Jesus fucking Christ. You really had me going there before."

Cassidy also was laughing, doubled over, clutching his belly and gasping for breath. "Your face," Cassidy whined. "You should have seen your face when we pulled up to the house." Laughter over-

took him and he collapsed onto the bed, panting
loudly.

Mark staggered toward Cassidy, laughter rolling
over him in great waves. He grabbed hold of Cassidy's
neck. "I should kill you, you crazy son of a bitch. I
really should strangle you." Mark was shaking so hard
from laughter he could hardly hold onto Cassidy.

Suddenly Cassidy grabbed Mark around the waist
and floored him. The two men rolled on the floor,
trying to wrestle one another but mainly roaring
and bellowing like two bull moose. They wrestled
playfully for several minutes. For the first time in
years, Mark felt as he had when he was a child, so
full of energy and joy it was almost painful. A whole
future he couldn't even begin to guess at lay ahead
of him. The bustle of days working on a secret experiment, the quiet of long evenings far away from the
city stretching in front of him for months, perhaps
years. It made him feel boyish, energetic, full of life,
and he realized just how much those feelings had
vanished out of his life.

The two men fell back, exhausted and gasping for
air. Mark couldn't believe he'd resisted Cassidy's plan.
He felt like running out of the door and howling
through the desert, stark naked. He felt like stretching out in the warm blue-black desert, letting the
night breeze ripple over him. Mark stood up and
stretched.

Suddenly there was a noise at the door. It opened
and the gorilla stood on the threshold.

"Hi!" said Cassidy matter-of-factly. Mark watched
dumbfounded as the gorilla closed the door and
shuffled over to Cassidy.

"This is Molly," Cassidy said formally. He could

have been at a dinner party at the White House. "Molly, this is Mark."

Cassidy again made hand signals to the ape. It watched Cassidy solemnly, then turned to Mark. In fact, the ape too was exhibiting manners worthy of a presidential audience. Only Mark was showing bad manners, standing in the middle of the room, his mouth gaping.

"You'll hurt her feelings, Mark. Say hello."

"Cassidy, get off it, okay? It's too damn late for any more games."

"I'm serious. You think gorillas don't have feelings? Molly does. Don't you, Molly? She's real sensitive. So wave hello."

"I will not."

Cassidy's voice grew serious. "I'm not kidding, Mark. Apes get depressed, and Molly can be as bad as a housewife with three kids in diapers. Now, wave."

Finally Mark waved, but it was a small one and full of irony, and he quickly retreated into getting undressed for bed.

"How much do you know about gorillas?" Cassidy asked as he followed behind Mark who entered the bathroom.

"Well, I don't think they like peanuts, they can be dangerous as hell, and Darwin says they're our ancestors." Mark found two toothbrushes and toothpaste. It was even the brand he used.

Cassidy laughed. "That's it?"

"More or less." Mark's mouth foamed with toothpaste.

"To start off, they do like peanuts, if they're raised right they aren't dangerous, and they're more like our brothers than our ancestors."

"Great. I always wanted a brother. I used to ask my mother for one all the time when I was a kid." Mark walked back into the bedroom.

"Did you know apes can talk?" asked Cassidy right at his heels. "Well, they can. Not with their voices. Unfortunately, their vocal cords aren't as well developed as ours. You can get a chimp to say 'Mom' or 'cup' but that's about it. It took a long time and a couple of psychologists named Gardner to figure out it was the pharynx and larynx and not their brains that were at fault."

Again Cassidy made several hand signals to Molly. "It's called Ameslan, that's short for American deaf and dumb language. And with the proper training chimps like Washoe and Lana and gorillas like Coco can talk. Not just a few words either but whole sentences, inventive ones, too. Lana once called her trainer a 'green shit.' Our Molly's been trained by the best. Her vocabulary is close to 200 words and growing every day. Watch." Cassidy's hands flew through the signals. "I just told her, 'This is Mark. Molly and him be friends.'"

Molly signaled back and Cassidy started to laugh. "Damn ape just corrected my grammar!" He shook his head, amazed. "Honest to Christ, she just signaled back 'Molly and he be friends.'"

"You mean you're really serious?" Mark asked incredulously.

"Absolutely. Molly can understand, speak, and like I said before, she can feel emotion. Sometimes pretty strong emotion. On top of that, Molly is so biologically similar to a human being that some scientists think it's possible to mate an ape and a man and produce a viable offspring."

"Now wait a minute, Cassidy. I know it'll be lonely out here, but that's going a little too far."

Cassidy laughed. "You idiot. I didn't spend $100,000 just to fuck her. She's our mother. There are only one or two amino acids that are different and their gestation period is a week longer than ours. But biochemically we're the same animal."

Mark lowered himself to the bed. "You can do that?"

"I'm banking on it. For years America's been transporting cow fetuses to Europe in the wombs of live rabbits. Easier than shipping the cow, you know. There's only one problem I can foresee, and that's the head. A human baby is born with an enormous one, big enough to hold that fabulous brain we've evolved. They say that's why women have trouble in childbirth and most animals don't. Anyway, we may have to take the baby Caesarean. Other than that, I can see nothing stopping us."

Mark looked at the gorilla, whose serious black eyes watched him from under the ridge of her forehead, her leathery hands hanging still by her sides. Molly moved away from Cassidy and began scooting around the room, her movements at once bestial and yet disturbingly human. Mark noticed that her belly was slightly distended and her nipples stood out, hard and rigid.

"Is she pregnant?" Mark asked.

"Not really. But her body thinks so. I've been injecting her with hormones to prepare her."

Cassidy saw a shiver pass through Mark. He couldn't really blame him. In the beginning, he too felt the revulsion. But it had only been for a short time, and now that he knew Molly, he thought of her as another person. In fact, he was beginning to like Molly a good bit better than most of the people he met. Except Schaftner. A wave of sadness swept over Cassidy when he thought of Schaftner. He couldn't get those eyes out of his head, the scared animal eyes, scanning the room.

"There are going to be things that bother you, you know." The understanding in Cassidy's voice surprised Mark.

"I hadn't really thought about it recently. Yes, I suppose there will be."

Molly stopped her investigation of her surroundings and stood in the middle of the room watching Mark. Gathering courage, she moved toward him, leathery knuckles scooting her along. She stopped in front of Mark and began signing.

Cassidy laughed. "She says, 'Mark, please tickle Molly.' She likes to be tickled. It's become sort of a sign of affection."

Molly stood close to Mark. He could feel her hot breath on his arm, he could smell her hot animal smell. She had her head slightly cocked, looking at him with curiosity mixed with fear. There was almost the feeling that she sensed she repulsed him.

Suddenly Mark realized it wasn't the fact that Molly was an animal that disturbed him as much as how human she was. Her eyes were small and her heavy forehead threw a shadow over them. Her nose was flattened against her face, so that it was little more than two large nostrils in a pad of flesh. Her mouth was a wide, lipless slash. Taken separately, each one of her features looked nothing like a man, and yet together it was the face of someone very human indeed. Even the thick black hair that sprouted from her skin and her black leathery hands were somehow human.

It reminded him of an exhibit he had seen as a child. Human fetuses from the age of one month to birth were enclosed in glass bottles, pickled in formaldehyde, ranged along a shelf. Real babies, curled tightly within themselves, their skin polished and green-white. If those babies had been made of plaster, even if they had just been pictures, he would have walked out of that museum and never thought of them again. But those babies had been real; they had all been alive at one time. Some of the older ones might have even had names and rooms waiting for them with musical mobiles over their cribs. "Is there no alternative?" he asked.

Cassidy shook his head. "She's our best shot. Actually our second best. The first would be a human subject. But that would be too risky."

The word *subject* jarred Mark in the same way the sight of Molly had. He knew scientists used it all the time, and yet the word kept coming back to him.

"Besides," said Cassidy, "we couldn't trust anyone else knowing. That's why I had to go to Mexico for the workmen and carefully planned the decor upstairs in the factory. As far as this area goes, we just don't exist."

"Why?"

Cassidy shrugged. "Like I said, we need privacy." But Mark's eyes were already back to Molly. Cassidy watched carefully. It was important that Mark begin to feel comfortable with her. She would know the difference.

"Why can't we use an incubator?"

"There isn't one in the world that's really good

enough. Besides, Molly's alive. She moves, her heart beats, her stomach growls, she has emotions. I don't know how important all that is to shaping a baby's personality, but it's gotta go for something. And we can restrict Molly, monitor her. So she's the best of both worlds."

"Was this the ape Schaftner was going to use?"

"Schaftner was going to use an incubator. But Schaftner would have failed." The moment Cassidy said this, he realized he'd known all along that Schaftner was going to fail. Had he also felt that it would be he who succeeded? Even then, had everything been working toward this conclusion?

Mark reached out tentatively and touched Molly's swollen belly. "I can't believe it."

"Don't worry about good old Molly. She'll be great. Look at her. Doesn't she seem happy to be pregnant? Next thing you know, she'll be calling for pickles and ice cream."

Mark shivered. "Not yet, okay, Cassidy? Let's just give me a little time on this one."

"No second thoughts?"

"Second, third, and fourth thoughts. But I suppose I'll get used to them. I may even get used to her." Mark smiled and slowly put out his hand to Molly. She waited a moment, as if trying to make sure the gesture was genuine, then tentatively she reached out her hand to Mark and touched his.

Cassidy watched them, then his eyes drifted around the room, taking in everything. Finally he turned back to Mark and Molly and smiled.

"We start tomorrow," he said softly. "Tomorrow is day one."

Chapter 5

Sy Sheinberg stood in the bathroom of the Sheinberg Diner, lining up his morning vitamins. Meticulously he placed 500 milligrams of C along the side of the washbasin; fifteen garlic pearls took the curve and blended into a regiment of E's, followed by A's, high potency B's, kelp, and brewer's yeast. He filled a paper cup with water and began mowing them down.

When he was finished, he splashed his face with cold water and wiped away the dust. Even though he hadn't been outside more than thirty seconds, he was covered with it. That was the way it was in the desert. Not the clean white sand people expected, but dirty, gritty dust. It got into your shoes, your hair, under your nails, in your eyes; he suspected it even got into your soul after a while.

Sy carefully wiped his face dry with a paper towel. As he glanced into the mirror, he saw another face behind his. It was a white, drawn face, even more wasted than his own, yet faintly similar.

"So you've come," he said without surprise, then looked out the window. His eyes moved through the early morning darkness over the 100 yards to what he called "the big house," a run-down clapboard affair that was neither big nor all that much of a house.

Still, since it and the diner were all he had to show for twenty years of work, he guessed he could call it what he wanted.

The door of the house opened and Sy's wife Sally bustled out toward the diner. A few seconds later, Becky, the waitress who had become more like a daughter to the Sheinbergs, loped out. Becky was wearing her usual ten-gallon hat pulled low, baggy jeans, and an old cowboy shirt which completely hid her seventeen-year-old body and made her look like an animated scarecrow. A great sadness came over Sy as he realized how much he would miss Sally and the strange tomboyish girl who was like a daughter.

Sy turned back to the mirror. "So this is how it all ends, eh?" Sy shrugged philosophically. The specter shrugged back, and Sy thought he detected a slight grin. "All right, then, do your worst. I'm ready."

Sy clutched at his heart and staggered over to the toilet, remembering just in time to lower the seat. He slumped into a sitting position and waited, certain that this time he'd bought it for sure.

Sy heard the screen door slam, then the clattering of Sally and Becky as they opened the diner for breakfast. He didn't bother to call out to them. They'd find out what happened soon enough. And somehow, now that the chips were down, he wanted these last few moments to himself.

Sitting on the toilet, waiting for the Grim Reaper, Sy tried to make his whole life play out before his eyes, like a TV rerun. But nothing happened. The faucet was dripping and the noise kept interfering with his thoughts. He felt like crying. It was bad enough ending his days in the can of a broken-down diner that was all he had to show out of life, but he wasn't even going to be allowed the dignity of a re-playing of his life or some last words; there wasn't even enough room to make a halfway decent fall.

Five minutes later, he was still waiting. Sy pulled himself up and walked back to the mirror. He squinted, and once again the white-faced specter squinted back at him. Sy nodded, in some strange way reassured, then staggered back to the toilet to wait.

Suddenly there was a knock at the door and Sally called, "You in there, Sy?"

Sy shook his head in anger at the disturbance but said nothing.

There was another loud knock. "The ice cream freezer's on the fritz again. I called Jim but he says he won't be able to make it out to fix it before late after-noon."

Still Sy remained silent. "Sy," Sally yelled, "the Rocky Road's running faster than the Colorado River in spring."

Sy felt the world closing in on him. There he was, facing the most important moment in a man's life, and instead of a choir of angels, he got his wife screaming about a busted ice cream freezer. He closed his eyes and tried to concentrate on the inevitable.

"Sy, are you all right?" Sally's voice was high-pitched and anxious.

Sy remained where he was, rigid, expectant, mutter-ing to himself, "I'm ready now. Do your worst."

Sally began battering at the door, crying out des-perately, "For God's sake, Sy, speak to me."

Sy's concentration was shot. "Dry ice, woman. Go get some dry ice!"

"I can't find none. You put it away last time Richard's delivered."

Sy got up, threw open the bathroom door, and glowered out. Sally stood in the doorway, her face red and tense. "You okay, honey?"

Sy pushed past her and walked into the dining room. "As good as I'll ever be," he grunted.

Sally followed behind him. "Maybe you need an enema."

Sy walked to the grill and switched it on. Perhaps he'd die later that evening. It was probably better that way. There'd be another day's receipts to help Sally and Becky over the hump.

That he would die, if not now, then within the next few hours, was unquestionable. Sy Sheinberg had a bum heart. He also had a bum liver, bum arteries, and bum bowels. In fact, there wasn't an inch of his body that didn't have something wrong with it. The only thing Sy didn't have was cancer, and he lived in mortal fear of it, investigating every mole, every pimple for signs of the end. That he hadn't croaked years ago and was still walking around, a pale stick of a man in his middle forties, was a source of constant amazement to him. Still, he was positive that every day was his last.

Sy greased the grill from the coffee can of drippings and placed the baskets in the deep fryer. It was getting hot already, and the sweat stood out on his forehead like blisters. He wiped his face with the back of his arm and silently cursed the desert which had been his home since he'd moved west from Brooklyn, a young man of twenty-three with one heart attack already under his belt.

Oddly enough Sy remembered that period of his life as the golden days. The minute he'd recovered from his attack, he sold the small shoe factory he inherited, rented a U-Haul, and he and Sally had headed westward. For two weeks they bumped through mountains, cornfields, and eventually salt flats, in a style not much above the original wagon trains, except they had Magi-Fingers in their hotel rooms and burnt almond Good Humors every afternoon.

Five miles outside Felicity, California, Sy's Dodge blew a valve. They took it as an omen. Felicity was a small desert town of less than a thousand people with two main streets, one traffic light, a five-and-dime, three banks, and what Sy considered to be a great future. Feeling the strong hand of destiny guiding him, he snapped up a diner just outside of town on what was then the major artery between Las Vegas and Los Angeles but what proved to be, within the next year, only an auxiliary to the freeway that was being built.

Within a few months, Sy began to realize that the diner he bought might not turn out to be the rousing success he had anticipated. But by that time he wasn't left with a multitude of options. He'd sunk just about every penny of his nest egg into the buying of the diner, and what hadn't been spent there had gone into replacing the old wooden tables and chairs with brand-new red plastic booths and matching formica tables. He had also spent money to replace the old sign with a flashing neon one that said Sheinberg's Diner. The grill had to be completely overhauled, new menus printed, paper napkins and mats bought. The meat man was a thief and the produce man wasn't much better. The result was that by the end of the year Sy found himself up to his Italian leather boots, the only thing left of his factory, in debt. The past twenty years had been spent slowly paying everything back.

Through it all, Sally had been a rock of strength. Sally Sheinberg was one of those robust, pink-cheeked, jolly women who are always smiling, always have a good word, and always have a pot of coffee going—a woman too good to be true. But behind those dimpled smiles, kind words, and everlasting pots of coffee was something worse than a person who was always grumbling—there was the professional martyr. She bore her misfortunes like a cross, always with a smile but with just that hint of sadness in her huge browns that told you you didn't know the half of it.

Sy shifted several bags of dry ice into the freezer and allowed the cool air to brush past his face. Once again he saw the shadowy head leering at him from the stainless steel.

"All right, all right, I know my number's up," he sighed. "But no one says I gotta see your kisser everywhere I look." He slammed the freezer shut and found Becky behind him, leaning against the counter in that funny, half-child, half-woman way she had.

"I saw a sports car up by the factory." She was trying to appear nonchalant, but Sy could see the excitement and curiosity all over her freckled face.

He shrugged and walked back to the grill, scraping back the brown bits from the last meal, but everything was collapsing inside him. That look of excitement could mean only one thing. He glanced over at Sally and could see she was thinking the same.

Becky walked over to the grill and stood over Sy's shoulder. "I told you something was going on at the

factory. Last time I went up there to shoot rabbit I
saw all those tire tracks and footprints. I knew something was going on. I knew it."

"The factory's been closed for twenty years."

"Not anymore."

Sy shook his head but didn't turn around. Becky
had been talking about people in the deserted factory
for weeks. And while he didn't believe a word of it,
he didn't at all like the idea that Becky felt the need
to make up tales. To him it spelled a desire to find
adventure and a meaning to life which could only
end in her leaving them forever.

Becky had come to the Sheinbergs two years ago,
a sullen, long-limbed girl who took the job as waitress
and quickly moved into their hearts. Where Becky
had come from, what her life had been like before,
was something she refused to talk about, but it hung
over the Sheinbergs like a cloud. They lived in mortal
fear that one day someone would knock on their door
and claim Becky as their own. They also lived in
mortal fear that Becky would fall in love with one of
the guys passing through in a semi. The possibility
that she would one day leave was a thought that tortured them constantly.

Until now their worries had been unfounded. Becky
showed no interest in the world beyond the boundaries
of the diner. She kept close to home and had no
friends. Boys didn't seem to interest her. All she
wanted was to work as little as possible, sit on the
porch watching nothing in particular, and go to bed
on clean sheets. It wasn't that Becky was feebleminded
or lazy; she was like an injured bird.

"Maybe we should go over there," said Becky brightly. "Bring them some menus. You know, sort of drum up business."

"Since when are you interested in drumming up business?"

"I'm just curious, that's all."

"Curiosity killed the cat." Sy emptied a bag of frozen french fries into the baskets and started them prefrying. He tried to appear as uninterested as possible, but his mind was reeling. It occurred to him that Becky's sudden interest in the world should please him. How often had he and Sally tiptoed into Becky's room and watched the sleeping little girl, shaking their heads in concern? How often had they planned short excursions to a Fourth of July parade or a county fair just to see her show only half the interest she was showing now? Guilt swept over him, but it was quickly replaced with anger. He liked things just as they were. Why did life always have to change?

"I'll bet they're burglars," said Becky as she jumped on the counter and swung her legs back and forth. "I saw this picture once where these aliens took over a town, and no one knew they were there except this little boy. And no one believed him until it was too late."

Sally shot Sy a meaningful look and sighed dramatically. This addition of burglars and aliens seemed to be the clincher. Still, there was nothing to do but play along and hope it was just a phase she was going through. "Maybe you better go down there and take a look."

Sy laughed. "Don't tell me you believe all that malarkey?"

"It can't hurt to take a look," Sally said, raising

and lowering her eyebrows with deep meaning. "Nine times out of ten it ain't nothing but some kids. But they shouldn't be allowed up there either."

"I ain't going nowhere. So let's have a little peace and quiet."

Sally bit her lip and lowered her eyes. "Anything you say, darling."

Sy went back to scraping the grill. Why was it Sally always called him "darling" at precisely the moments when he wasn't?

Becky jumped off the counter; never had Sy seen her look more like a five-year-old picking a fight. Again the guilt and the anger.

"I think you don't want to go 'cause you're scared," she said.

"Like hell I am," growled Sy. But deep down he knew what she said was true. Sy's friend, the specter, scowled back at him from behind the shiny grill; he knew it too.

In truth, Sy was scared all the time. The heart attack he'd had did more than scar his heart, it scarred his whole outlook. Illness had spread through his life, bleeding out into the corners until death was everywhere, frosting his hair, stooping his shoulders, seeping darkness into light, and leaving him no peace from the first light of dawn until the sweat-soaked nightmare-filled night.

He looked over at Sally, who had averted her eyes as if she'd just seen something she couldn't face. Becky was staring up at him. "All right," he said at last. "I'll go up after dinner." He turned back to the grill, telling himself he could only die once. The reflection of his friend nodded in agreement. Sy almost threw a spatula at him.

"I want to go too," Becky said with excitement.

"Over my dead body," snapped Sy, noting grimly that this was a very real possibility, then rushing over to the fries, which had a heavy cloud of smoke rising from them.

While Sy was battling with the baskets of burning potatoes, Cassidy, in a pretty fair imitation of Humpty Dumpty, sat perched on the lab bench, looking around at the $2 million worth of equipment just itching to be used. Every inch of his body was alive and expectant; his mind was racing weeks, even months ahead; it took a monumental effort to drag himself back to today, day one, the morning of the beginning.

"Okay," said Cassidy, "I've broken down the experiment into five stages. The first stage is simple. We're going to take epithelial cells—those are mouth cells—from each of us and culture them."

"Any particular reason we're using epi . . . mouth cells?" Mark was really trying, bent over a steno pad like an eager student. Again Cassidy felt a strong tie to his frail partner.

"Good question," said Cassidy enthusiastically. "We need cells that have a rapid turnover. There are other kinds of cells we could've used like liver cells or bone marrow or even cancer."

Mark shivered.

"Yeah, I know. That's why we're using mouth cells. They're easier to get at, and anyway, how can you tell a kid that his dad was a cancerous mole?"

"He's not going to be too pleased he was a mouth either."

"We'll let his shrink work that one out, okay? Now, next we culture the cells. Do you know why?"

Mark shook his head. For a moment he looked panicked, like a school kid being asked a question to which he had no answer.

Cassidy smiled reassuringly. "Remember I told you all cells have the entire programming of a human being in them? Well, there's one catch. That program is in sort of a holding pattern. Otherwise we'd be growing new bodies all over the place. And instead of your toes growing more toes, it might get down to work on brain or thyroid. So the rest of the program is shut off by biochemical suppressors. Our problem is to switch on what was switched off. We do that by culturing. For some reason, the next generation and the one after that have a better chance of being undifferentiated."

Mark's hand was flying across the page. While Cassidy waited for him to catch up, he again looked around his supersonic laboratory. In his mind he was already working away, jabbering to himself like a monkey as he always did, throwing the switch on the centrifuge, holding test tubes up to the light, shaking them gently, and seeing the whole universe in one gray ghostly cell.

Mark's eyes were on Cassidy and again he was dragged back. There was no question Cassidy was having a problem with the here and now. He continued, "When we get our undifferentiated cells, then we move into Stage Two. That's where I break the backbone of the DNA with the restriction enzyme I told you about before, unite the two portions of our DNA into a new cell, and make the Mark-Cassidy cell."

"More likely the Cassidy-Mark cell if I know you."

Cassidy nodded. "Petty but true. After that we take

a live human egg, suck out all its genetic information, and stick our cell in there."

"And then?"

"We bite our fingernails and wait. If we're still on target, it shouldn't take long to get to the blastula stage. That's when we have thirty-eight cells with trophoblast cells, those little pincer-type things that help the embryo attach to the lining of the womb."

Mark looked up amazed. "You mean it will be an embryo?"

"By that time it will be a he."

"Alive?"

"Of course alive. What do you think we're doing, growing potatoes?"

Mark shook his head. But in truth he suspected that until now he hadn't considered this experiment as anything more than an extremely expensive lifeboat. He looked around at the sparkling glass and futuristic machinery and felt a trembling deep within his body.

Cassidy jumped down from the lab bench and started to pace with electric energetic movements. "Stage Three is implantation. Now I gotta admit, I'll be sweating that part. Although I know that Molly and I are biochemically almost the same animal there may be some crazy difference I know nothing about. Anyway, next is Stage Four, the growth period."

"That at least sounds straightforward."

"Don't bet on it. I plan to do a lot of things to help the baby along in that stage. Then Stage Five is birth."

Mark stopped him, not quite ready for Stage Five. "What kind of things?"

"Growth hormones, oxygenation, things that are going to make little X better than the sum of his parts. But I'll explain all that when we get to it."

Mark watched Cassidy for a long while. There was something in his face he didn't like, a coldness, a hard determination. It was the face of a man who, in order to accomplish something great, had to make himself less human. He suspected God might have had just such a look when he was planning the earth.

"Hey," said Cassidy reading Mark's concern, "we aren't going to do anything terrible. Believe me."

Mark forced a smile. "It's just everything seems so . . . I don't know if bizarre conveys the meaning."

Cassidy wasn't listening. His eyes were on the future. "It'll be terrific. Don't worry about a thing." Cassidy clapped his hands together as if he were getting ready to sit down to a bang-up meal. "So, are you ready?"

Mark nodded slowly. In the end, it was Cassidy's experiment. It was impossible for him to make judgments on something he knew nothing about; making judgments on the known was difficult enough. Finally Mark put out his hand and said, "Good luck."

"Luck has nothing to do with it," answered Cassidy. He didn't see Mark's extended hand. He was already headed for his lab gown.

The setting sun cast a pink haze over the desert, turning dried shrubs and pale earth a glowing pink, softening everything so that the ugliness and barrenness seemed to disappear and the land was more beautiful than any Mark had ever seen.

Lying nude in the still warm sun, a gin and tonic in one hand, nothing on his mind, exhaustion relaxing his body, Mark felt almost whole. True, he had never been so tired in his entire life, but it was a satisfying tiredness. His feet hurt, his mind was spent from thinking and listening, his back ached from bending, but he had done more in this one day than he had in the entire twenty-four years he'd been pissing and moaning around this earth.

A breeze kicked up, nudging tumbleweed, rustling the dried scrub. Behind him, Mark could hear Cassidy bounding through the factory, on his way outside to share the last little bit of sunlight.

Cassidy raised his arms over his head and stretched to release twelve hours of tension, then lit up a joint to speed the process along.

He stopped. Far out on the horizon was a faint haze of dust, rising from the flat wasteland like a line of smoke. Cassidy stood, rigid and alert, like a dog scenting an intruder. "Someone's coming. We better get inside." Cassidy's voice was hard-edged and insistent.

Mark opened his tired groggy eyes and glanced at Cassidy. "Why? What's the problem?"

"I told you I want privacy."

Mark shrugged. "They'll see my car anyway, so we might just as well stay here."

Cassidy kicked at a rock, sending it spinning out into the flat desert. "Jesus, how stupid can I get? How the hell could I forget about the car?"

"I don't understand. What's the difference if people know we're here?"

"They might be just a hair curious about what we're doing here. You want to try explaining it?"

Mark thought about that. "It sounds a bit crazy, I guess."

"Remember your first reaction to the experiment? Well, take that and multiply it by an IQ of seventy-five."

"Oh boy. Shades of Frankenstein. So what do we do?"

The question hung in the air like the line of dust which was slowly materializing into a red pickup truck bumping through the grooved path. A few seconds later the truck drew up to the factory in a cloud of choking dust and stopped.

Cassidy was walking toward the intruders when Sy shouted from the safety of the truck, "Stop where you are." There was unmistakable hostility in his tone, and Cassidy obeyed, standing hands on hips, eyes screwed up against the red sun.

Becky rolled down her window, stuck out her head, and waved. All Cassidy could see was a ten-gallon hat, a crooked smile, and a slim young arm. "I'm Becky, from the diner up the road."

Without giving Sy a chance to react, she threw open the door, jumped out, and began walking toward Cassidy. Just as she reached him, she caught sight of Mark, lying face down, hugging the ground to hide his nakedness. She stopped, startled more by his handsomeness than his nudity. He reminded her of one of those smooth marble statues that you wanted desperately to touch, though you knew the feeling under your fingertips would be cold and lifeless.

Sy's body stiffened as he saw Becky staring at Mark. "Leave her alone," he yelled.

Becky didn't turn. "They ain't doing nothing."

"I don't care what they're doing. Get back in here!"

Sy sat stewing in the truck, watching the men

through infuriated red-rimmed eyes. He told himself to get out of the car and show all of them a thing or two, but his muscles felt like Cream of Wheat and there was a lump in his throat the size of a regulation football. He was scared, and to make matters worse, he didn't know why.

Cassidy began walking toward the truck again. "Hey, we aren't doing anything wrong."

"Stop where you are!" Sy repeated. His hand reached up to the rifle on a hook above his head. Cassidy caught the gesture and froze.

"Now, Becky, get in here!" This time his voice carried more authority and Becky slowly backed up toward the truck. She hesitated, then reluctantly got in, slamming the door sulkily. "Roll up the window!" barked Sy. Becky pouted but rolled it up, leaving a crack open so she could hear.

Sy slipped out of the truck cautiously, keeping his rifle ready at his side. "All right, you two. Get your hands up!" Sy smiled to himself as he saw Cassidy's hands shoot into the air. In all his forty-five years, he'd never felt so in control. Sy gestured with the rifle. It was an imposing gesture and he delighted in the forcefulness of it. So this was what the National Rifle Association was talking about.

Mark continued to hug the ground. "I'm naked," he whimpered plaintively.

Sy ignored him. "What the hell are you doing here?"

Cassidy tried to keep his voice reasonable. His mind was racing, trying to figure out how he was going to get them out of this one. "It's our land. We bought it last month."

"This shit patch? You think I'm an idiot?"

Cassidy had the urge to laugh. It was not a healthy urge, he decided. "You don't believe me, talk to Quinn Savant in Lancaster. He sold it to us."

"Like hell. Now, up against the wall. And that perverted bare-assed friend of yours too!"

Cassidy glanced at Mark whose desperate eyes were pleading with him to say something. "No. It's our land," Cassidy said softly.

"What's that, punk?" Sy shifted the rifle until it was pointed at Cassidy's head, but he could feel his jaw quivering. Everything was beginning to disintegrate. He had no intention of using the rifle, and even if he had, the fact that it wasn't loaded would have presented a slight problem.

Cassidy, noticing Sy's hesitation and feeling the tide shifting, began walking toward him. "You're trespassing," he said.

Sy's hands were trembling. "I told you, up against the wall." The implied threat seemed as limp as two-day-old parsley. Still, he clutched the rifle, hoping that something would come up to save him. Perhaps this would be a good time to die.

Once again Cassidy sorted through his brain, this time emerging with a plan. All at once his face became a solemn confiding mask. "If I was you, I'd be careful where I aimed that thing. My friend's . . . nervous. You know what I mean? You see, he just got over, well, you know. He had a nervous breakdown." Cassidy had lowered his voice to almost a whisper.

Sy froze. His fingers were dripping moisture and he could feel the butt of his rifle slipping in his hands.

Cassidy shot Sy a confidential look. "Nothing to

worry about, you understand. Still, he does get so upset." Cassidy yelled back to Mark. "It's okay, buddy. Nothing to get uptight about. Just some neighbors paying a little visit."

Mark caught on immediately and whined back, "They're trespassing, Cassidy." Mark would have loved to drool, but decided that was going a shade too far.

"Now, now, Mark. We've got to be neighborly."

"Some neighborly," growled Mark. He allowed his eyes to roll in his head. "That guy's got a rifle. I saw it."

"No, no," Sy said quickly. The corners of his mouth were drawn up so high they almost touched his anemic eyes. "This is just for rattlers."

"Some neighbors," Mark spat out. "And me, as naked as a peach."

Cassidy held up his hands. "Now, calm down, Mark. This nice man doesn't mean any harm." He turned to the nice man in question, who suddenly had to go to the bathroom with a vengeance. "You don't mean any harm, do you?" Cassidy finished off with a glance that was meant to convey the fact that Sy had better humor Mark.

Sy, however, needed no prompting. His lips curled back and he flashed a friendly smile. "Hell, no." He was laughing amiably. "No harm. No harm at all."

"See," said Cassidy to Mark, "now just sit back and relax, old buddy."

"Sure, Cassidy." Mark's head bobbed up and down like a marionette. "Okay, I'll just sit here and look at the pretty sunset. But you'll tell them to go away, won't you?"

"Sure thing, pal. Don't you worry." Cassidy turned

back to Sy. "My friend needs lots of peace and quiet, if you get my meaning."

Sy whispered hoarsely, "Is he dangerous?"

Cassidy hesitated ever so slightly. "No, no, I can't say he's really dangerous. Just a bit touchy. Actually, you could say he's as good as gold most of the time. He only gets testy when he thinks people are taking advantage of him."

Mark picked up on it. "Why is it everyone always takes advantage of me?" His voice was high and shrill.

"Easy, Mark. Easy."

"Easy there, Mark," echoed Sy.

"I think it would be better if you left," Cassidy said significantly.

Sy nodded vigorously, then started backpedaling to his truck.

"See," Cassidy called to Mark, "the nice man is leaving. I told you there wouldn't be any problem, didn't I?"

"Is he really leaving now, Cassidy?"

"That's right, Mark. See how he's moving back to his truck? A real nice man, Mark. Very neighborly."

"He's trespassing!" Mark screamed.

Sy reached his truck, leaped in, and threw the lock. He stuck his head out the window as he started it up. "He won't be coming into town and making no trouble, will he?" Sy felt a lot better with a couple tons of steel around him.

Cassidy felt a stab of icy pain through his heart as he realized he might have talked himself into more trouble than he thought. He laughed quickly and shook his head. "Believe me, all he wants is to stay away from people. As long as we're left alone, I can promise you won't hear a peep out of us."

Becky watched, wide-eyed. She leaned over Sy and asked in a quivering excited voice, "Did he murder anyone?"

Sy pushed her back into her seat, threw the truck into drive, and took off in a cloud of dust.

Mark jumped up, smiling. "Brilliant. Absolutely brilliant. A beautiful weaving of fact and fancy."

Cassidy nodded, but he was watching the receding line of dust. "I think we better get a dog."

"Hey, relax, they won't be back."

"Maybe." Cassidy continued to stare at the horizon and there was a look of something pretty close to fear on his face.

The molten sun slipped away, leaving blue-black evening shadows everywhere. A cool breeze kicked up. Without another word, Cassidy broke off and walked back to the house, leaving Mark feeling slightly jumpy in the quickly falling night.

"Cassidy, please tickle Molly. Please tickle Molly."

It was late at night and Cassidy and Mark were both asleep, exhausted from a week of work that began at five in the morning and didn't end until seven at night. Only Molly was awake, sitting in the middle of her cage room, making hand signals to the wall.

Molly knew Cassidy was asleep and all the hand signing in the world wouldn't bring him to her, but she did it anyway. It made her feel better to at least express what she felt.

Quickly Molly tired of signing and grabbed the bar over her head for a few good swings. She was hungry. She checked her bowl lying below her, but it was empty. It was her own fault. She always ate everything up quickly, hunched over her bowl possessively, and then the long night would stretch on with nothing to eat. She saw herself hiding a bit of banana away. But she'd seen that image before and done nothing about it.

Molly sighed and let go of the bar, allowing herself to drop to the floor. She touched her belly. It felt slightly rounder than it used to be. It had been like that for some time. How long she didn't know. Cassidy had tried to explain time to her, but she couldn't quite get a hold of it. You couldn't touch time or see it, but Cassidy said it was there. It didn't matter anyway because she had forgotten what she was thinking.

She felt bored. Bored was a new word. Cassidy was always saying it to her when she wanted a tickle or a hand talk. He would sign, "I am busy. You are bored." After seeing the new sign repeated again and again, Molly began to associate it with feeling sad.

Yesterday when she felt bored, she'd tried to hand sign to BooBoo, the new Doberman, but BooBoo was stupid and didn't understand. Cassidy said he'd never understand. There was a time when she was stupid and couldn't hand talk either. Time. There it was again.

Suddenly Molly remembered what she'd been thinking. Her stomach felt funny. But there was something else, something frightening and close to pain.

Molly concentrated on the feeling that sometimes was making her dizzy and scared. She had tried to tell Cassidy about it, but she didn't know the words, like when she was stupid. It was bad not to have a word. It made her feel lonely.

Molly scooted over to her toy box and started

rummaging through it. She found her ball, then remembered, no ball at night. She put the ball back and pulled out her picture book. Picture books couldn't talk, but she could look at them for company. She plopped down on the floor and leafed through the pages.

She found a picture of a monkey and pointed to it, then she signed, "Me, picture. Me, picture." She pretended Cassidy was behind her laughing. "Funny," she signed, spreading her lips and trying to imitate his laugh. "Me, funny." Then she nodded like Cassidy always did, and again felt sad. Pictures couldn't talk. Dogs couldn't talk. They were stupid.

Molly sat there for a long while, but it was still night and she was still alone. Molly wanted Cassidy to come out and tickle her. There was a new man with Cassidy now. Mark. Mark let her eat all the time. He talked to her a lot. Cassidy was always busy, but Mark got out the picture book and sat with her while she hand talked to the pictures.

Molly threw her book aside. She was bored and her stomach was round and sometimes she didn't feel well.

Then suddenly it was there, the feeling that scared her. Molly felt a wrenching in her heart. The dizziness swayed her body. She began to sign, "Molly feels not well. Molly feels not well." But no one came.

Molly put her arms around herself and clung tightly. She felt scared and she wanted Cassidy. There was a strange feeling inside her chest, as if it were moving. After a while the feeling passed but not the fear. It clung to the darkened walls, leering at her with sparkling jungle eyes.

Molly stood up shakily. Maybe if she bounced her

ball Cassidy would come out. He would get mad, but he would come out, and then he would be there, and she wouldn't be so frightened.

Molly scooted back to her toy box and pulled out the red ball. She hesitated, thinking how angry Cassidy would be. But the loneliness seemed even greater than the punishment he would give her, and she bounced the ball again and again.

Finally Mark came out of the bedroom, groggy, his blond hair standing on end, his eyes two slits in his tired, sleep-puffed face.

"Stop that noise, damn it!" Then, remembering Molly didn't understand voices, he signed for her to stop.

Molly looked at him innocently, but Mark knew that she was faking it. He was gaining a healthy respect for Molly's intellect. He opened the lock on Molly's cage, walked in, shoved the offending ball under his arm, and walked out, slamming the cage door angrily.

He glanced back and saw Molly signing to him. "Mark tickle Molly? Mark tickle Molly?"

"No!" signed Mark, but he smiled fondly. Cassidy had been right. Almost immediately, any revulsion he'd felt had disappeared and he was deeply interested in Molly. What could she tell him about? What other worlds did she live in? What did sex feel like to her? And love, did she feel love like human beings?

Molly was sitting in the middle of her cage like a great overgrown baby, signing. "Mark, please tickle Molly." But it was clear from her face that she had little hope of any tickling going on.

Mark put down the ball and walked back into her cage. Molly's face lit up. "Mark tickle Molly?"

Mark found himself laughing as he reached down to tickle Molly, though whether he was laughing at himself or Molly he wasn't sure.

Murphy's Law states: 1. Nothing is ever as simple as you think it will be. 2. Everything takes longer than you expect. 3. If anything can go wrong, it will, and at precisely the wrong time.

Cassidy sat hunched over the microscope. He could feel the blood coursing through his veins. Hot flashes of anxiety swept across his body, and he felt like he was going to vomit at any minute. Stage One of the experiment was a simple, straightforward procedure, a mundane culturing of epithelial cells in ordinary tissue culture medium. Any high school student could do it, and in fact Cassidy had done it so often it was almost second nature. And yet below him were petri dish after petri dish of spoiled cultures.

Cassidy remained motionless, straddling his chair, staring down into the microscope. Behind him, the wall clock was ticking loudly; he could hear Molly in the next room, jabbering and bouncing up and down.

It hardly took much thought to know that the cultures were spoiled because Mark had been careless. Perhaps he had forgotten to wear rubber gloves or hadn't exactly followed the procedure for autoclaving glassware. Any number of tiny mistakes would be enough to start bacteria on that first commandment of life: Go forth my children and multiply. Which they had, with a vengeance.

Of course the mistake could be easily rectified. They would lose some time, but at least Mark would have learned a valuable lesson at one of the easier stages.

A mistake later would be much more crucial. There was really nothing to get too upset about.

Nevertheless, Cassidy didn't move. He heard Mark enter the laboratory and move from vat to vat of EcoRl, feeding the bacterial menagerie its evening meal. Cassidy had to hold himself down; at this point, nothing short of the death sentence would satisfy his anger. Yet he knew if he so much as yelled at Mark, he'd reduce him to a quivering mass of hysteria. Mark was scared enough as it was, tentative, shaking. The slightest criticism could reduce him to tears. Never had Mark cared so much about anything; never had he felt such a need to please. He was like a child.

That thought didn't help much. Cassidy still felt like strangling him. Then, quickly following the anger, the real feeling lurched up at him, grinning like a hyena. Cassidy was scared. It was a new feeling, and Cassidy turned it over and over in his mind with disgust and fascination.

As much as Cassidy had talked about the possibility of failure, he'd never really believed in it. But now he could feel failure pulling up a chair and sitting down next to him in the lab, dipping its spiny fingers into the cultures, putting its moth-eaten head close to the microscope and delighting in the damage.

If Cassidy couldn't even make sure that the simplest part of the experiment proceeded well, how the hell could he hope to perform the greatest scientific feat in the history of man?

The sands of hysteria shifted, and mountains slipped back down to molehills. Still the possibility that he might fail sat with him. Certainly Cassidy had always been aware what success would mean. All his life he'd shielded himself against pain by telling himself that

one day he'd be important, special, probably even
great. What did it matter if he was disliked or ignored?
What did it matter if he was a bastard or poor or had
acne or if he'd blown it by puking on his date's lap?
He would be great one day. Suddenly he realized
just how much of life he had postponed, bargaining
on his ultimate success. But Cassidy was mortal. People failed. Cassidy could fail.

He glanced at Mark, who smiled a greeting, then
began readying the centrifuge for what was supposed
to have been the culture cells. Mark was watching
him, unsure what was going on, suspecting he'd done
something wrong but hoping against hope that he
hadn't. "Is anything the matter?" he asked softly.

Cassidy's resolve weakened. He heard the tentative
quavering of Mark's voice, felt Mark's attempt to hide
his fear, and went nuts. He whirled around in his
chair and blew his stack. Mark had introduced him
to something he had never felt before, failure, and
once introduced, it would never entirely leave him.

It was getting dark and Mark was drunk. His foot
felt like a cement block on the accelerator, his mouth
was dry and dusty, but the feeling of opening the
Porsche up and racing it through the quickly falling
night was dangerous, tilting, breakneck adventure
that Mark had missed since he'd resolved to try to be
sane.

The faster he went, the better he felt, in control,
sure. Holding the steering wheel, a couple of drinks
in him, he was an astronaut, a mountain climber, a
deep sea diver, a man of command and purpose. He
pressed even harder on the gas.

As he turned onto the dirt road leading to the

factory, there was a sudden burst of color, a startled face, a scream. Mark jerked the steering wheel around, sending the car spinning out, catching in one of the deep ruts in the road, jolting forward, then spinning around in the opposite direction.

Flashes of Joshua trees, boulders, sand, the front of his car, tipped and whirled madly. The thought that he was about to die, the irony that it was happening just when he was beginning to get it together, drummed slowly under the panic. The idea that he couldn't stop thinking even when he was dying appeared, burst, and was replaced by the knowledge that this was the big jolt.

The car slowed and the landscape reassembled. Mark heard himself say, "Jesus!" but it sounded like someone else's voice. He didn't know how long it took before he began to become aware of his body. His head was resting on the steering wheel. Pain came next. He touched his forehead and felt blood.

He jerked his head up and glanced in the rearview mirror. It was just a scratch. He wondered vaguely about the rest of his body, but he didn't try to move. Everything had happened too fast; he needed time to catch up. Then Mark remembered the face and the scream. How much of what he'd seen and heard was real he didn't know. But the memory of the pale startled face and the terrified scream kept coming back.

He looked around and saw emptiness. The Joshua trees stood out, gnarled silhouettes against the deepening night. There was a terrible smell of rotting cantaloupe. It took Mark some time to remember the groceries he was carrying in back.

It was obvious there had been no face, no scream.

Whatever it was that caused him to panic was in his own booze-soaked neurotic mind. He saw himself, hands grasping the steering wheel, his foot pressing the accelerator and his scrambled brain filled with dreams. He decided once again he really was an asshole.

Suddenly he felt someone watching him. He whirled around and saw a small, young face at the window, pale and ghostly in the rapidly falling night. Smeared with dirt and what looked like blood, the face seemed to belong to a savage. The savage's hands were pressed to the window and Mark caught a glimpse of a rifle and the limp body of a dead jackrabbit in them.

It took close to a minute before Mark realized the face was real. He rolled down the window and saw a small frail girl watching him, terrified. Her face was indeed covered with dirt and traces of blood.

"Oh God," Mark gasped. "Your face."

Becky wiped her face with the back of her arm. "I just tripped. I'm okay."

"Running from me." Mark felt like he was going to puke from the drink and his own nauseating, self-destructive personality. "I was driving too fast. It's one in a long list of unattractive qualities of mine."

Becky didn't move. Standing in the darkness with the rifle and dead rabbit, there was a brutality to the young girl that startled yet intrigued Mark. "It was my fault," she answered. Her voice was haunting.

Mark reached over and opened the passenger door. "The least I can do is drive you home."

She hesitated, caught in the headlights like a startled fawn.

"If you don't mind," Mark continued, "I'd prefer if Bunny stays behind."

Becky looked down at the limp body she was carrying, then back up at Mark, confused. "I only kill to eat."

Mark shivered. "That is hardly reassuring. Either for Mrs. Rabbit and all her little orphaned babies, or, for that matter, me. In truth I like to think that meat is born in the supermarket in nice, neat, bloodless plastic."

Becky watched him, wide-eyed, the profusion of words overpowering her. Mark saw her shrink and hated his cleverness. Word upon word, piling up, meaning nothing.

"Come on. Get in."

Becky dropped the rabbit, still staring at him in that crazy, trancelike way, then hobbled to the other side of the car.

"I thought you said you were okay."

Becky shrugged and got in, cowering into her seat. Mark looked over at the slim, young girl with auburn hair, startled green eyes, and a faint sprinkling of freckles across the bridge of her childish nose. He realized both that she was extremely pretty and that she looked familiar.

"I know you, don't I?" he asked as he started the car.

"Sy and me came by the other night."

"That's right! The kid."

"I'm not a kid. I'm seventeen."

Mark laughed and turned to find Becky watching him seriously. There was no way to read the look on her face, yet Mark was surprised to find himself unsettled by it. He quickly threw the car into drive and drove back to the road.

There was silence, Becky neither daring to look nor

speak to him. The memory of Mark with amber evening light on his body had stayed in her mind as something to take out at night and look at. Men like
Mark were not only unattainable; they were from a
different galaxy. And yet underneath it all was the
knowledge that she had caused this meeting and
everything that was happening now was of her own
making. She trembled as she thought of how she had
dreamed of meeting Mark and had actually gone onto
the land knowing she'd see him.

Becky's hand went to the door handle. "You can stop
here. I live nearby."

Mark slowed the car but there was no house in
sight. "Where?"

"Just down the road."

"Then I'll take you just down the road."

"You'd better not. Sy'll get upset."

Mark smiled. "Daddy's little girl?"

"He's my boss. I don't have a Dad."

"We all have Dads. Only some of us are lucky and
never meet them."

Becky didn't answer and once again Mark regretted
his flippancy. "How about your Mom?" he asked. "Do
you live with her?"

Still Becky didn't answer. Visions of her mother,
pressed tight to a wall by a man, her torn dressing
gown open to his probing hands, flashed through
her mind. Cold, dark, empty corridors, her mother
coming home angry and tired from work at a coffee
shop; being hurt and vowing not to cry yet wanting
to kill until she actually wished her mother dead
and had to run in case it ever happened. She shook
the thoughts out of her mind. That was the past.

"You like chatting about your family, don't you?"

Mark glanced over at the young girl, but she was staring down at her hands. He could see how sensitive and shy she was and found something charming in that.

Finally she looked up at him and asked softly, "You're laughing at me, aren't you?"

"Not in the way you think," Mark answered. He was enjoying sitting in the car next to her. There was something clear and fresh about her innocence. It made all the sophistication and grace he was used to seem overripe. But underneath the soft childlike freshness was a sad, tortured look. It had been there when she insisted the accident had been her fault and it was there now. It was profoundly moving.

Mark stopped the car at the diner. Inside he could see Sy working over the hot grill and Sally ringing up a check. They both kept glancing out the windows into the black night.

"Would you teach me to shoot that thing?" Mark indicated the rifle, wondering why in the hell he was saying that.

Becky shook her head and seemed to shrink even deeper into herself. "I'm trouble." Again her face had that haunting look.

Mark laughed. "First you cause the accident, now you tell me you're trouble."

"It's true. I have dreams and . . ." Becky stopped. There was no way of explaining what she meant; she hardly understood it herself.

"We all have dreams."

"Mine happen."

"So?"

"I caused the accident. That's all." Becky began

to open the door, but Mark stopped her with his hand. He turned her toward him.

"Well, well, I never thought I'd meet someone with a bigger guilt complex than I."

"It's true," she insisted.

"Of course it isn't."

"You see, I always have these dreams, and they come true. One time . . ." She stopped, turning away.

"One time?"

"Nothing." She again tried for the door, but Mark was holding her hand, and when she turned back the look on his face made her continue. "I've even wished bad things."

Mark smiled. "Welcome to the human race."

"I mean like people getting hurt."

Mark felt her trembling under his hand, but her eyes were wide and innocent and clear. "And what happened?" he asked. He was almost afraid to hear the answer. He remembered the rabbit.

Becky hesitated, then started to giggle. "Nothing."

Mark looked over at Becky's freckled face, lit up with delight. He was thrown off balance, and searched her eyes to see if she was making fun of him. He decided she was not. He shook his head. "You're a strange one, aren't you?"

Becky turned away and he sensed there were tears in her eyes. "Hey, come on," he said. "No one is stranger than yours truly."

"Are you really crazy?" The words were out of Becky's mouth before she had a chance to censor them and she blushed and shifted in her seat. She saw the look of surprise on Mark's face and continued quickly. "I mean, that's what your keeper said, didn't he?"

"A keeper is in the zoo."

Becky wanted to jump from the car and run. For a brief moment, she had felt comfortable and sane. The years of anger and abuse with her mother, the years of hiding away at Sheinberg's had all fallen away and she'd felt secure. "I don't go around people much," she said softly. "And when I do, I always say the wrong thing. I'm sorry."

"In answer to your question . . ."

Becky interrupted. "Oh, please, don't answer it. That was a crazy thing to say. You see, that's what everyone used to say to me. That I'm crazy. And they were right. I mean, not dangerous, but crazy. You know what I mean?"

"In answer to your question," Mark continued, "it's tough for me to admit, but I'm afraid I'm certifiably sane. Weak undoubtedly, lazy certainly, but sound of mind. And I've got a feeling the same goes for you."

Again Becky's face lit up. "You do?"

Mark laughed, but he was disturbed by the smiling wonder on Becky's face. He felt a strong urge to take her in his arms but restrained himself. "Come on, I'll help you to the door." Mark got out of the car and opened Becky's door. She climbed out stiffly and Mark was surprised to find himself shaky on his feet. He put his arm around her waist and together they limped to the brightly lit diner.

Shuffling around the kitchen the next morning, stirring pots, separating strips of sizzling bacon, measuring coffee, Mark felt whole. At first he'd resented the fact that most of the cooking fell to him; now, walking around the bright cheerful blue and white kitchen with its tiles and scrubbed wood furniture, he realized he enjoyed it. Twice a week, he'd leave the house early in the morning and drive to a supermarket in an out-of-the-way town. He loved pulling tins from the shelves, poking at chickens, plotting out the next week's meals, then bringing his treasures home and arranging them neatly on the shelves and in the refrigerator. It made him think of generations of men, hunched over fires, roasting sizzling flesh, telling great tales.

Cassidy was down the hall in the bedroom, still asleep. Mark decided to surprise him with breakfast in bed. The thought of bringing in a steaming mound of buttery yellow eggs delighted him. He pulled the eggs out of the refrigerator and cracked them against a bowl, filled with the wonder of how much he'd changed.

As Mark was beating the eggs, his eyes caught sight of one of the ten Geiger counters placed throughout the basement. It was registering right off the dial. He walked over, picked up the sensing device, and checked his hands, then the kitchen counter. The needle fell quickly until it registered no radioactivity. "Damn machine," he muttered, making a mental note to tell Cassidy it was broken.

Mark was about to turn back to his eggs when he stopped. There was the feeling that something was moving near the Geiger counter, something very small that he only caught out of the corner of his eye.

He slowly scanned the kitchen counter. A long line of red ants moved along the floor and up to the wall. Mark cursed to himself. Red ants were bigger than the black variety and their bites packed a hell of a wallop. He reached under the sink for the bug spray, and wasted a good thousand of them, smiling with vengeance as the army fell defeated. He wiped up the dead bodies with a paper towel, and was about to left-hook them into the garbage when his hand passed over the Geiger counter. The needle shot up. Mark stopped where he was. He picked up the sensing device and slowly moved it over the entire kitchen. It registered minimal radioactivity, until he passed the wadded-up paper towel with its ants who were beginning the process of returning to their maker. The needle went right off the dial.

Mark ran to the bedroom. He grabbed Cassidy by the shoulders and shook him awake. Cassidy growled, pulled his pillow tight over his ears like a bonnet, and rolled onto his stomach. Mark shook him even harder. "Something's wrong. There're red ants in the kitchen . . ."

Cassidy interrupted. "Who gives a shit?"

"Cassidy, I think they're radioactive."

Cassidy rolled over and squinted at Mark. "I told you not to throw any radioactive diapers in the kitchen garbage."

"I didn't."

Cassidy pulled himself out of bed, not quite believing Mark, and followed him into the kitchen with a sullen look. Mark walked over to the paper towel and pulled it open, then moved the Geiger counter close. The needle went off the dial.

"You're sure you didn't bring anything radioactive into the kitchen?" Cassidy was watching Mark, anxiety beginning to make a meal of his guts.

"I'm sure."

Cassidy stood, stunned for a moment, then turned

and ran to the lab, Mark just behind him. "You take the right half, I'll take the left," he yelled.

"What are we looking for?"

"Ants, for Christ's sake. They picked up the radio-activity from somewhere."

"Jesus, Cassidy, what if they got it from here?"

"You better pray they did. 'Cause if they got it from the inner laboratory, there's no telling what damage they've done."

Cassidy scoured every inch of the floor, then turned to the ceiling. After several minutes he stopped in the middle of the room, his eyes wild and frightened. His heart shivered and shook his chest; fear clutched at his throat until he felt like he was gagging. He stood, swaying and trembling, his startled eyes seeing nothing. Then, suddenly, he rushed through the darkroom door into the inner lab. Mark followed behind.

The ants started at the back wall and moved in a straight line across the floor, up the wall, making a perfect corner and finally ending in a circular loop that covered the perimeters of the lab bench.

Cassidy rushed to the incubator and pulled out one of the cultures. Floating inside was a dead ant. He threw the culture to the floor, sending liquid and glass crashing around the room. Then he pulled out another. Inside were more ants, radioactive ants, killing everything around them. Again he pulled out another petri dish, but all the cultures were the same, and Cassidy threw them against the floor violently.

Finally he stopped and stood in the middle of the lab, his shoulders heaving. "If I hadn't slept late . . ." he broke off; his voice was expressionless and his face a rigid mask.

Mark looked at Cassidy, crushed and terrified, standing amidst the broken glass. He held out his hand. "Cassidy, there was nothing we could have done. It wasn't our fault."

But Cassidy walked past him. "From now on, there'll be no more mistakes. I'll make sure of it." Cassidy entered the black drum, slid the panel shut with a loud slam, and passed into darkness.

Chapter 6

Cassidy sipped a cup of foul dishwater coffee and stared out the window of the twenty-four-hour coffee shop in downtown L.A. Street lamps splashed liquid pools of light onto the black streets. Once in a while, an old lady, immune to the revving motors of cruising kids or the leers of men on the prowl, would walk by the window. For the most part, though, the sidewalk was deserted.

Cassidy looked up at the clock. It was after midnight. Leeland was almost an hour late. Every time the door opened, Cassidy looked up anxiously, but it was always a hooker in a green afro or a pimp in a pink suit.

Cassidy ordered a slice of apple pie, more out of boredom than hunger. It looked like the glue he had used in grammar school. He played with it for a while, then ate it. Panic was rising inside of him. Maybe Leeland wouldn't come. No, he told himself, he'll come. Although Leeland was never terribly reliable, utimately he usually did what he promised in his own good time, especially at the right price.

Cassidy tried to empty his mind and concentrate on his breathing, but the panic kept pushing through

in brilliant agonizing flashes. Ever since the radioactive ants and the subsequent loss of another two
weeks, Cassidy had been getting the crazy sharp anxiety
stabs with increasing frequency. Suddenly he'd feel
his heart pounding and his fingers shake, perspiration would flow, and beads of it would stand out all
over his chilled face. He tried everything he could
think of to gain control over them. It seemed a simple thing; everyone knew the mind could control the
body. And yet those stabs were there to remind him
sometimes it was the other way around.

Cassidy took a deep breath and reviewed his reasons
for being uptight. Except for such earthshaking questions as will the experiment work and what right had
he to make the experiment at all, he found none. He
had lost a few weeks, but in the end, he'd success-
fully cultured the cells. Then, in a feat not unlike
the creation of the world, he had broken the back of
the DNA, tested that he had the right parts of the
molecules by gel electrophoresis, and placed the two
different segments of DNA in petri dishes with some
plasmids, *E. Coli,* and culture medium. All he could
do now was wait. He'd made twenty-five separate little dishes of Cassidy-Mark. He'd be happy if one of
them took.

The door of the coffee shop opened. It was a couple
of truckers, and once again the panic gripped him.
Cassidy began to talk to himself reassuringly. "Now,
don't worry, he'll come. Have another piece of pie
and by the time you're done, good old Leeland will
walk through the door and everything will be okay."

But even this brought little relief, and by the time
the door opened and Leeland finally loped in, Cassidy's body was a quivering mass of tension.

Leeland looked around the coffee shop with red, swollen eyes. He was a tall, rangy man with a greasy ponytail and thick curly sideburns that melted into three days' growth of beard. He wore ripped jeans, a psychedelic T-shirt, and the expression of a man who'd gone way beyond the limits of stoned to a brand-new territory.

Cassidy smiled and waved to him. In the five years Cassidy had known Leeland, he had hardly changed at all. Cassidy doubted he ever would. He could imagine him as an old man, the top of his head bald but a scraggly gray ponytail hanging down his back. He'd be another one of those men that haunt the health food shops of L.A. buying kelp.

"Hey man, how ya doin'?" Leeland slapped Cassidy's palms and flopped down opposite him, tucking his knapsack under the table. Without waiting for an answer, he reached across the table and drained Cassidy's cup of coffee, then made a face. "Swill!" He motioned to the waitress to bring him his own cup. "So, where ya been?"

Cassidy shrugged. "I'm living out in the country." He was trying to slow himself down; it was a losing cause. "Have you got them?" he asked impatiently.

"Hey, relax, ole Leeland ever let you down?"

Cassidy repressed "all the time" and nodded.

"Even threw in a little treat. Sinsemillia. Far out stuff."

"Where are they?" Cassidy could feel his leg moving up and down, doing the nervous rag.

"Whew!" Leeland snickered. It was a stoned snicker, and Cassidy was wound tighter than the hair of an afro. It was not a winning combination. "What's the matter, coked up?"

"Yeah, yeah, that's right." Cassidy thought that was a better explanation than the real one.

"Far out. Got any more?"

"No. Listen, I really want to see the . . ." Cassidy felt an overpowering urge to turn around and see if anyone was watching. He knew it was ridiculous. All he was buying was live human eggs. But while Cassidy knew what he was doing was not strictly illegal, he could hardly classify it as altogether ethical.

Leeland worked in a hospital where it was easy to procure all manner of supplies and equipment not ordinarily found on the shelves of supermarkets. There were a lot of Leelands around. Whether the hospitals and morgues knew about them or not, Cassidy didn't know. He suspected they did.

Leeland took a large gulp of coffee and shook his head. "Jesus, man, how can you drink this shit?"

"I'm in a rush Leeland, okay?" Cassidy's face was an intense knot.

Leeland watched him a moment. "Yeah, sure." He reached into his knapsack and pulled out a small parcel. "It's on dry ice but get it into the frig ASAP."

Cassidy put the package on the seat next to him and counted his money under the table.

"What do you need them for?" Leeland was watching Cassidy with curiosity, but Cassidy's mind was elsewhere.

"Morgue or hospital?" he asked abruptly.

Leeland looked hurt. "Hospital, man. I only deal in the best stuff, you know that. Ole Leeland doesn't dig that graveyard scene." He let out a huge horse laugh. "Get it? Dig? Graveyard?"

Cassidy tried for a laugh. "Great, great. How old are they?"

Again Leeland pulled a face. "Hey, fresh. Like you reached up into some chick in the back seat of a Ford and pulled 'em out yourself. I told you, ole Leeland only deals the best. Matter of fact, I'm thinking of branching out. You know, diversifying. Sperm, eggs, all them small supplies don't pay me enough to live on hardly. And you know me. I got my eye on a really far out eight-track system and a pair of Bose speakers." He leaned over the table and whispered to Cassidy. "I got a job at County now. Possibility of some organs, if you need 'em." Leeland paused. Underneath the ponytail and orange T-shirt beat the heart of a businessman.

Cassidy handed him the money under the table.

Leeland took the money and recounted. "Livers are pretty easy. So are glands. Jesus, they just throw 'em out over there. I figure to a guy like you, glands would be pretty interesting. Fair amount of uteruses . . . uteri?, too. Not in such great shape, though. But maybe for research. Hey, you never told me what you need them eggs for."

"Oh, just a little dissecting. I've pretty much given up science. I just like to mess around once in a while."

Cassidy got up to leave, but Leeland stopped him with his hand. "Hey," he said, "what's the rush? Come by my place. We'll have a smoke, listen to some sounds. Like the old days."

"Sorry, next time." Cassidy was shifting his weight from foot to foot as if he were marching. Leeland's hand felt like a manacle.

"Jesus, Cassidy, that stuff must be cut with speed. Well, all right man, take it easy." Leeland released him.

"Yeah, okay, sure. I'll take it easy." Cassidy made for the door. He could feel his heart pounding just under his skin. Taking it easy hardly seemed a possibility. He had to cool out a good deal just to get to raving paranoia.

At one thousand times life size, the cell was still an insignificant circle of transparent matter. Faint and pale, it floated under the microscope, a gray ghost moving in a gray sea. And yet contained within its thin colorless walls was all the potential for a man. Arms, legs, brain, heart, everything was there already, waiting.

And not just one man but all men, past, present, and future. That one insignificant cell held the remnants of eons of man. For while it came from Mark, it came also from Sol and backwards, through *Homo sapiens* to *Homo habilis* to *Homo erectus*. The discovery of fire and tools, a world of dragons and demons where men huddled in dim caves, was all written there. And still farther backward down to one ghostly cell alive in the sea.

But also it was the future. Once activated, it would begin its move forward, evolving, mutating out into infinity. The ghostly cell slipped quietly through its gray world, seeming to displace nothing around it. But within was the parent, the parent of the parents, and also the child. It was the chicken and also the egg. Looked at in the proper way, it was even the coop.

Had Cassidy been tempted to consider God, he might have seen within the cell all the earmarks of that personage. The eternal spiraling, forward and

backward, the constant unrelenting movement on-
ward, with as much heart as a ten-ton bulldozer.

Holding the universe in his hand, Cassidy slipped
the disk of culture cells from under the microscope,
chose one cell, transferred it to a marked test tube,
and placed it on the trolley.

He slid a new glass disk under the microscope,
hunched low over it, and checked the next sample.
Close by, he could hear Mark slipping on his gown
and booties and sliding open the darkroom door to
the inner lab. Once again there was silence, only the
ticking of the wall clock and the occasional clink of
the glass test tubes as he transferred them from the
petri dish. But inside his head a concert of sounds
raged, and Cassidy began jabbering to himself like a
monkey.

Cassidy wheeled the trolley through the darkroom
door and over to the centrifuge in the inner lab. He
set the dials for speed and temperature, placed the
test tubes into the holders, and threw the switch. The
spinning started that would force the nuclei out of
the cells and into a tight nugget at the bottom of the
tubes.

"How come you're doing ten of them?" asked Mark.

Cassidy whirled around. He'd forgotten he wasn't
alone, and Mark's voice sent a bolt of fear through
his body. Cassidy smiled at himself, but still his heart
beat and flickered like a dying moth. "The next part
is risky as hell. If we get one cell to unite with an
egg, we're lucky."

"But what if we are lucky? What if two cells unite
with an egg? Or three? We're only going to implant
one embryo. That makes it death, doesn't it?"

"You're asking one of the most controversial questions in all of science." Cassidy fell silent. Behind him the timer shut the centrifuge off and the spinning began to slow. "I don't have an answer," Cassidy said finally. "Maybe it is death. Yeah, I guess it is. I never lied to you about that. Death will be a possibility from now on. But so will life."

Cassidy turned back to the centrifuge and removed the test tubes. Mark walked over to help him, but the idea of death lurked deep in his mind and he couldn't shake it.

"You ever knock someone up?" Mark asked after a while. He didn't wait for an answer.

"There was one lady who I'd known for years. I remember she showed me in a book what the embryo looked like. I remember being surprised that it didn't look like a mass of cells or a fish or any of the other things you expect. It looked like a tiny baby, pretty close to human. I remember she was crying and I didn't want to look. The truth was, it really didn't mean anything to me. Only an inconvenience, that's all."

Cassidy paused, then, "I don't know what you want me to say."

"I don't either. Probably nothing. It's just that I never thought about it before. Life, death—those are the biggies, Cassidy. It's different for you, I suppose. You're a scientist."

Cassidy smiled. "Even we have our moments." He turned back to the test tubes, shaking them, holding them up to the light, then transferring them to a refrigerator that would cold shock them into life. Mark laughed at the incongruity of what Cassidy said and what he did. Yet there was a reassurance about Cassidy's detachment.

Cassidy removed a glass container from the refrigerator and placed the ten shimmering eggs he'd gotten from the scientific underground on separate petri dishes. Next he carefully autopipetted polyethylene glycol, a chemical to help fusion, into the dishes. There was nothing for Mark to do but watch; it was often like that.

Mark shifted uncomfortably, glancing at the wall clock. "I'm going out."

There was a long silence and Mark wondered if Cassidy had heard him. Finally he said, "Not tonight."

"I made plans."

"Cancel them."

Mark was silent for quite some time, feeling an argument warming up on the sidelines and dreading it. "Do you really need me to stay here?"

"Are you kidding? First I have to incubate the petri dishes, varying the temperatures, and that'll take hours. But I'm also going to operate microsurgically on one of the cells. It's likely as hell to be a wipeout because I'm no microsurgeon. But if it works, we've really got something. You don't have to use as many chemicals. And it'll be like I made the baby with my own hands."

"And what will I be doing while you're playing God?" Mark flushed with anger, then instantly relented. "I'm sorry. I didn't mean that." Cassidy's eyes were on him, hot and furious. He wanted to run from them, and at the same time, wished he could stand up to them. He hated the power Cassidy had over him.

Cassidy shrugged and waited for Mark to say he'd

cancel his plans. Mark was surprised that he didn't,
surprised and scared, like a newborn, standing on awk-
ward, shaky legs.

"I'll be back early." Mark walked to the black cylinder and pulled open the door. "Probably before midnight." He quickly entered and slammed the door;
he felt as if he were escaping.

Cassidy whirled around and called after him,
"Where are you going?" But Mark was already gone
and Cassidy didn't really need Mark's answer. He knew
instantly that Mark was going to meet that girl from
town.

Cassidy wanted to run after him, grab him by the
arm, wrestle him to the ground, anything to make him
stay. More and more, he was becoming attuned to what
discovery would mean to them, and with the awareness
came terror. Even a line of dust rising in the horizon
made him feel sick to his stomach. It was getting to
the point where leaving the house was impossible.

But beyond Cassidy's fear of Mark saying too much
was an even greater fear, the fear of being left alone,
exposed. Exposed to what? He suspected himself. He
needed Mark, not to help him with what he was about
to do, but for reinforcement, to stop the noise that
grew louder in his head, the fear that was wriggling
in the pit of his stomach and making a meal of his
insides. His entire body was racked by anxiety attacks
that stabbed constantly at him, holding him both night
and day in their icy grip.

As Cassidy sat shaking in the laboratory, his breathing fast and short, it occurred to him that he might be
going crazy.

"You're going nuts," he hissed to himself. He caught

a glimpse of his image reflected in the glass walls. "Look at yourself," he said, baiting himself, pushing his already strung-out mind to new heights of fear and grief. He felt that if he could just take himself over the edge, the fall would be a relief.

Quickly Cassidy turned back to his work, jabbering to himself loudly, keeping his hot needy eyes on his work in front of him.

Sitting at the controls of the microsurgery theater, the pumping of atmosphere making a whooshing sound that was as calming as the rhythmic beating of a mother's heart, Cassidy felt his sanity return. Stability, wonder, vividness lay beyond, in the glassed-in box, and he bent to it with relief.

Cassidy concentrated on the magnified egg, shimmering oily yellow, and next to it the waiting nucleus of the body cell. He set the controls to deamplify his movements, slowly lifted the tiny nucleus from its culture medium, and moved it toward the egg.

Stretched out on the warm desert floor, the hot late afternoon sun glistening on their limbs, their minds open to the quiet emptiness, Mark and Becky felt like two lizards on a rock. Becky was wearing cutoff jeans and a halter. Mark tried to imagine her smooth, brown skin and the way her hipbones would be raised above the soft flesh of her belly. The round, small breasts he couldn't even begin to imagine. She would be athletic and slim, he was sure. But he knew he mustn't touch her. To touch her would be dangerous. There would be a great deal of power to it.

As they lay out in the warm glowing sun, Mark wondered what Becky was thinking, then guessed correctly that she wasn't thinking at all. Her mind had shut down and the dark secret places fell open to the hot desert sun and bleached into nothingness.

Becky rolled over and looked down at Mark, then moved under his arm. Mark smiled. She was like a fawn that wanted only warmth and comfort. It occurred to him that perhaps that was all there was in the end, that all the sophisticated compatibility and sameness of goals had nothing to do with anything but self-love, a desire to make the best of oneself by admitting that someone else was almost as good.

Mark's mind began to slow down. Erratic flashes of thought came and went, until there were no thoughts at all. Instinctively he reached over to Becky and touched her thigh. Heat radiated from it, and he felt her body stir slightly under his touch. He lifted himself up on his elbow and looked down at the slim young girl who lay opened out to him. There was no defense in her wide green eyes or tanned upturned face. Mark's hand slowly moved over her thigh, past her slim hips, and toward her breasts.

She didn't move but looked up at him, her trusting eyes opening into his, revealing everything. Her innocence awed Mark. Of all the multitude of life's experiences, innocence was one he'd never had, and it peeled back all the layers of civilization until he felt raw and exposed.

As Mark's hand moved to her breast, Becky closed her eyes and became blinded to everything but the call from within. He unbuttoned her halter and it fell open, revealing her pale tiny breasts, so fragile against the tan of her body. Her nipples stood out, delicate and brown, reaching up to him.

Mark didn't touch her for a long while. He just

watched her, lying beneath him, all of her seeming to reach toward him though she didn't move at all. Then softly he moved his hand over the small delicate bones of her chest and down over her stomach, past her childish cotton pants to the warmth of her.

He lifted her slim hips with his other hand and slid her shorts down her legs. Gently, he rolled over her. A vague instinct told him she was a virgin and that he should be gentle.

He felt Becky's body blending into him, her thighs tightening around his hips. Then the warmth and incredible smoothness of her enveloped him and held him in darkness.

He felt like crying out in pain and sorrow and joy. It crowded out all the mechanical fantasies he usually played out for himself as he lay with other women.

Becky whispered in his ear, "I love you." The words overpowered him, sweeping him away, calling up more feeling than he'd ever experienced.

"I love you," he said in return. It came out easily, naturally. "I love you," he said again and again, the swelling of sex making his words almost a cry, not unlike the cry of birth.

Cassidy was sprawled across a hard-backed chair, asleep in the laboratory. Beads of sweat stood out on his forehead. His head moved from side to side jerkily; every once in a while his arms would thrash outward. He hit his arm on the chair and woke up with a start. Almost immediately he was out of his chair and over at the incubator. He was still wearing his rubber gloves and quickly stripped them off, pulling on a fresh pair.

He flipped on the microscope and slid one of the petri dishes under it. There was nothing. He glanced back at the clock and noted it was ten o'clock, though which ten o'clock he wasn't sure for quite some time. Then the long night of checking and rechecking came rolling back on him.

Cassidy continued pulling out petri dishes, checking them under the microscope, then replacing them. The results were all the same. He slumped back into his chair, his head between his hands. He felt feverish, and the skin on his face was puffed and tender under his fingers. He sat still for only a moment, then slammed his fist violently against the hard wooden arm. Pain radiated through his hand, but there was some relief—at least this pain was something he could understand.

It had been eighteen hours since he'd combined the genetically engineered cells with the eggs. Something should have happened by now, some furrowing of the cell wall, a bulging in the nucleus. At least the cell should have grown, a sign it was taking in nourishment. Instead he found nothing.

Again Cassidy glanced back at the clock. It was ten minutes past ten. He hadn't seen Mark since five o'clock in the afternoon. Several times Cassidy had found himself with his finger in the dial of the telephone, calling he didn't know where.

He tried to empty his mind and began breathing slowly, deeply. Images shifted like shadowy phantoms, then they too faded away and Cassidy fell asleep.

At noon he woke, his muscles tight painful knots, his head aching and empty. Ignoring everything, he rushed to the microscope, pulling the dishes from the incubator, slipping them under the lighted lens.

Cassidy gritted his teeth against the anxious worm

that was making a mush of his insides. It occurred to him that part of the problem might be that he hadn't eaten since the previous afternoon. It also occurred to him that the few hours of sleep he had gotten had been under glaring fluorescent lights and filled with shadowy nightmares. But the major portion he ascribed to his new friend, failure, who'd been keeping a vigil by his side for the past twenty hours, gloating and chattering on endlessly.

Finally Cassidy pulled himself together, stripped off his gloves and lab coat, and climbed to the factory. He stopped at the top of the stairs. Brilliant light slanted through the boards, and he could feel the heat hanging as heavy as a drape. He couldn't bring himself to go outside.

Suddenly he heard a car door slam, then the factory door opened and the slim shadow of Mark fell across the lines of light.

There were tears in Cassidy's eyes. "I've failed," he said, his voice quavering with emotion. "It's been close to twenty-one hours and nothing has happened. I've failed." Cassidy stood, shaky and weak. He didn't pound his fist or yell. There was nothing left inside him. Even the anxiety had fled, and all he was left with was emptiness.

It wasn't until five o'clock in the afternoon that Mark was able to force Cassidy to eat a dish of scrambled eggs and take a shower. But he couldn't keep him away from the laboratory for more than an hour, and by six o'clock Cassidy was once again switching on the microscope, sliding the specimens under it carefully.

As Cassidy put the last specimen under the microscope and bent over it, a tremor went through his body, then he froze.

Suddenly he leaped back, his eyes two startled flashes of light, his hair standing on end as if he'd been electrocuted.

He switched on the intercom and located Mark in the kitchen. "Get in here, you asshole!"

"Are you all right?" Mark's voice crackled with apprehension. Cassidy switched off the intercom and waited. It took Mark less than twenty seconds to come through the door, yet Cassidy felt he'd never waited so long in his life.

"Now what the hell's going on?"

Cassidy pointed to the microscope. "Look!" His face was so knotted and lined with tension that Mark couldn't even begin to imagine what difficulty they'd run into. He half expected to see a nine-pound cancer cell as he bent to the lens.

Cassidy leaned over his shoulder and Mark could feel his breath, hot and urgent, against his neck. Below him, under the microscope, was an egg cell. It looked very much like the rest of the cells he'd viewed before.

"I don't see what you're getting at."

"Look again!"

Mark tried squinting. "I still don't see anything." He hesitated. "Well, maybe it's a bit bigger."

"Like twice its original size?"

"I don't know. Maybe."

"How about the wall of the cell? Anything there?"

"Yeah. A little ridge. One on each side, like a notch was taken out of it. What does that mean?"

"It means that the centrioles are being drawn away

from one another. And the fine lines of the centromeres are stretching."

Mark shrugged and shut off the microscope. Cassidy leaned over him and switched the light back on. "Don't you know what you're seeing?" Cassidy stood back from the microscope, his eyes electric with excitement. "That cell is going into anaphase. It's dividing. Life! We have life!"

"Life," Mark repeated, staring into the lens, stunned, barely able to breathe. That thing, that floating gray ghost was alive, and it was him, him and Cassidy. He couldn't take his eyes away from it. He felt as if he were viewing his own body dividing, pulling apart, and recreating itself.

The phantomlike cell, transparent and colorless, seemed to Mark to be the most beautiful thing he'd ever seen. He clung to the lens spellbound as the furrows on either side of the cell grew deeper. The nucleus continued to stretch until there were two nuclei divided by a thin strand of matter, which began to pull apart.

"It was the cell I worked on surgically," Cassidy was almost yelling. "The others haven't divided yet. I don't think they will." His lips were dry and he licked them with his equally dry tongue. "I felt it would be this one, Mark. I swear I could feel it under my fingers. I knew it would work."

When Mark finally turned from the microscope, his eyes were wide with excitement and, beneath it, fear. He was silent a long while, then he said softly, "Is it wrong, Cassidy? Is what we're doing wrong?"

Cassidy laughed, though in truth it was a question he had repeated to himself until it burned into his soul. "Of course it's not wrong," he answered. "After all, it's not all that different from what's happening all over the world. Nature's just come up with a more fun method."

"You believe that?"

Cassidy smiled wryly. He looked very old and very calm. "Okay. I guess I'm kind of scared too. I keep looking at it two ways. Maybe what we're doing is wrong, but maybe not doing what you're capable of is an even greater wrong, a sin against nature. I swear to God, I just don't know, and in the end I don't care. We've got life!"

The two men stared at each other for a long while. Finally Mark walked over to Cassidy and put his arm around him. "Congratulations," he said. "What you did was fabulous."

Cassidy grinned boyishly and raised his hands above his head in the sign of victory. "Hell, what can I say, it was brilliant. As a matter of fact, what you just looked at under the lens would bring me the Nobel Prize, if I was into talking this around, which I most definitely am not. Still, I know it. And that's all that counts." For a moment Cassidy believed this.

Cassidy replaced the dish in the incubator, then threw open the darkroom door. "Come on, Dad," he said to Mark, his face lit up with an otherworldly glow. "Let's go have ourselves a little birthday party for Adam."

Mark laughed. "We're calling him Adam?"

"You got a better name?"

Mark shook his head. "No, not really. I suppose I should be pleased you didn't call him Jesus."

Cassidy winked at him as he closed the door. "Don't think it didn't cross my mind."

* * *

Molly was sitting in her cage, crushed tightly into the corner of it. It was night and she was scared. She was going to go to sleep today, and when she woke up, she'd have a baby in her stomach. Cassidy had come into her cage to tell her and sat with her for a long while. He'd shown her a picture of a big monkey and a little monkey in her book. The tiny baby clung to its mother's breast with greedy persistence while she kept a cautious eye on the green leaves around her. Molly had stared at the picture for a long time, understanding little but listening to the call from within.

Cassidy had promised her that going to sleep wouldn't hurt. That had made her feel a bit better, because Cassidy never lied to her. She knew she had lied to Cassidy. Once she'd told him she'd eaten all her food and was hungry, but she'd hidden a bit of banana for later. Cassidy had found it and punished her with no treats for a long time. Lying was bad.

Molly scooted over to her toy box and opened the lid. But she didn't feel much like playing because she was going to sleep today and she was scared.

The hall lights went on and Cassidy yelled, "Mark, wake up. It's five o'clock." Although Molly couldn't understand what he was saying, she knew what it meant. She made her arms into the hands of the clock. Five o'clock was a good time; it meant food at night or time to get up. This five was time to get up.

But Molly didn't rush to the bars of her cage to rattle them as she did every morning. Instead she clung close to the wall, feeling her heart pounding in her chest.

When Cassidy came in he was wearing a lab coat and his hands were covered with plastic gloves. She thought she saw him hiding something behind his back. Molly pushed closer to the wall, pressing tightly to it. Her whole body was shaking, fear and anger rising until she was weak from it. Cassidy signed, "Good morning." He was smiling.

Molly couldn't sign back. Her body was like a dead-weight and her brain whirled with fear. Yet she knew Cassidy loved her and wouldn't hurt her. She was squeezed so tightly between love and fear that breath seemed to stop in her lungs and her body was immobilized.

Finally she regained movement and signed, "Molly scared."

Cassidy sat down next to her and held her shaking body. "Cassidy will not hurt Molly," he signed.

"Please, no sleep."

"It won't hurt Molly. Molly will sleep. Then wake up. Then Cassidy will tickle Molly and Molly will eat."

"Where is Mark?"

"Mark will be here."

"Now?"

"Mark will be here."

"Future?"

"Near future. Soon."

"Molly doesn't understand future."

"Molly will."

"When?"

"Near future."

Molly sat still for a moment, thinking, trying to understand a world her instincts told her was changing. "Will sleep make Molly understand future?"

Cassidy hesitated. It would be simple to lie to Molly. It would certainly calm her. Cassidy winced, then signed, "Yes, sleep will make Molly understand."

Molly relaxed and Cassidy pulled out a needle. She felt a sting and tried to pull away, but Cassidy was holding her tightly. There was a moment of pressure and then it was over.

Cassidy signed, "Lie down."

Cassidy was still holding her arm tightly; she didn't know whether she wanted to run or be close to him. There was the click of a door and she whirled to see Mark, but everything had started to move under her, fast and scary. She heard Mark's voice and tried to see him, but suddenly the world collapsed into blackness.

"So you did it." Mark remained in the doorway, not even daring to look down at Molly.

"It won't hurt her," said Cassidy. "I told you that."

Mark shook his head. "I hate doing this to her. She's so trusting, so like a child."

"Mark, she's an ape. You think it's going to ruin her social life or something?"

"You know what I mean. We're using her. It isn't like she's just some lab animal. She thinks and feels and even talks, for Christ's sake."

Cassidy put his hand on Mark's shoulder. "It'll be over soon."

Mark nodded solemnly, then helped Cassidy roll Molly's inert black body onto a stretcher and carry her into the lab.

Everything had been set up the night before. There was a clean operating table with straps suspended over it, a lab bench with scalpels, clamps, cotton, and the incubator holding that tiny swimming cluster of cells. Cassidy wheeled the intravenous apparatus close to Molly and slid the needle under the thick skin of her hand. Then he attached her to several monitoring machines.

"All you gotta do is watch the machines like I showed you." Cassidy injected a syringe of sodium pentathol into the intravenous bottle of glucose solution. "If there's any problem, just yell out."

Mark felt a shiver run through him as he took his place in front of the machines. "You sure you can handle this?"

"If everything goes as it should."

"And if it doesn't?"

Cassidy was silent for a while. "I'm no doctor."

Mark looked at Molly's motionless body. "Trust you not to lie."

A stab went through Cassidy as he remembered the lie he'd told Molly. He wondered if that counted. He suspected it did. He watched the clear liquid dripping through the fine plastic tubing and down into Molly's hand. Then he walked to the side of the table and lifted her heavy legs into the leather straps.

"Tie her arms down."

Mark looked at the leather straps, hesitated, then leaned toward them.

A minute later, Molly lay clamped open, her soft dark insides revealed. Mark kept his eyes on the dials, unable to look at Molly. Yet his eyes drifted back to the dark legs suspended in the air and Cassidy standing between them shining a bright lamp into her body and placing the little naked mulberry of life deep into her darkness.

Suddenly Mark cried out, "Cassidy, something's wrong!"

Cassidy didn't look up but his face was tense, his voice urgent. "What's the matter?"

"I don't know. Her heart. The line is erratic."

"Do you want me to come over there?" Cassidy was

working to keep his tone controlled, but there was the tightness of fear in it.

"I don't know. I just don't know." Mark paused. "Wait a minute. Now it's back to normal." Mark let out a deep breath as the signals crossed the screen rhythmically. "I think it's okay now."

Cassidy's face was a tense knot of concentration, trying to shift his mind back to what he was doing and away from the irregular signals on the monitor. He wished he could have brought in a doctor, or even a vet, but they tended to ask questions, and questions were not exactly what he felt like dealing with at this point.

Cassidy glanced up. "Are you keeping your eyes on the monitors?"

"Where the hell do you think I'm keeping them?"

Cassidy tried to sound optimistic and calm. "It'll be okay. I'm almost finished."

Molly's belly rolled and surged beneath him, everything inside her still working, though in slow motion because of the anesthesia. Cassidy was hunched above her womb. In his mind he could see it swelling into ripeness. Molly's organs would shift and press tightly against one another as they were pushed brutally aside by the growing child. He quickly came back to reality. He had to get her off the table before anything happened or there would be no swelling, there would be no growing seed, all there would be was death. The urge to rush gripped him. He stopped himself. That too could spell disaster.

"It's happening again!" Mark's voice shattered the quiet.

"Just keep watching. I'm almost done."

Perspiration was dripping off of Cassidy. He wiped

his arm across his face, then continued stitching while a vision of TV doctors with big-titted nurses mopping their brows presented itself to him. He laughed.

"What's going on?" screamed Mark furiously. He wanted to kill Cassidy for laughing. He couldn't even begin to imagine anything funny in what was happening.

Cassidy was chattering to himself as he worked quickly, trying to block out the fear and urgency, ignoring Mark's anger.

Suddenly he jumped back. "That's it!" He rushed in front of Mark, removed the anesthesia syringe from the intravenous setup, and checked Molly's eyes.

Almost immediately, the blips on the screen returned to normal. "Thank God," Mark gasped.

Cassidy stood over Molly, watching her. "The question is, what caused her heart to do that?"

Mark turned away from Cassidy and Molly, stripping off his gloves and walking to the washbasin. He lathered his hands and held them under scalding water, though he knew they were clean. "I told you she's been complaining about something in her chest. Now maybe you'll listen."

"I checked her heart. There didn't seem to be anything wrong with it."

"Seem?"

"That's right, seem."

Mark turned off the hot water and wiped his hands dry, but he remained where he was, staring at the water as it swirled down the drain. He couldn't bring himself to look at Molly. "We better get her to a vet."

"We can't risk it."

"She's sick!"

"We'll be careful."

"Don't you understand, for Christ's sake? She could die!"

"You're hysterical." Cassidy peeled off his gloves and threw them in the wastebasket marked for biohazard, then walked to the door of the lab and passed through.

When Mark heard the click of the door, he whirled around. Molly was lying motionless on the operating table, helpless, exposed. He cried out hoarsely, "At least help me take her legs down. Goddamn you! At least take her legs down."

Chapter 7

Schaftner looked around the white room and caught sight of a large-boned, redheaded woman sitting at a desk, writing on what looked like a chart. It took very little time for him to recognize he was in a hospital room and, from the way he felt, it was undoubtedly his. He didn't realize that to feel anything was amazing.

Schaftner wondered who he was. Certainly he was an intelligent man. Everything he saw around him had a name, many of them in Latin. He was also a very ill man. Perhaps discovering what he was ill with should be the first thing on his agenda. He smiled to himself. Yes, whoever he was, he was an intelligent man, also a relatively detached man. He could imagine most people waking from coma and going crazy with fear. He was not afraid. There was a tube in his neck. A tracheotomy would have been necessary. Next to the bed was an intravenous setup. He noted with satisfaction that they were using a good food substitute. Though wasted, his arms still had some flesh around the bones; his muscle tone was acceptable. His skin had broken out into a terrible rash; he could almost smell it decomposing.

The big question was, would he have another

stroke? Yes, he said to himself, that was what it had been, a stroke. He wondered about his heart; was it weak too? He suspected not. It was strokes he had to be concerned with.

Suddenly his mind flashed on something important, something he must do. But he couldn't remember what.

He pulled himself back to the problem at hand. The important thing now was Schaftner. Again the internal smile. That was his name, Irwin Schaftner. He had always felt his first name didn't really belong to him. The odors of clover and cut grass came rushing back to him, and he saw a group of boys teasing him for being Irwin. There was a moment when he couldn't tell if he were the little boy or the frail man in the hospital, then the flash was gone.

Again the thought that there was something he must remember came to him. He knew it had something to do wih a dark-haired man and wondered if this man was his son. No, he could feel he had no children. No wife either. That Schaftner was one selfish, self-contained bastard. He decided he rather liked Schaftner, flawed though he was.

Still there was no question that Schaftner was a very ill man; he doubted he'd have much time to become acquainted with himself. From the incredible weakness in his body, he had to assume Schaftner's number was about to come up in the not too distant future. He tried to decide whether he cared but wasn't sure. He kept getting the feeling that there was something urgent. Perhaps he should ask Cassidy.

And suddenly it was there, clear and whole. As Schaftner lifted up his arm, the nurse caught sight of it in the mirror and gasped. Schaftner laughed to himself; he guessed his prognosis hadn't been too good.

Finally the nurse composed herself and walked over to the bed. Schaftner pointed to the breathing tube, then moved his mouth. It was slow, painful work, and he felt dizzy. He really was in terrible shape, but he had to find out if he could talk.

The nurse understood. "You want to talk, do you? Well, there'll be plenty of time for that." Schaftner opened his eyes wide and kicked his weak legs. "Hey, calm down," the nurse said. "Let me just unhook the trach and we'll give it a try."

She slipped the tube from the metal holder buried in his neck and covered the opening with her hand. He could hear a hissing of air. "Try to talk now."

Schaftner opened his mouth and an airy growl that sounded nothing like language came from deep inside him. His throat hurt like twenty workmen had been going over it with rough sandpaper.

"Try again," said the nurse.

"I . . ." Schaftner stopped. Had she ever understood that one word?

"I," repeated the nurse.

Relief swept over him. "Want . . . ," he continued. It sounded like another growl to him, but the nurse nodded her head and repeated the word to him.

His lips were unbearably dry and his throat felt as if it would explode. "Cassidy," he struggled.

"Cassidy?" The nurse looked at him with no understanding.

Schaftner waited a moment, gathering his strength. "Richard Cassidy," he hissed out.

"Is he a doctor?"

Schaftner shook his head. Again he tried to pull himself together, but the room was starting to whirl, and he felt himself slipping into the world where everything was black and white, receding like an old snapshot.

The nurse replaced the trach tube, picked up his chart, and started for the door. Just as she was leaving she noted a phone number at the top of his chart.

Schaftner had fallen back toward the darkness, his eyes closed, his body limp. But he could still feel the air hissing into his lungs and the cool sheets against his aching body. He was just falling asleep..

"Sorry, Sy, but you can't kick a man outta town 'cause he smiles at your daughter. Or maybe I should say waitress. Because in the end that's all she is." Sheriff Anderson looked at Sy, who was slumped in a chair across from his desk, with a combination of pity and condescension.

Sheriff Anderson was a big man with a belly that hung like a fleshy shelf over his belt and a head that was much too large for his body. Anderson kept his thinning, greasy hair short partly because of the heat but mostly because he thought it made his head look smaller. In fact, it made it look like a large torpedo.

Anderson wiped his face and head with a handkerchief that was so wet you could wring it out. It was close to 120 degrees, and he pictured himself sitting at home with his feet in a tub, his face in an electric fan, and his hand around a beer.

"It had to happen sometime," said Anderson. "Besides, it ain't even happened yet. After all, what would a city boy want with your Becky?"

This was hardly reassuring to Sy. He passed his frail hand over his heart which was doing the "Colonel Bogie March" in his thin pigeon chest. His mind was racing way ahead of the facts. Inside his head, Becky had already left them, had already fled into the night, leaving behind an aching dark emptiness. He could hardly bear to look at her anymore. "I think she sneaks out with him."

"Are you sure?"

"I ain't got proof if that's what you mean." Anderson's face seemed to be shrinking right before Sy's eyes. And it didn't take very long for Sy to recognize in it his ghostly old friend. "I think she's been seein' him regular for some time."

"But you ain't got no proof."

"What's he doing up here? That's what I want to know."

Anderson sighed. He was having trouble feeling Sy's problem very deeply. First of all, Sheinberg was a Jew, and everyone knew what they were like when the chips were down. Then there was the fact that Anderson didn't have any children. On top of that, he was sweating bullets. Hell, he was sweating A-bombs, and it was only three o'clock. There were still two hours before Wilt Cason, his deputy, took over. By that time, there was a very good chance he'd have melted down like that little nigger boy his mother used to read him about. Cason would come in and all he'd find was a pool of melted butter on his swivel chair.

Anderson turned his clear blue eyes on Sy, indicating that their chat was over, but Sy just hunched over even farther, locking his hands between his legs in a gesture of meekness.

Anderson buried his handkerchief deep in his shirt and wiped his armpits. "You got no evidence against them boys," he grunted, shifting his handkerchief to his ample chest. "My advice is go back, fry yourself a couple of eggs, and forget it." Anderson's stomach started to growl—he was planning to do the same thing.

Still Sy didn't move. "You're thinking me and Sally don't deserve nothing so good as little Becky."

Anderson started to protest, but Sy waved it away. "It ain't no more than I been thinking myself. And it's true. Gentleness and beauty ain't something that happens often. Especially to folks like Sally and me. But I'd do anything for that little girl, Anderson. And maybe that's why she's been given to us. Because we'll protect her."

Anderson regarded the poor crumpled man sitting in front of him. He put his big, meaty hand on Sy's scrawny arm. "Maybe it's about time you laid down the law up at the diner. Tell her she can't leave without your permission. Work her so hard she ain't got enough energy for no hanky-panky. Throw your weight around a little." He looked at Sy's matchstick body and added, "If that don't work, find me a reason and I'll kick their asses outta town faster'n you can say jailbait."

Sy would have been happier had Anderson offered something more positive in the way of action, like a lynching party, but he had to content himself with this. His feeble face wrinkled into a smile, and he left the sheriff's office feeling somewhat better. He would have a talk with Becky that evening and let her know who was boss. If he failed, he'd fall back on the might of Anderson.

It was only as Sy drew back up to the diner that he put two and two together and came up with the disconcerting answer that Anderson had promised noth-

ing but to do his job. Sy touched the mole on his chest
with grave foreboding and entered the diner.

The barking of BooBoo made Cassidy's heart con-
tract into a tight ball. He swung around, then stood
frozen to the spot, listening. He heard nothing and
decided it had been his imagination. It had been a
while since Cassidy had had one of those crazy anxiety
attacks, but the threat of them hung over him always.
The moment Molly's urine test was positive, he'd
begun to cool out, and for five months life had been,
if not peaceful, at least bearable, as Molly grew
rounder and bigger.

Again there was a barking and Cassidy's heart was
pounding so hard he could hear the sound of his blood
in his ears. Cautiously he opened the door and slid
through.

But already there was a figure there, standing in
the darkness, small and afraid. Becky didn't move or
speak for a minute, frozen by the glimpse of incredibly
bright light from within. There had seemed to be glass
everywhere, reflecting light sharply as from a thousand
prisms, and through the glass, a huge, black inhuman
figure.

"I've left home." Becky's eyes were on the ground,
her voice shaky yet full of resolve.

Cassidy didn't answer, but his mind was a cacophony
of sound. He noticed the small plastic overnight bag
she was carrying. It was not a happy sight.

"I want to see Mark."

"Go home. He'll call you." Cassidy turned back to
the door.

"No. I want to see him now."

Cassidy had to admit that for a shaky little girl she

had a lot of guts. At this point he would have liked to
see them spilled all over the floor.

"I love Mark," she answered simply.

"And I'm sure he loves you," answered Cassidy with
a sweetness that made him want to puke. "But you're
under age. All you'll be doing is making trouble for
Mark. So do everyone a favor—turn around and go
home."

"It's too late. I left already."

Cassidy recoiled. "You didn't tell anyone where you
were going, did you?"

"I'm not crazy."

"Great. So go back and tell them you've changed
your mind."

"But I didn't change my mind." She hesitated, seem-
ing to shrink into herself, then continued. "Sy suspects.
He won't let me out anymore. I'd do anything to have
Mark. I love him. Can't you understand that?"

Cassidy expected tears at this point and was surprised when there were none. "Sure, sure," he answered. "I've been in love."

"Have you?" Becky's tone implied that she didn't
believe him, and Cassidy began to wonder if she
wasn't smarter than she let on.

Becky remained silent for a long time, and when she
spoke, it was so softly that Cassidy wasn't quite sure
he had heard what she said.

"I'll tell them. I really will."

Cassidy laughed. "You'll tell who what?"

"About all the glass. About the black shadow I just
saw. I'll tell them all about it. I'm not sure what
you're keeping in there. It looked . . . I don't even
know what it looked like. But something's going on.
Something you don't want anyone to know about. And

if I can't stay, I'll tell Sy, Sheriff Anderson, everyone."

Cassidy tried for a shrug or a smile but came up empty-handed. "So?"

"Someone will listen."

"To what? Black shadows? Glass?" This time he came up with a fairly creditable laugh which he most definitely was not feeling.

"They don't trust city people here."

"Why, you calculating little bitch!" Cassidy hissed.

Becky sighed deeply. "I'm desperate."

Cassidy's face was a tight mask of anger. "And what if Mark doesn't want you?"

A shiver ran through Becky. "He loves me. I know he does."

"And if you're wrong?"

Becky's face went blank. For a moment Cassidy saw a hardness in it that spoke of years of mistreatment and anger and a will that had come through battered but still solid as steel. "Then I'll tell them for sure."

She saw Cassidy's shock. "Desperate," she repeated.

"You're crazy!"

"Isn't that what you told Sy? That Mark was crazy?"

"You don't think it's the truth?"

"Yes," answered Becky softly. "I think you told him the truth. I think we're all crazy. Mark, you, me. Now are you going to open the door and let me in?"

Cassidy didn't answer for a minute. He stood clinging to the cool steel door, watching the little girl with freckles who was standing next to him, then slowly he opened the door and let Becky inside.

"Of course they'll be coming." Cassidy could feel his mouth twitching with tension.

Mark ran his hands through his hair until it stood

away from his head in spikes. Becky sat hunched over the kitchen table, eating a bowl of cereal, her eyes focused straight ahead, her overnight bag next to her. She looked like a passenger in a bus station.

Mark closed his eyes. He couldn't stand Cassidy's furious eyes glaring at him or the sight of Becky, terrified yet determined. Becky had been innocence and purity to him. Their long walks had been silent, their lovemaking soulful and profound. "What can we do?" he asked at last.

"She's left us no choice," Cassidy answered. He hesitated, and the thought that Cassidy would kill her passed through both Mark's and Becky's minds.

"You'll show her everything, explain it to her," Cassidy continued. "But for now we've got to get her out of here."

"I won't go!" said Becky, looking from Cassidy to Mark.

Cassidy strode over to the table and glowered down at her. "Oh, yes, you will. The first place they're going to look for you is here."

Becky shook her head and went back to her bowl of Rice Krispies. Cassidy hated her a great deal, and every snap, crackle, and pop went through him like a spike. "We'll have to put her and Molly somewhere. Then set up the lab like we're doing research on sweet peas or fruit flies or whatever people think scientists do."

Becky looked up. "Who's Molly?"

"Spare me the jealous act, okay? She's a goddamn ape!" Cassidy stopped, bringing his hot, angry eyes close to her face.

Becky was quivering like a frightened animal. Mark hated seeing her this way. All equivocation ceased and he wanted to take her in his arms and protect her. "Leave her alone, will you, Cassidy?" he said angrily.

Cassidy turned on Mark. "I should leave her alone?"

"Can't you see she's about to cry?"

"I'm about to do a lot more than cry!" Cassidy slammed his fist against the table. He moved away from the table and started to pace. "We gotta get her and Molly out of here."

"Where?" asked Mark.

Cassidy whirled around. "Good question. Excellent, Mark!"

"Hey, I'm not thrilled about this either."

"You think with your cock."

"This arguing isn't going to solve anything."

"Okay, okay. Any suggestions?"

"One of the outhouses. We could move my car out and put Becky and Molly in there for a couple of days until things cool down."

Cassidy shook his head. "I'm going to have to give those insects from town free run of this place. Like your girl friend over there said, they are suspicious of us city folks."

"I have a friend back in L.A.," suggested Mark.

"I can just imagine someone taking a look into our car on the freeway. And good old Molly signing, 'Please tickle Molly. Please tickle Molly.' "

Cassidy fell into a chair and turned his desperate eyes on Mark, who wasn't in any better shape than he was.

Finally Mark flopped down into a chair next to Cassidy. "So what do we do?" he asked with no expectation of an answer.

Cassidy sighed. "I have a friend in L.A., too."

* * *

"Schaftner came out of coma," Lenny said, walking to the stove for more coffee, though Cassidy hadn't touched his. Cassidy looked up surprised. "Remember, you left my number with the nurse?"

For a moment, the anxiousness in Cassidy's face faded and he looked delighted. "How is he?"

Lenny sighed in answer, then said, "He asked for you. But I didn't know how to reach you." She too was working hard to down the coffee. "I was worried about you."

"Well, you can see for yourself, there's nothing to worry about."

Lenny surveyed the dark circles lining Cassidy's eyes and his frantic haunted look and answered, "I'm glad you're here."

"It's good to see you, too." Cassidy leaned back to his coffee, trying to avoid her probing black eyes.

"Why did you come?" asked Lenny.

"I need a favor."

Though Lenny had expected that was the reason, she hated to hear it. "What do you want?" She sounded hurt.

"Can you do something for me and not ask any questions?"

"Probably not. At the best of times it's hard for me not to ask questions. Right now I can think of about a thousand, and that's just scratching the surface." She saw the look of fear cross Cassidy's face and put her hand on his arm. "But I'll try, all right?"

Cassidy shook his head. "That's not good enough."

"Then I'm sorry. More than that you'll never get from me, Cassidy. At least not anymore. Maybe once . . ." She thought for a moment. "No, not even then. Not even when I needed you so badly that I even considered having a kid with you." She laughed sadly. "Can you beat that? Thirty-five and I was thinking about starting a family." There were tears in her eyes, and she wiped them away quickly before Cassidy could see them. "I needed you, friend. I knew you didn't care, but that didn't change anything."

Cassidy was staring into his coffee, hearing very little of what she was saying. "I need the favor badly."

"That I can see." Lenny's voice was cold and hard.

"You're still angry that I left, aren't you?"

"Cassidy, sometimes I think you're from another planet." But it seemed futile to try to explain. "Look, I can't promise to do what you want unquestioningly. All I can promise is silence."

Cassidy nodded. At this point his bargaining power wasn't exactly good. "I want you to put two people up. Actually, one of them isn't a person at all. And I want you to do it for two days."

"Who?"

"The girl of a friend of mine and a gorilla."

Lenny started to laugh, then caught the look on Cassidy's face. "You're serious."

Even Cassidy had to smile. "Yes. A gorilla. We call her Molly."

"What do you call a gorilla?" asked Lenny, her eyes dancing. "Anything it likes."

"Don't worry. She's not dangerous. In fact, she can speak in sign language."

"Cassidy, stop it. It's not funny."

Cassidy turned morose. "Sometimes I wish I were kidding," he muttered.

Lenny had never seen such unhappiness on anyone's face before. "Tell me about it," she said softly.

Cassidy turned his pleading eyes toward her. "Will you do it?"

Lenny sighed. "What does King Kong eat? Human flesh?"

"You'll like Molly. She's a lot better than a human. All you have to do is feed her once a day. I've written down what she eats." He reached into the pocket of his filthy Levi's, pulled out a torn piece of paper, and threw it on the table. "The girl's name is Becky," Cassidy continued. "I don't give a damn what you feed her. Just keep them both in the house and don't let them out of your sight."

"Even for me it's hard to misplace a gorilla, Cassidy. Oh, by the way, I lost my car again. I took it to a gas station for an oil change, and when I went to pick it up, I'd forgotten which station it was at. All I knew was it was in the Valley. It took me three days to find it."

Cassidy smiled feebly; once again the nervous energy had taken over. "Molly's been sick. She isn't supposed to move around too much."

"In here? She'll be lucky if she can stretch her arms."

Cassidy touched her face. "You're being a good sport."

"When do you want me to do this little baby-sitting job?"

"They're downstairs in a truck I rented."

"I see. Pretty sure of me, weren't you?"

"That you'd save me? Yes."

Lenny hesitated, surveying Cassidy's ravaged face. "It is a matter of saving you, Cassidy, isn't it?"

"Yes."

Cassidy got up from the table. Lenny stopped him with her hand. "Wait a minute. I want you to tell me what's going on." Cassidy just stood there. "I'm not a fool, you know. You're doing the experiment again, aren't you?"

Cassidy didn't answer for a long while. He looked around at the familiar blue and white tiles and copper pots but saw nothing. Finally he said, "The fetus is five months old."

"And what do you do when you have the world's most perfect ape?"

Cassidy sighed. "It isn't an ape."

Lenny could feel her body shaking underneath her. "Oh, Jesus, Cassidy." She clutched the table tightly, feeling doom and awe at the same moment. Her heart pounded frantically, and there were tears in her eyes. Finally she said, "On one condition. I want in."

Cassidy looked up startled, and even Lenny was surprised by her words. "I'm a nurse. You'll need me."

Cassidy's foot began its nervous shaking. His stomach was a knot. "We'll get by."

Lenny shook her head. "I want in, Cassidy. Those are the terms."

Cassidy didn't answer, and Lenny sat in stunned silence, watching him. She'd always wondered what she'd do if a spaceship landed and they asked her to come along. Now she had her answer. But as she looked over at Cassidy, she knew that was only a half-truth. She still loved him, his burning, insatiable ambition, his daring. Only Cassidy could perform an experiment like this; only Cassidy could succeed. Standing next to him, she'd feel touched by the power of his destiny.

* * *

It was late afternoon and an orange-brown drape of poisons covered Los Angeles like an atomic mushroom, turning stoplights a strange iridescent color, swallowing everything and everyone as their air became choked off and they committed voluntary genocide.

Cassidy closed the truck windows and turned on the air conditioner. The heavy smoke hanging over Los Angeles only served to confirm what he had been doing for the past months. Now Lenny had told him that Schaftner was out of coma, and once again Cassidy felt as if he were flowing with the stream of what was already planned and good.

Cassidy felt better. Molly and Becky would be safe with Lenny. He had to admit he even felt better that Lenny would be helping them. It was true; he did need her. And now he was on his way to see Schaftner.

He could hardly wait to tell him about Adam. Perhaps if he was well enough he might even be included. The thought of meeting problems with the ever-cool Schaftner by his side was such a relief that he let out a delighted yell. Of course, including Schaftner in the experiment would include him in the credit for it also. Until now, the experiment had been all Cassidy. But so were the fear and the loneliness. It was a difficult decision.

Cassidy pulled into the hospital parking lot and took the familiar, antiseptic journey up the stairs and down the long pale corridor to Schaftner's room. He paused, remembering the weeks of agony he'd spent there, then threw open the door.

Schaftner was lying in bed, motionless, still attached to the breathing and intravenous apparatus. Cassidy felt like screaming; after all his years of work Schaftner had died without knowing about Adam.

There was a flutter of Schaftner's eyelids. Cassidy rushed to the side of the bed. "Goddamn it, Schaftner. You scared the hell out of me!"

A wry smile passed over Schaftner's pale lips. He pointed to the trach tube, then his mouth. His frail hand reached up and pushed the buzzer for the nurse, then he turned his eyes on Cassidy. It was a fatherly look, filled with more emotion than Schaftner had ever shown.

Cassidy felt tears come to his eyes. He loved this thin, stooped man. The two men looked into one another for close to a minute, and when the large, carrot-headed nurse lumbered in they only left off looking at one another reluctantly.

"The professor is able to talk," said the nurse briskly. "All you have to do is unhook the breathing tube and place your hand over the opening." The nurse removed the tube and placed her hand over the opening.

Almost immediately Schaftner wheezed, "Well . . . look who's . . . here!" He was anxious to use every second.

"How long can we talk?" Cassidy asked the nurse, equally anxious. The nurse smiled, revealing two deep dimples in her pale, freckled face. The sight of the two of them had reached through her tiredness and touched her. "He still needs the trach to breathe, so don't unhook it from the respirator. Only keep the tube out of his neck a minute, then replace it. You can do that a few times, but not too many. The professor is still very weak. Also be sure you don't remove your hand from the opening except to replace the trach." She smiled. "You two have a nice chat." She placed Cassidy's hand where hers had been and quickly left the room.

Now that the two men were alone, neither of them spoke, their eyes locking in fondness, probing each other gently.

"I . . . was . . . worried . . . about . . . you," Schaftner gasped finally.

Cassidy could feel the air pulsing under his hand as Schaftner spoke, and the vulnerability of it seemed tragic to him. "Yeah, well, I wasn't resting real easy about you either."

"I'm . . . all right." Suddenly Schaftner's eyes became sharp. "3476 . . . ," he paused, moistening his dry lips.

"Destroyed," answered Cassidy. He was surprised by Schaftner's question. 3476 seemed so long ago he had almost forgotten about it. The gap of time had opened between the two of them, and Cassidy began to realize the distance he had come since they worked together.

"Now there is Adam," said Cassidy. "Adam is 3476 redone." He beamed down at Schaftner, his excitement returning with every word. "I got financing and resumed the experiment. And it's working! I've implanted and it held. Adam is five months old. He's got fingernails, hair, genitals, everything." He laughed at himself. He hardly had to explain a five-month-old fetus to Schaftner. God, he missed him.

Schaftner's airy voice hissed out. "No!" It was a command and also a plea. "3476 is evil!"

"You don't understand. 3476 is dead. And there's nothing evil about Adam. Wait till you see what I've done. It's nothing short of spectacular."

"No!" Schaftner repeated. "Experiment . . . evil."

Schaftner wet his lips, resting, trying to gather his strength.

Cassidy saw him struggling for speech and nodded. "I better put this thing back for a while."

Schaftner reached out his arm to stop him, but Cassidy had already locked the snakelike tube in place and sat down on the chair beside his bed.

Schaftner's eyes moved to Cassidy and revealed the horror he was feeling. Happiness drained from Cassidy. Watching Schaftner, all he could see was the insane rolling on the sweat-soaked bed and the wild, fearful eyes of coma. Schaftner had regained consciousness, but he hadn't regained his mind. Cassidy wished he had died. Schaftner without his mind was only an animal passing time, checking off the hours until it finally checked out. Cassidy often thought of animals walking around the earth, living only to eat, eating only to live, until they dropped and decomposed. It seemed so pointless. Occasionally, mostly when he was stoned, he saw human beings like that. But he knew that wasn't true. Men were working toward something, though what they were working toward was somewhat unclear. At one time he'd been tempted to believe it might be a showdown between good and evil, but he'd dropped that along with his baby fat. Still, driving through the smog-covered city, it had seemed like that and from the looks of things, evil was making a strong bid for first. One thing was for sure, if it was a fight between good and evil, God must be sitting on the sidelines, drinking a beer and watching one hell of a contest.

Schaftner gestured to his neck, but Cassidy shook his head and pointed to the clock.

Schaftner was in agony. How could he, a sick, used-up old man who could barely speak, convince a young man to destroy what he must consider to be the greatest scientific feat since man dropped out of the trees? It was a feeling he well remembered, that overpowering excitement that overtook you, driving you forward until you felt like you were climbing all the way up that staircase of clouds and sitting down at the right hand of God. And yet he must convince him. Schaftner knew now that he'd been fighting to stay conscious for this one moment.

It occurred to Schaftner that there'd be other Cassidys. Even if he managed to stop this one, there'd be dozens just like him. Still, there was nothing he could do about the other Cassidys. That would be someone else's job or perhaps no one's job. Perhaps it was inevitable. Well, so be it, he thought; his job was now.

When Cassidy finally removed the trach tube from Schaftner's neck, the look of desperation was gone. "You . . . must . . . listen!" Schaftner didn't give Cassidy a chance to interrupt. "Just . . . before . . . stroke . . . ran . . . computer . . . program. Extrapolate . . . personality. 3476 . . . evil." He stopped, looking into Cassidy's eyes. For the first time he noticed the dark circles, the lines of tension, and was appalled by how old he had become. Cassidy's eyes were now avoiding Schaftner. It was a sign that he believed him.

"No . . . compassion. Emotions . . . but . . . no compassion. . . . Inhuman. Perfection . . . is . . . evil."

Cassidy laughed. It was a strained, choked-off laugh and Schaftner didn't like the sound of it.

"I don't believe that for a second."

"I . . . think . . . you . . . do."

"I'd better replace the trach."

Cassidy quickly put the thick plastic tube back into Schaftner. He was tempted to leave. He'd expected to share his dream with Schaftner, and instead he was greeted with the same kind of closed thinking the two of them had often ridiculed in outsiders. What had happened to Schaftner in the dark reaches of coma?

Cassidy waited for a minute, then removed the breathing tube. He could see Schaftner was weakening from the ordeal and was relieved to see it. He would leave very soon. The two men no longer had anything to say to one another. The delight and love he had felt before had drifted away.

Schaftner watched him, his face contorted from the effort he was making, but his eyes were bright and intense. "You must . . . destroy!" he gasped.

Again Cassidy laughed. Destroying Adam wasn't even within the realm of possibility. "I can't do that. Adam will be born."

"Must!"

Schaftner's wispy voice cut through Cassidy; he could imagine what an effort it took for him to speak. "I'm sorry," he said. His body tensed, ready to leave.

"If . . . you . . . don't," Schaftner's voice was little more than a growl. He struggled for the next words with what little energy he had left. "I . . . will . . . tell!"

Cassidy stood over Schaftner, his eyes wild and furious.

"No! You can't tell anyone!"

Schaftner could see that Cassidy was no longer the man he knew; he wondered if he was any longer even a man. "Must!" Schaftner's face was tight and resolved; in its own way, as mad as Cassidy's.

Cassidy could feel Schaftner's throat pulsing under his fingertips and the thin rattling of the sick man's breath. If Schaftner told others about the experiment, he'd be believed. Cassidy could see the bleeding fetus being torn from Molly, leaving it quivering to die. Looking at the brittle man, lying just beneath his hand, he could see Adam being destroyed. Schaftner's eyes were two hard, angry rocks. Cassidy knew he would tell.

It would be easy, so easy. All Cassidy had to do was unhook the tracheotomy tube from the respirator and let the air escape from his lungs. There would be seizures and, after a short time, nothing. Cassidy could then run for the nurse, distressed, and explain that Schaftner began to lose air and there was nothing he could do. Schaftner was a dying man. It would be so easy.

Suddenly Schaftner saw his death in Cassidy's eyes. He started to scream, but Cassidy removed his fingers from Schaftner's neck and all sound was gone. It took only a second to remove the tube from the respirator. Schaftner was flailing at the air desperately, feeling air and life hissing from inside himself, pitching him quickly into the black hole of death.

Cassidy rushed to the window and clutched it like a man drowning. His eyes were closed, but he could sense Schaftner's struggle as surely as if he were watching him, and could feel life ebbing from him in a hissing of air, seeping out into nothingness. The hissing seemed to grow louder and louder. Cassidy wanted to cover his ears and go running from the room. He grasped the window even tighter. If he left, the nurse would know what happened. What had happened? He was killing a man. But his mind blacked out at the thought and he held the window, struggling to stay on his feet.

Schaftner's thin, wasted arm was struggling upward toward the buzzer for the nurse. Pain seared his chest until it felt like a burned paper, blackened and weightless. His arm was extended only halfway, yet the effort it was costing him was total. He could sense he was blacking out and struggled to keep hold onto the light, which was growing dimmer with every passing second.

Schaftner pushed his arm higher. The cord was three inches above his fingertips, but his arm was shaking violently and his chest felt as if it was in flames.

Schaftner fought for consciousness like an animal fighting for its life. He felt the cord touch his finger-tips and reached even harder, everything directed toward that one movement, seeing and hearing noth-ing else but the struggle. His fingers closed around the string.

Suddenly there was a shock of blackness. Cassidy stood over Schaftner, knocking his arm away and with it all hope. Schaftner released his hold. Pain more intense than any he had ever known exploded through his chest, and then there was no pain. Schaftner floated into blackness.

Cassidy stood over Schaftner for a long while until he was sure his inert body and wide-open, terrified jungle eyes were dead. Cassidy felt nothing, not fear or remorse or even shock. There was only a clear un-derstanding of what had to be done next.

Efficiently Cassidy replaced the trach in Schaftner's throat and rearranged his covers. Suddenly Schaftner's chest began to expand. Cassidy recoiled, sweat pouring from his face. Schaftner's chest contracted, then once again began to expand. But it was like air rushing in and out of a bladder. Schaftner had already slipped into a place where no amount of air would help. Cassidy walked to the door, opened it mechanically, and screamed. It was a terrified, ear-piercing scream, the scream of a man who had just seen a loved one in his death throes. All at once the scream became real. He was terrified as he reached down into the heart of himself and found only emptiness, torture, and damnation.

Chapter 8

Molly lay, black and glistening with sweat, under the plastic bubble of the Haynes decompression chamber, just as Adam, himself, was lying in the amniotic sac. She was eight months pregnant and had the swollen ridiculous look of a pheasant under glass, yet there was a magnificence to her, a radiance that reached through to everyone in the room.

Lenny walked over to Cassidy, feeling a tenderness and peace she had almost forgotten existed. "It's pretty powerful stuff," she said.

Cassidy smiled and nodded. He too was feeling the peace. It had been three months, three months of relaxing peace. Having brisk, efficient Lenny there, the long nights working with Gilda, the IBM computer they were programming for Adam as a mother prepares her layette, and the quiet, softness of Becky and Mark had helped make the horror of Schaftner's death recede into something that had happened to another. The ghastly nightmares and the torment had begun to fade. And now, standing in front of Molly, he felt almost sane.

A low growl came from Molly. Her face contorted as the spasm rolled across her body. Lenny checked her watch. "Every five minutes. Now she should be getting into the big cramps."

Lenny put her cool hand on Molly's head, but Molly didn't notice; she was concentrating on the pain that reached from her chest to her legs. The pain slowed and faded, then once again Molly's face contorted. Lenny checked her watch. Only thirty seconds. Either labor was progressing faster than usual or it was the other pain.

She tried to get Molly's attention. "Where does it hurt?" But Molly's eyes were shut tightly against the pain, and when Lenny touched her arm, he got no response.

"Oh God," Lenny yelled. "I think it's her heart!"

Molly let out a loud howl as the pain spread across her chest. Suddenly the other pain grabbed at her stomach and pulled the flesh into an agonizing rock.

"Get ready for Caesarean!" There was none of the usual brisk efficiency in Lenny's voice. She was almost yelling.

But no one moved. They were held by the sight of Molly, her face twisted in agony, her eyes glistening sightlessly, filled with a panic that was contagious. Suddenly her arms flailed out and she kicked violently, as if trying to run from the pain.

"Hold her down!" Lenny grabbed Molly's arm, trying to keep the struggling ape from hurting herself. Mark and Becky also clamped onto Molly. Only Cassidy didn't move. He was watching Molly's belly, paralyzed with terror. His lips were blue and he was shivering violently.

"Cassidy, come on. We need you!" Lenny's voice was almost drowned out by Molly's anguished squeals.

Suddenly Cassidy shrieked. "Adam's dying!" Cassidy's hands went to his head and he doubled over screaming.

"Oh my God, Cassidy, stop!" The violent pulling of Molly, the sounds of her agony, and Cassidy's horrified scream were stoking Lenny's own fears. She could feel panic choking off her air until she too wanted to scream.

Cassidy staggered around the room, his body hunched low to the ground. His wail knifed through them all. "He's dying! I can feel it! He's dying!"

Mark and Becky were frozen, unsure of what to do, unable even to ask.

Then suddenly Molly went limp. Lenny grabbed onto her wrist. "There's still a pulse. Cassidy! Do you hear me? There's still a pulse."

But Cassidy was beyond hearing anything but the howling of his own terror.

Lenny whirled on Mark, trying to block out her own fear. "Quick, Cassidy's going into shock. Try to get him down. Cover him up. And for God's sake don't let him near Molly until he's okay." Mark nodded and moved toward Cassidy.

"We're going to have to carry her into the lab," Lenny said to Becky. She lifted the top of the bubble that enclosed Molly, but Becky just stared wide-eyed at the black, still figure.

"Move, Becky. Goddamn it. Move!"

Suddenly Cassidy caught sight of them and pulled away from Mark. "No. Don't. I'm going to do it!" He rushed over to Molly. Just as he reached her, Mark grabbed hold of his shoulders and pulled him away.

"Let go of me," Cassidy screamed. "Me. I have to. Me!"

Mark tightened his grip, tearing Cassidy from Molly.

"No!" Cassidy wailed.

Again Lenny yelled. "Becky! Now! Lift!"

Becky looked up at Lenny, her eyes no longer terrified and wild. "I'm sorry."

"Never mind that now. Just lift."

Lenny and Becky heaved Molly up and started to the door. Just as they were passing through, Cassidy saw them leave and his wail became an appalling howl. It was the howl of an animal.

Becky shouted. "I can see the top of his head."

Lenny didn't answer. She bit her lip as she picked up a scalpel and brought it to Molly's vagina.

"What about Caesarean?"

"Too late. Just watch the monitors."

"I don't know what I'm seeing."

Lenny didn't look up. "Do your best."

Carefully Lenny cut the perineum, then held the two sides with cotton. "Hold on, Molly. Please, hold on," she whispered.

Molly lay motionless, her legs hanging from the straps like a grotesque marionette. Her huge stomach heaved up and down, her breathing labored.

Lenny pushed her hands into Molly's swollen bleeding vagina and touched the head of Adam. Carefully clasping his crown, she began pulling gently. Adam slipped under her fingers but after a while he began to slide toward her. She stopped and touched his temples. There was a pulse. Again she took hold of Adam's head and helped him toward her. Molly's rich red blood oozed down Lenny's gloves and up her arms. Adam moved outward. Lenny could see eyes, then miraculously a nose, a tiny mouth, and a chin.

She stopped, her breath coming fast from the concentration and the fear. Looking down at the membrane-shrouded child, it occurred to her, what did she hold in her hands? Then once again her mind returned to helping him on his journey, bringing his shoulders to Molly's opening.

A shout from Becky. "Something's happening!"

"Tell me." Lenny kept her eyes on the baby.

"I think her heartbeat is irregular. I don't know. I told you I just don't know."

"Keep a watch on it. We're almost there."

"I'm scared."

"So am I."

There was a knock at the door, then it opened. Mark and Cassidy stood in the doorway.

"I can take over now." Lenny glanced up and saw Cassidy calmly walking to Molly's side.

Lenny continued working the baby toward her. She didn't lift her eyes. "No, I'll do it. It's going okay."

"I want to." Cassidy pushed Lenny's hands from the child.

"Are you crazy?" Lenny screamed. Mark started toward Cassidy, but Lenny stopped him. "For God's sake, don't. He's holding Adam!"

Cassidy touched Adam's head, cradling it in his hands. "He's beautiful," he breathed. "Look at him, he's beautiful!"

Becky yelled, "It's getting worse!"

Lenny hissed, "Get away! Do you want to kill Adam?"

Suddenly Cassidy looked down at his hands covered with blood and membrane. He shuddered violently. For a moment he was torn between wanting to breathe life into Adam and wanting to kill him. He looked around terrified, then quickly backed away.

Lenny grabbed Adam's head. The pulse was still there. Molly's belly still heaved with breath. "Okay," she whispered, "we're okay." She began pulling again, twisting the little form of Adam back and forth, rocking him as she brought him toward her and into the light. Adam's shoulders pressed tightly to the birth canal, resisting. She pulled harder. Suddenly Adam slid free, spilling toward her.

Lenny gathered him in her hands, blood and membrane covering them both. Suddenly Adam started to breathe on his own.

He cried, loud, shattering the room with its power. It was a cry of pain and joy and greed, the cry of life.

Book Two

ADAM

Adam felt a burning warmth spread out from him to the bedclothes. He had wet his bed again. He threw back the covers angrily and sat stewing in his own dampness. Being four years old was no great shakes, that was for sure. A child's world was dangerous and frustrating, a world of legs and hems, unreachable doorknobs, unopenable locks, shelves that were too high even with a chair. On the other hand, it was warm, soft, and filled with colors, tastes, and sounds so new and startlingly vivid that sometimes he wanted to scream out with happiness.

Adam flicked a switch near his bed and a four-foot remote TV screen lit up, showing the land that lay just outside his door, a concession to the windowless basement they all lived in.

It was dawn and the orange sun sat atop the mountains. Everything was hazy blue, cool, and peaceful. But that rising orange ball held the promise of the glittering heat that would come later.

Adam stared with wonder at the flat emptiness with its sprinkling of Joshua trees and dried shrubs. Beyond that small parcel of land were oceans and mountains, lakes and forests. Paris was out there, 6,000 miles away. Paris was the capital of France and had a population of over 9 million, including its suburbs. One day Adam would see Paris and eat snails and frog's legs. India was in the opposite direction and was a very big country, over 1 million square miles. They spoke many dialects there, most of them originating from Sanskrit, but Hindi and English were the primary languages. He decided he'd visit a guru when he went. One day he'd do everything—climb mountains, eat frog's legs, swim the oceans, maybe even see the universe. But for now, this was his world. Adam looked around at the colorful circus wallpaper and the mobiles trembling from the ceiling. Gilda, the massive home computer, completely covered one wall, a giant toy box the other.

Adam felt a chill pass through him as his damp bed became room temperature. There was no question, it was a drag being a kid, and while Mark said adulthood was no party either, it looked pretty good from where Adam sat. At least you didn't have to walk around with your underpants stiff with peepee or go to bed when everyone else was just starting to have fun. And, anyway, Mark admitted his judgment wasn't always accurate. He said he was neurotic. The dictionary defined neurosis as an emotional disorder in which feelings of anxiety, obsessive thoughts, compulsive acts, and physical complaints dominate the personality. Mark said it was like trying to open a door with your foot.

He slid to the floor and walked off to the bathroom, leaving moist footprints behind him. He pulled on a pair of corduroy pants and a T-shirt, then glanced at the digital watch. It was almost six o'clock, and he'd have to rush like mad if he wanted to get in any time with Molly before breakfast and lessons.

When Adam walked into the cage room Molly was

already jumping up and down, holding onto the
bars and rattling them happily with her huge, leathery
hands. She lifted Adam to her thick black neck and he
buried his face deep into her, clinging tightly, taking
in big drafts of her warm animal smell. Molly sighed
deeply. She loved feeling the little fingers exploring
her neck, trusting and fragile fingers that held onto
her hard, muscular body like roots to the earth. She
knew she had to be very careful with Adam; she was
big and strong and any careless move could hurt him.
One time, when Adam was a baby, she had pulled at
his arm too hard and he'd cried.

Molly had shrieked and hidden herself in the corner,
neither eating nor sleeping for days. Something happened to her when she heard Adam cry out, something
that twisted her soul and left her breathless with des-
pair. After that time, Molly reminded herself every
morning to be careful of the porcelain boy with the
big, fringed, blue eyes, and whenever she touched him
she always checked his face for any sign of pain.

Molly felt Adam's body tense, and she sensed he
wanted to be let down. She allowed the sturdy little
body to reach the floor, then stood, watching and
waiting to see what Adam wanted. Immediately Adam
began signing to her. Molly understood very little of
what Adam was saying, but she watched with fascination. Of everyone, Adam seemed least able to understand that Molly wasn't human. And in the end, it
didn't matter what he was saying; all that really mattered were the tiny, quick-moving fingers and the
solemn, blue eyes. Molly found it hard to imagine not
being able to play with the small boy, sense his whims,
breathe in his familiar smell.

Adam saw the faraway look in Molly's eyes and

pulled at her arm. "Today I dissect a frog," he signed proudly.

"Dissect?"

"Cut up."

Molly looked at Adam, puzzled. She knew food was cut up, and sometimes knees became cut up if you fell down hard. "You will eat?" she asked.

Adam laughed. It was a tinkling laugh that lit up Molly's soul. She loved it when Adam laughed, though she knew the humor often lay in her being stupid.

"We cut up the frog to learn all about it."

"Why?"

"Y is the twenty-fifth letter of the alphabet."

Molly watched Adam, confused, and Adam giggled and jumped into her arms, tickling her warm, hairy chest. Molly sighed deeply and stared straight ahead in wonder and delight.

Once again Adam glanced at his watch and Molly felt a weight falling across her. It was time to go and she wouldn't be seeing Adam again until late afternoon. The few precious minutes she spent with him were never enough. She turned to the wall so she wouldn't have to watch him leave, listening to the loud, final clank as he closed the heavy iron door and skipped off to breakfast. Then she sat down and stared at the wall, trying to wait out the day.

When Adam walked into the kitchen, everyone was already at the table, passing around a huge bowl of steaming scrambled eggs and a platter of bacon. The kitchen was warm with the smell of cinnamon and coffee and full of the sounds of raucous laughter and morning groans.

Lenny helped Adam onto a telephone book they had placed on a chair, tucked in his napkin, and handed him a strip of bacon. She gave a sniff, then smiled. "I guess we haven't quite got this bed-wetting licked yet."

Adam pulled a face. "Freud says you shouldn't tease kids about that." He smiled slyly, then bit into the bacon.

"Nobody likes a smart-ass kid," said Lenny, trying to stifle her laughter. "Just remember that."

"Is my ass smart?" Adam's eyes were full of wonder and newness.

"Not this morning it wasn't," Mark answered with a wink.

"Don't listen to them," growled Cassidy. "There isn't a bone in your body that isn't smarter than any of them."

"Even you?"

Cassidy glanced up from his buttery eggs and shot Adam a withering glance. "Nobody likes a smart-ass kid," he muttered, then went back to attacking breakfast.

Adam clapped his greasy hands together in delight while everyone around him laughed. Cassidy, Lenny, Mark, and Becky exchanged proud parental looks, full of softness and contentment.

Four years had hardly aged them, yet there was something older, deeper about them. The everyday work of caring for a child had started the process, but it was the four years of discovery and wonder that taught them a lesson in love and trust and bound them to Adam and each other. Everything else began to recede, until none of them left the compound for more than a few hours at a time. It was hard for any of them to imagine a time without Adam.

Becky pushed back a stray hair from Adam's eyes and gave him a kiss. Sitting in the warm kitchen with

its smells of food and its light and laughter, Adam
thought there could be no finer family around.

"Where did I come from?" Adam was sitting at the
console of Gilda, the computer, but his eyes were on
Cassidy.

Cassidy flicked through the trigonometry book he
was holding and laughed nervously. He could see what
was coming and wanted to avoid it.

"Didn't I tell you all about reproduction?"

"Yes." Adam continued to watch Cassidy.

"So what do you want me to explain?"

"I understand reproduction, but it's other things,
things I can feel."

"Like?"

"Who am I?" Adam's voice was chilling.

"You're Adam, that's who you are."

"Why do I look like Mark and act like you?" Adam
was pressing. The childish pout and lisp were gone. He
looked like a wizened old dwarf.

Cassidy stood up. "I'll go get the others."

"Why do we need the others?"

"We're all involved. We should all tell you together."

Adam shivered. "Is it that terrible?"

Cassidy sat back down, taking Adam's little hand in
his. "Terrible? It isn't terrible at all. It's wonderful.
It's the most goddamn wonderful thing in the world."

Adam searched Cassidy's face for signs that it wasn't
true. All he found was the awe of the artist, the pride
of the creator, a cosmic wonder. Adam smiled up at
Cassidy. "I'd rather you told me."

"You got it." But having said that, Cassidy became
silent, holding Adam's hand in his, trying to make

some kind of sense out of the months of confusion. He would have given a lot for Mark's quick tongue or Lenny's sensibility or even Becky's dark intuition.

Suddenly Adam sat up straight. Sparkling glass and steel flashed through his mind, and across it all, a stain of bright red blood, pulsing and warm. He covered his eyes with his hands and the flashes stopped.

"What's the matter?" asked Cassidy, trying to take Adam in his arms.

Adam's body stiffened. Something inside warned him that he shouldn't tell Cassidy about the flashes. It had been the same kind of feeling that told him not to tell anyone about the time he knocked over the milk carton in the refrigerator or took candy from Lenny's room. But this time the feeling was stronger, more urgent. Adam didn't know where the flashes had come from or what they meant, although there was the feeling that somewhere inside himself he did, that he was hiding their meaning from himself.

"Nothing's the matter," Adam said and smiled calmly.

Cassidy relaxed. "Do you remember when I explained to you about genetic engineering? Well, it was like that with you. It's true, you do look like Mark and act like me. You're parts of both of us. I took cells from both Mark and me and engineered them."

Adam interrupted, "Which cells?"

"Epithelial."

"I see. And then what?"

Cassidy was amazed at the cold detachment Adam was showing. He glanced at Adam but could read nothing from his face. Whatever it was that Adam was feeling, Cassidy could imagine it must be pretty powerful. He had been through somewhat the same thing, though his experience had been limited to printing on the schoolyard fence and the snickering of his friends. Learning he was a bastard had hardly been a high point in his life. Was Adam a bastard too? In a sense he was. Cassidy held his little hand tightly. "After I cultured the new cell, I placed it in an egg voided of its genetic coding and allowed it to grow."

"Where?" The question came out with the same clinical detachment as before, but inside Adam's head flashes of bright blood and the black heat of Molly's delivery burned.

"Why are you asking me all this now?"

"I want to know now!" Adam's voice was hard and impatient. The bloodstained images were still reverberating in his brain, and the black inert form still imprinted on his mind. Somehow he understood everything. "I came from Molly, didn't I?"

"What makes you say that?"

"I feel it."

Cassidy looked away. "And if I told you that you were wrong?"

"I wouldn't believe it. You put me in an ape."

"All her body did was hold you. You were complete long before we implanted." He paused, again trying to read what Adam was thinking. "You love Molly."

"Yes." Adam's voice was tense and faraway. He sat in his chair, his eyes turned inward, focusing on the flashes that pulsed in his brain. He tried to imagine the liquid floating world, dark, red, and muffled, and the twisting tube that led to the black animal center of Molly. It was a graphic picture he received back but one that didn't really belong to him. He wasn't sure what did belong to him. If Lenny's flat, tanned belly had held him, would he feel any better? Everything and everyone came from somewhere, Adam knew, though he'd never known it with such force until now.

"I'm sorry," Cassidy said at last.

Adam tried to smile. "I'm not."

Cassidy wanted to believe this more than he'd ever wanted to believe anything, but he couldn't. Everyone was always sorry about where they came from. When Cassidy was a little boy, he used to dream he'd been born of a prince and princess. Later, he realized, even that would have been a disappointment to him. In the end, no one ever seemed worthy enough of bearing you.

"Remember I told you about the Greek gods and how some of them came from animals? It's like that with you. You're made from everything, part man, part woman, and even part animal. That makes you very special."

Adam's eyes broke into planes of glittering light. "The most special boy in the world! I'm perfect," he said proudly.

Cassidy smiled. "Yes. Adam is perfect."

Adam checked his watch. It was close to five o'clock, almost time for free-play hour. Adam thought about what he and Molly would do with the only time in the day when someone wasn't asking questions and expecting answers.

"Your mind isn't on Milton," said Lenny, pushing the button on Gilda and illuminating a new page.

"Even Homer nods," answered Adam.

Lenny laughed and ruffled his head fondly. "Very funny, smarty-pants."

Adam was confused. "Why is it funny?"

Again Lenny started giggling. "Comparing yourself to Homer. It's funny."

"I could be Homer if I felt like it."

The smile faded from Lenny's face. "Yes. I suppose you could."

There were whole days when Lenny forgot who Adam was, but then, all at once, the reminder, always unsettling. Adam was so sweet and loving, so like a real child, but behind the pale soft skin and enormous blue eyes was a brain so powerful and complete within itself that she wanted to run from the sight of him. Adam was just four years old, but mentally he was somewhere in his twenties, a gifted, intuitive person. Why that unnerved her, she didn't know. Cassidy said it was man's primitive fear of anything he doesn't understand. Lenny didn't know what she thought.

"I don't think I will be Homer, though," Adam said seriously.

"Oh, really? Who will you be, then?"

"You!" Adam jumped onto Lenny's lap and threw his arms around her neck in a big, giggly bear hug. "I love Lenny," he said happily.

And once again Lenny was holding a child of flesh and blood, not the marble or clay creation she sometimes felt Mark and Cassidy saw, but a living, breathing child.

Adam glanced at his watch. "Free time!" he announced and climbed off Lenny's lap.

"What will you do today?" Lenny asked, smiling.

"It's a secret. I only just thought of it."

"Will you tell us all about it at dinner?"

"Only if it works."

"And if it doesn't?"

"Then it'll stay a secret until it does."

"Okay, okay," laughed Lenny. "Just be sure you're back on time."

"What's for dinner?"

"It's a secret," Lenny teased and started gathering up her pencils and notes.

Adam walked to the door. Lenny reached to open it for him but he gently nudged her away. "I'll do it." He turned the knob until the door clicked free, then called to BooBoo, the Doberman. Together they went to get Molly.

Adam applied fifty volts of electricity to the headless body of a frog he and Cassidy had been working on earlier. It jumped and Adam giggled, trying it again. It occurred to him that in France people ate frogs. The frog looked horrible and felt slimy, and he couldn't imagine eating one of its legs. He decided he might not go to France after all.

"BooBoo, stay!" Adam held up his finger. "I'll give you a treat later."

BooBoo sat, looking at his master, obediently awaiting further instructions, his black tail swishing happily. Molly sat on the floor, one eye on Adam, the other on a picture book. She was looking at the picture of the big monkey and the little monkey. It had become her favorite because it reminded her of her and Adam.

Adam signed to Molly. "Does Molly understand the word *secret*?"

"Secret means no hand talking," Molly answered.

"Ever," amended Adam.

"Yes. Molly understands."

"This is secret."

"What?" Molly looked around, confused.

"What Adam is going to do."

"Future?"

"Near future. Starting now."

"Yes."

Adam looked into the glove box, then carefully opened a large glass bottle. He took a rag from the drawer in Mark's lab bench and soaked it.

"BooBoo, come here."

BooBoo walked to Adam and gently licked his face. Adam giggled, wiping off the wet with his shirt sleeve, then clamped the rag over BooBoo's muzzle. BooBoo shivered for a moment, then slipped to the floor. Adam resoaked the rag, placed it over BooBoo's face, and tried to lift him up. The huge dog hardly moved.

Adam signed to Molly. "Put BooBoo on lab bench."

Molly got up and walked over to BooBoo. "Dead?"

"Sleeping."

Molly shivered, remembering her own sleep. She looked over at Adam but he seemed calm.

"BooBoo is okay," signed Adam.

Molly stood where she was for a while longer but eventually stooped and lifted the dog to the lab bench.

"No, no, on his back."

Molly tried to put BooBoo on his back, but he kept rolling to his side.

Adam laughed. "Okay, Molly. It's fine." He watched as Molly let go of BooBoo and shuffled back to her place on the floor. For a moment what Cassidy had told him about his birth lit up his mind, and the bright red-and-black flashes unsettled him. But they were soon gone and he turned back to BooBoo, his mind calm and practical.

Adam pulled a footstool over to where BooBoo lay and climbed up. He found the knife they'd used

earlier on the frog and stood holding it in his tiny
hand, looking down at BooBoo.

Adam knew what hearts were supposed to do and
had seen many pictures of them, but he'd never held
one in his hand. He wondered how it would be to hold
the pumping bundle of muscle and feel the twitching
at it pumped blood to the rest of the body. He imagined it would tickle.

Adam moved the knife to where his hand was, then
pressed down hard into BooBoo's tough dog flesh. He
felt the blade begin to slip through and pressed down
even harder. Suddenly blood spurted out all over his
hands and shirt. Adam recoiled in terror. The frog
hadn't bled like that.

Molly stood up instantly, the smell of blood filling
the air.

"Get a pan," signed Adam. He wished he had
thought of the pan before. What if he couldn't catch
all the blood? Already much of it was lost on his hands
and shirt. But then he remembered how new blood was
manufactured by the bone marrow and decided that
BooBoo would be fine.

Molly brought the pan and stood like a shadow over
his shoulder. Adam turned and signed, "Go!"

Molly hesitated, the smell of blood making her fearful and agitated, but eventually she moved back,
watching from the center of the lab, alert and rigid,
shrinking from the warm, sweet odor that meant danger to her.

Again Adam pushed the knife deep into BooBoo.
The blood no longer spurted but oozed out all over his
hands and dripped into the pan. The thick skin resisted the knife until finally Adam had to saw back
and forth to get through. After a minute, he had made

a bloody flap of skin and hair. Adam lifted it up and looked inside. All he could see was more blood.

He reached over for a paper towel and left a great red smear on the dispenser. He'd have to clean that up before Cassidy found out. Then it occurred to him that he'd forgotten to bring a needle and thread to stitch BooBoo back up. He'd have to sneak into the utility cupboard of the kitchen to get it, which would be no easy thing to do without someone seeing him. But he knew he'd figure something out. He was good at figuring things out.

Adam placed several paper towels over the wound. They quickly soaked up the blood, but everything was still liquid and red. He saw a patch of white and decided it must be bone. Adam put his hand on BooBoo's rib cage. It felt smooth and slippery to the touch; underneath it something quivered. Adam wasn't sure whether he was touching the lungs or the heart. Everything was so slimy and wet, it was hard to know where things were.

Adam pushed his hand in deeper; the soft lung tissue moved, and finally he felt a tough knot of muscle, jerking violently. He slid his fingers around it and tried to pull the pumping muscle out so that he could see it.

All at once BooBoo twitched. Adam recoiled, pulling his hand from the dog's chest. He caught himself just before he screamed. Then, quickly, he climbed off the stool and rushed back to the glove box for more chloroform.

Molly didn't move, but her watchful, terrified eyes darted from BooBoo to Adam.

"Secret," Adam signed.

"Adam hurt BooBoo?"

"I promise to put BooBoo back together again."

Adam brought the soaked rag back to BooBoo but just as he reached down to him, the dog convulsed, his twitching legs clawing the air. A terrible howl came from him and suddenly he sprang from the lab bench, blood pouring from his chest, bright red organs sagging outward.

"No!" yelled Adam. "Stay!"

BooBoo lurched around the laboratory, desperately searching for a way out, screeching out in pain as he spilled his life all over the floor.

Adam rushed after him, yelling, "No! Stop! I want you to stop!"

Suddenly BooBoo turned. Adam stopped, seeing the enormous dog's teeth bared, his horrifying growl of agony and rage filling the room. Adam screamed, pushing himself tightly against the lab bench, watching the dog as he poised, ready to strike.

There was a moment of frozen terror, then Molly grabbed BooBoo by the neck and jerked him up into the air, bleeding and howling. BooBoo thrashed out, struggling against the black shadow that held him. Molly was breathing heavily, her black, gleaming eyes senseless with rage. Suddenly she smashed BooBoo against the lab bench. There was a loud crack as the dog's head hit, splintering his brain case into a thousand pieces. Then there was silence. Molly let BooBoo drop from her grasp.

Adam was crouched in the corner, crying. Molly scooted over to him and lifted him to her great warm chest. Adam clung to her tightly, his small body shaking against the furry softness. It took several minutes before Adam's body began to relax and he lay still in Molly's arms. Then he turned to the broken bleeding mass on the floor that was BooBoo. Confused and angry, he clung tightly to Molly but his eyes were on the dog. "Bad BooBoo," he said. "BooBoo wanted to hurt Adam. Now I won't put you back together again."

Just then, Cassidy walked into the laboratory.

"He doesn't understand death." Cassidy looked around at the others who sat at the dinner table, unable to touch the steaming meal that lay at its center. Only Adam was missing from the table, but his presence hung over all of them.

Lenny blew up. "For Christ's sake, he understands quantum mechanics. How come he doesn't understand a simple one, like dog dies?"

"He understands the word," Mark said wearily, "but not the reality."

"What you're saying is, he doesn't care." Lenny's words were directed to Mark, but she was staring through Cassidy.

"That isn't what he means," said Cassidy. "Adam thought he could put BooBoo together again like a clock. I confused him by showing him how frogs can live even without their heads for a while."

"Some living," said Becky.

"Well, he didn't think about that," said Cassidy quietly.

"Oh yeah?" Lenny's voice was brittle with anger. "Did you ask him how it would feel if he had to live without his head?"

"You can't expect a four-year-old to reason all that out, you know."

Lenny banged her fist on the table. "How come Adam's always four years old when you want to pro-

tect him, and mature and responsible when you think
he should gain an extra privilege?"

"The question is, what do we do about it?" said
Mark.

"At this moment I can't think of a punishment that
would satisfy me!" Lenny felt bloodless and a chill
passed through her.

"He's bad," said Becky.

"Well, he certainly wasn't what I'd call a good boy,"
said Mark.

"That's not what I mean."

Cassidy whirled around. "What do you mean?"

Everyone was watching Becky, Mark's eyes full of
warning. Becky's fear of Adam was something they had
discussed in the dark warmth of their bed. While Mark
had never believed there was any truth to what she
said, he'd always been there to listen. But that was one
thing. Exposing it to the light and especially to Cassidy was another thing entirely.

Becky looked around at them all. For a moment it
seemed that they knew what she was thinking and
agreed with her. Then she decided they were all just
lost in their own thoughts and she turned away, her
jaw tensed, holding back the words she wanted to
say.

"I'll go talk to him," Cassidy said at last.

"Talk!" Lenny laughed angrily. "Talk has no place
here. We have to punish him or he'll do it again."

Cassidy smiled. "He can't. We've run out of dogs."

"I ought to rip that smile off your face." Lenny's
voice crackled. "You have some weird sense of humor.
How would you like it if Adam decided to take a
closer look at your heart? Anything in the interest of
science, huh?"

Cassidy didn't answer. There was a part of him that almost agreed with her.

Lenny turned to Mark. "You talked to him. Is he sorry?"

"He said he was sorry." Mark avoided her eyes.

"But is he?"

"I don't think he understands being sorry."

"What, in good Christ's name, does he understand?"

"Look, I don't know. Maybe he does. He understands that BooBoo could have hurt him, and he's sorry about that. He understands now that he can't go around carving up animals."

"I asked, is he sorry?"

"It's a difficult question . . ."

"In other words, he isn't. He's just disappointed that dogs die and he can't put them back together so he can have another go at butchering them later."

"He's a child," said Cassidy. "Children don't understand things like that. It takes years to build up a child's morality."

"We don't have years, Cassidy. In case you hadn't noticed, he's already a grown-up mentally, and a damn smart one at that."

"But he's still a child," Cassidy insisted. "We knew it was going to be difficult with all his different parts growing at different rates, but it's nothing we can't handle."

"Maybe. If we let him know right now what is right. If not, we're going to get ourselves into a heap of trouble."

"Okay, what do you suggest?" Cassidy challenged.

"I'm glad you asked because I've got a couple dozen suggestions, starting with punishing him for what he did and ending with some nice reading in the Bible."

"The what?" Cassidy laughed. "You can take the girl out of the church, but you can't take the church out of the girl."

"Don't be an ass. I'm not asking you to sign him away to the Catholic church. You know how I feel about that. But there are some good things he can read in the Bible, some lessons he ought to be learning."

"There's a lot of bullturd, too."

"Oh yeah, like 'do unto others.' Is that your idea of bullturd? Because that's exactly the opposite of what you're teaching him."

Mark interrupted. "There can't be any harm in what Lenny's saying. We can cram it into his schedule. He's already learning faster than we could have projected. At least he is in history, geography, and science."

"Don't worry," said Lenny. "We can use my English time. None of it would come out of your precious science lectures."

Cassidy held up his hands. "Okay, okay, Adam will learn the Bible."

"Good. And you'll punish him?"

"Reading the Bible sounds like punishment enough."

"Shut up, Cassidy. No one's laughing."

"You're so big on punishing, you do it," said Cassidy.

"No. We have to all be in on it together," said Mark. "Otherwise Adam will learn to go to those of us who won't punish him and avoid those who will."

"Okay, Mark," snapped Cassidy. "What kind of punishment do you suggest?"

Lenny interjected. "I think we should take away

Adam's free hour for a month. Or better yet, until we feel he understands what he did."

Cassidy shook his head. "Adam isn't going to like that."

"He's not supposed to. I think it's about time Adam began to experience some things he doesn't like. I think it'll be good for him. In fact, it'll probably be good for all of us."

"What's that supposed to mean?" Cassidy asked angrily.

"I call for a vote," said Mark. "Everyone ready?"

Cassidy glanced angrily at Lenny but nodded.

There were three votes to punish and one against. No one heard, but down the hall a door clicked closed when the vote was finished.

Adam woke up at 5:45 and switched on his remote TV. It was another hazy morning, the sun riding the crest of the mountains as if it was floating on a blue ocean. Adam felt a wet chill around him and realized he had wet his bed again. He jumped to the ground, angrily pulled his wet pajamas off, and threw them into a pile on the floor.

He grabbed his clothes out of the dresser, pulling on his pants and his T-shirt with hasty, jerking fury. The T-shirt ripped and he tore it off, throwing it onto the pile of wet pajamas and stomping on them.

Suddenly he began to cry. Tears of frustration and rage coursed down his cheeks. He hadn't meant to hurt BooBoo. He'd only tried to do an experiment, just like Cassidy always did. It hadn't occurred to him what would happen if he failed. And yet they were punishing him.

Adam didn't want to be punished. It wasn't fair. But

more than that, Adam felt the power of everyone's rejection. Suddenly love and warmth and comfort were eclipsed by the chill black shadow of anger and it left him shivering. They were angry with him. No one had ever really been angry with him before, and to him, it looked the same as hate. Adam stood in the middle of his room, half dressed, the tears rolling down his face, balanced between agonizing sadness and rage. They were new emotions to him, powerful and debilitating. The anger was like a blinding light that left him hollow and twisted inside. It filled his stomach with a tight pain and his head echoed with the flashing images of everyone's faces. The need to strike out at those faces was so overwhelming that he felt every muscle in his body cry out, leaving him with a pent-up energy that tingled electrically. He felt more alone than he ever had before.

Finally Adam calmed and opened his door. He looked out cautiously, but everyone was still asleep. He turned toward Molly's cage room, his pace quickening until he tore at the lock and rushed to Molly's arms. She swept him up and Adam clung to her, crying.

Suddenly Cassidy rushed in. "Get down," he yelled to Adam.

Adam looked around surprised, still holding tight to Molly's warm comfortable body.

"I don't want you going near Molly for a while. Now get down!" Cassidy walked over and took Adam from Molly's arms. Molly didn't resist but watched Cassidy, surprised and hurt.

"Why Cassidy take Adam from Molly?" she signed.

Cassidy lowered Adam to the floor. "Go into the kitchen."

"I want my time with Molly."

"Not now!" Cassidy's voice was sharp. Adam had never heard Cassidy speak that way to him and again the tears and the anger welled up. He watched for a moment longer, then let himself out of the cage.

Molly touched Cassidy's arm. "Cassidy angry at Molly?"

"No. Not angry."

"Molly hurt BooBoo and Cassidy angry."

"No. Molly was right to hurt BooBoo. Molly was protecting Adam."

"Then why Cassidy take Adam away?"

"Just for a while."

"Why?"

"Just for a short time." Cassidy turned from Molly quickly and left her cage without looking back. He knew he had no real reason to be scared of Molly. But the reminder of her power to hurt was too strong, and it would take a while for him to feel comfortable enough to let Molly touch Adam. It occurred to him that perhaps he'd never be able to allow it again. Seeing Adam clutching tightly to the huge black shadowy creature had terrified him, and all he wanted was to tear Adam from her and get him as far away as he could.

Molly watched Cassidy leave and heard the kitchen door slam. It was quiet. She sat down on the floor of her cage and picked up a bit of half-eaten banana, but she wasn't hungry.

Molly didn't understand. She'd only done what she was supposed to do. Cassidy had told her long ago to protect Adam. How could she have done something wrong if she was only doing what they told her to do? And now Adam was gone. She didn't even know for how long. What if she was never allowed to play with Adam again? What if they took him away forever and left her all alone in her dark empty cage?

A howl of mourning came from deep inside Molly, and she hugged herself, rocking back and forth. What if she wasn't allowed to see him anymore?

The flashes started again for Adam that afternoon. They began slowly, distant and unintelligible, a series of faint flashes that he didn't understand: an old man gasping for breath, reaching up toward something above his head, breath hissing from a steel-rimmed hole in his neck.

Adam was sitting at Gilda's typewriter. He stopped, trying to make sense out of the disjointed images. Then he heard a voice, garbled and faraway.

Cassidy was pacing the room behind him, cold and distant. Cassidy turned and saw Adam staring into space. "What's the matter?" he asked curtly.

Adam didn't answer, unsure whether the voice he'd heard came from Cassidy or his own head. It was a similar voice, perhaps even the same.

Cassidy walked to Adam and stood over him. "Is there something you don't understand?"

Adam looked up and smiled. "No. It's easy. I was just thinking."

"Try thinking about what you're doing!" Cassidy recognized in himself all the condescension of the black-moled, sagging-breasted teachers he'd had to put up with from kindergarten on. Becoming an adult was full of discovering people inside yourself you would have hated as a child.

"You're angry at me. Why?" asked Adam.

"Didn't Mark explain it to you?"

"Mark explained why he was angry. I don't think it's the same reason."

Again Adam heard the voice, still faraway but coming closer. He closed his eyes, trying to concentrate. His efforts were halting and not very productive, and the images kept interfering: an old man dying; Molly, her giant black arm raised threateningly; a long dark corridor in a basement apartment with two people Adam had never seen; and a dark, angry young boy hiding in the shadows, crying.

Cassidy's voice stopped the flashes. "I guess I'm angry at you for making everyone else angry. I know you didn't mean to hurt BooBoo. I understand why you did it, too. But no one else does."

"We can get another dog."

"That's not the point."

"Yes, it is. What's the difference if one dog dies? Look what I learned from it." Adam had a feeling that only seconds before, the voice had told him that. He recognized the voice as Cassidy's.

Cassidy shook his head. "That's not the way you should be thinking."

"That's the way you're thinking."

Cassidy recoiled. "What made you say that?"

Adam felt a burning sensation in his fingertips. They felt cold and sensitive. It was a sensation similar to fear, yet he wasn't scared himself. He looked into Cassidy's eyes and found the fear he was seeking.

"I'm sorry I hurt Booboo."

Cassidy relaxed. "Promise you'll check with me from now on before you do any scientific experiments?"

"I promise."

Adam felt his body relax. Once again the relaxation

wasn't his, any more than the fear had been. Suddenly Adam realized that the voices, the flashing images, the emotions were all coming from Cassidy. There was a moment of fear, then a feeling of solidity and power. As the images throbbed in his mind, he sensed long gray corridors opening to him, filled with electric pulses, pictures past, present, and imaginary, snatches of music, the smell of food and flowers. He wondered if he could travel into the heart of Cassidy's brain. He concentrated on the face he knew so well, his mind making a fine point of light. The gray corridors seemed to open before him. Adam closed them off, sensing that he had better wait for another time, eager, confused, terrified, and expectant.

"We should get back to work," Adam said brightly.

Cassidy smiled. "My sentiments exactly."

As Adam leaned back to his work, all the sorrow he'd been feeling disappeared, and he knew he was very special.

The human brain, rutted, shriveled like a walnut, an undistinguished-looking gray mass, shimmered on Gilda's screen, followed quickly by side, then cross-sectional, views. Adam pressed a button and the brain was replaced by words.

"The human brain is divided into two hemispheres, the right and the left. The left is the source of cognitive knowledge, logical, sequential thinking and language. The right hemisphere is the seat of inspirational, intuitive thinking. Shadowy and mysterious, the right hemisphere accounts for those flashes of thought that, while often not logical, are powerful and comprehensive. In children the transfer of information between hemispheres is more complete, and any damage to one can be compensated for by the other. This ability quickly disappears and most adults rely primarily on left hemisphere thinking."

Adam leaned back in his chair and tried to reach into the right side of his brain, then tried to make contact with his left side. It felt the same.

He turned back to the console. "How do you make contact with the right hemisphere?"

Gilda responded instantly. "Go to sleep."

"Stupid!" Adam banged on the keys angrily. Then he tried again. "Name possibilities."

"Sleep, especially dreams, meditation, possibly ESP."

"Define ESP."

"Extrasensory perception. The ability to exercise precognition, psychokinesis, mind control, prophecy, telepathy, levitation, and other psychic phenomena."

Adam became excited. That sounded pretty close to what he was experiencing. "How does someone get ESP?"

"No definite information on source of ESP. Theories hold that everyone has it to some extent."

"Why doesn't everyone use it?"

"Unknown."

"Speculate."

"The mind may become too cluttered with everyday thoughts. Flashes of ESP become inundated and eventually drown."

"In other words, children have more ESP than adults."

"Possibly. There is less going on in their minds to distract them."

"And there is the greater connection between the right and left hemispheres."

"Unknown."

"But it is possible."

"Anything is possible."

Adam realized that every time he asked Gilda if something was possible, the answer was always the same. He rightly reasoned that this was a Cassidyism inserted into every program and wondered if Cassidy really believed this. He decided that he did. And perhaps he was right. Adam himself was an impossibility, and yet he could hardly question his own reality.

"Start all available information on ESP."

"No available information."

"Damn it!" Adam pushed his chair back from the console. Cassidy hadn't programmed Gilda for ESP. Adam wondered whether that was because Cassidy didn't consider it worth learning about or because it was too powerful for Adam to know.

It left Adam with two choices. Either he could forget all about ESP and continue his work on the digestive system of the segmented worm, or he could ask Cassidy to program Gilda for it. The second course of action could be dangerous. If Cassidy hadn't programmed for ESP because he felt it was something Adam shouldn't know, then Cassidy might become suspicious. If he thought it was not worth learning, he'd simply refuse. There was a slim chance Cassidy would relent, not wishing to stifle any inquiry by Adam; it was hard to tell with Cassidy. The thing to avoid was suspicion. It occurred to Adam that if he truly had ESP he'd sense Cassidy's suspicion immediately and be able to divert him with answers he would want to hear. And if he didn't have ESP? Well, then it would make no difference if he became suspicious.

Adam rolled the alternatives over in his mind for a moment longer, then smiled. ESP or not, he loved the inner workings of his mind.

"It's a load of rat turd," answered Cassidy, his mouth full of mashed potatoes. He glanced around the table, then went back to his copy of *Lancet* propped in front of him.

"I don't agree," said Mark. As always, his table manners were impeccable. He was the kind of man who used a cloth napkin to eat a candy bar.

Adam made another stab at getting a forkful of potatoes to his mouth. Sixty percent landed on the table in a gooey blob. Becky sighed and wiped up the mess.

"I came across ESP when I was doing some reading on the brain," said Adam casually. "But when I tried to find out more about it, Gilda said no more info."

"Good for Gilda. She's a nice obedient computer."

"Why?"

"I don't want you wasting your time."

Lenny pointed to a spear of broccoli on Adam's plate. "ESP is knowing what's going to happen before it does," she said.

"How about mind reading?"

"That too. Now open your mouth and start stuffing. I want you to eat all your broccoli before you leave this table."

"How about moving objects with your mind?"

"You seem to know a lot more about the subject than you say," Becky answered.

Adam avoided her eyes, shrugged, and picked up the broccoli with his hands. He took a bite, hated the taste, and spat it out.

Lenny tried not to laugh, though her entire childhood seemed to have been spent sitting at a table, staring down at one soggy green mess or another. "Eat it," she warned.

"It tastes terrible."

"It's good for you. Now eat it."

Cassidy glanced up. "Leave him alone. You want him ending up on a psychiatrist's couch just because of a lousy stalk of cellulose?"

Mark laughed. "Living in this family, his chance of avoiding the couch is a little under nil."

"I'll eat my broccoli if you'll promise to tell me about ESP."

Lenny held the broccoli up to Adam's firmly closed lips. "No blackmail. Eat."

"Why do you want to know about ESP?" Becky was still looking at Adam sharply, and for the first time he realized how rarely she looked at him.

Adam allowed a small amount of the broccoli into his mouth and struggled to get it down, but in his mind he was zeroing in on Becky's face and her keen eyes, on the dark rutted corridors and the flashing electric pictures. He felt fear clutching at his body, then suddenly realized the fear was his own. The corridors of his own mind were opening like a fan. He shifted his great blue eyes to Becky's and saw the answer to his question.

"Why shouldn't I want to know?" Adam asked.

Becky turned away quickly. "Because, like Cassidy says, it's stupid. ESP doesn't exist."

"I just like to know things, that's all," answered Adam.

Cassidy looked up from his reading and repeated, "Waste of time."

"I had an ESP experience once," mused Mark.

"You've had just about every experience known to man," said Lenny, again inclining her head toward the neglected broccoli.

"And some unknown to man. That's why you find me in the state I'm in."

"I hadn't noticed," answered Lenny.

"Don't you want to hear about my ESP experience?"

"Not particularly."

"How about you, Adam?"

Adam nodded but his face reflected little interest. He was watching Becky, who kept her head turned from him.

"I bet Becky has ESP," said Adam. "She's so quiet and mysterious. I bet she's got a lot of eerie secrets, don't you?"

"I think that was very rude," snapped Lenny.

"I wasn't being rude. I just said I bet Becky has ESP. Do you Becky?"

"I told you I don't believe in all that psychic stuff," she said.

Adam could read the lie in her every movement. "Well, if I had ESP I wouldn't tell anyone either," he said smugly.

"If you had ESP you'd know I'm becoming pretty angry at you," growled Lenny.

"Why can't we have a dinner without an argument?" Cassidy asked.

"Good God, Cassidy, you really are beginning to sound like my mother," said Mark.

"I am your mother. And your father."

"Heaven forbid," answered Mark. "Can you imagine having Cassidy for a mother?"

"I can." Adam smiled wryly at everyone. He glanced

over at Becky, but she got up abruptly and began clearing the table.

"Hey!" said Cassidy, grabbing his plate back. "I'm just warming up." He reached for another slice of roast beef with his hand. Lenny slapped his fingers, but Cassidy only laughed and grabbed another piece. Lenny shook her head fondly.

"Will you get me some info on ESP?"

Cassidy turned to Adam and looked at him shrewdly. "Why this sudden interest in psychic bullshit?"

"Because everyone seems like they don't want me to know about it."

"Personally, I don't give a damn," said Lenny.

"Me either," said Mark. "Let Adam know what he wants to. Most of what we learn is totally useless anyway."

"Wait a minute," said Cassidy. "I want to know why."

"Because he wants to use it on us." Becky was standing by the stove, watching them all.

"Hostile, Becky. Very hostile." Mark wagged his finger at her.

Everyone turned to Becky, but her back was to them, stacking dishes in the sink. Lenny shrugged and looked around the table at Cassidy and Mark, who just shrugged back.

Adam had obviously touched a nerve.

"All right," sighed Cassidy. "I'll set up a program for psychic research. You'll find it under the call letters BS, short for bullshit."

"No, don't!" The words escaped from Becky's mouth and even she seemed surprised at the power in her voice.

"What's the matter with her?" Lenny whispered to Mark.

Mark shrugged and got up from the table. He walked over to Becky. She didn't turn but stayed hunched over the sink, her hands filled with greasy dinner dishes. Mark put his arms around her. "Hey, what's going on?" he asked softly.

Adam watched the two of them whispering on the other side of the kitchen. In his mind, he heard Becky tell Mark that nothing was wrong, and Mark insist that something was. Adam stared at Becky intently. Flashes of the diner and two middle-aged people flickered across his mind, then a woman in a torn housedress and pink fluffy slippers leading a man into the bedroom while he cupped her buttocks. Adam felt the contours of Becky's mind opening to him. She was no match for him, he decided. Hers was only the dark, secretive mind of a young girl.

Becky picked up another stack of dirty dishes and began walking them to the sink. Adam stared at the dishes, wondering what would happen if they all fell from her hands and broke into a thousand pieces. He imagined the sharp bits of china scattering all over the kitchen floor.

Suddenly Becky turned, her eyes alive with fear. The dishes crashed from her hands to the hard kitchen floor.

Chapter 10

Sy Sheinberg woke up and once again found himself among the living. He was certain it was a short-term lease, however, and crawled out of bed with the same dark foreboding that met him almost every morning of his life. Only now it was worse than ever before. Ever since that day five years ago when Becky left, there was a dark hole in his center, a purposelessness that made him feel like a lifer on his first year in the pen.

Sy couldn't begin to imagine how Sally felt. A profound, enduring sense of loss? Undoubtedly. It was just one more thing that held them together. He looked at her, still asleep, her mouth wide-open, snoring, her soft, down-covered chins quivering.

Sy padded down the hall. He knocked on the door of the new waitress Lillian, then slipped into the bathroom. He turned the lock, cleared his sinuses in the toilet, and took his morning shot of Alka-Seltzer, which had replaced his vitamins. He glanced out of the window at the orange morning sun rising behind the slate-colored mountains. It was close to impossible to tell if the sun was rising or setting. He noted the significance of this with some pride.

Sy threw cold water on his shriveled face, brushed

his teeth, took a leak, then hustled out, again rapping on Lazy Lillian's door.

This time he heard the rustle of sheets and a groan. "I hear ya."

He nodded, then continued to the bedroom where Sally was waking up with a smile. It was inhuman the way she smiled in the morning. If God had meant people to smile like that, he wouldn't have made morning breath.

As he reached for his shirt, Sy felt his back muscles pulling tightly, as if he'd been doing strenuous exercises the day before. A picture of he and Sally dancing together around the diner came to him. Since he hadn't danced with Sally since their junior prom, and then only once around the floor, he dismissed it. But oddly enough the back of his legs also seemed stiff, and as he pulled on his trousers, he groaned from the pain.

"Are you all right?" Sally's soft face wrinkled into concern.

Sy grunted his answer which Sally took for a yes.

"You won't believe what a silly dream I had," she said.

Sy interrupted. "I knocked twice on Lazy Lillian's door, but you'd better go in there and hustle her up."

"I was dancing with you. Around the diner, yet." She laughed gaily. "Isn't that funny? Reminded me of the junior prom."

Sy whirled around and stared at her. "Why'd you say that?"

"Because I dreamed it. I told you."

Sy's voice was small and quavering. "I was just thinking the same thing."

"Well, I guess you got ESP." Sally rolled out of

bed. As she pulled off her nightdress and slipped on her clean Sheinberg diner whites, she felt a twinge of pain in her back.

Sy was staring. "Now, why should we both be thinking the same thing?"

"Great minds, I guess." Sally walked to the door and was about to open it.

"Wait," said Sy. "Was there anyone else in your dream?"

"I don't remember."

"Think, woman!"

"Yes, I believe Lillian was there. And she was dancing by herself. You know, one of them new dances you don't need anyone else for. Just dance all by yourself. No wonder there's so many divorces these days."

Sy ignored Sally's sociological interpretation. "Anyone else?"

Sally tried to remember the dream, but most of it was very hazy. "I don't think so. No. No one."

She stopped. Maybe there was someone else, but she couldn't get a picture of him. All she could sense was a laugh, high-pitched and soft. It was the laugh of a little boy. But it was just a dream, and dreams never made any sense.

Sally bustled out of the room and down the hall. Sy heard her bang on Lazy Lillian's door. He felt a pinching of gas in his gut. "Damn Alka-Seltzer ain't worth shit," he muttered. He forced his weary body out of the bedroom and down the short walk to his life's work.

Adam tried not to yawn. He was bored and glanced at his watch, noting with relief that it was almost time for his recently restored free-play hour. Lenny sat on the edge of his bed, reading the Bible to him. Adam knew it made Lenny feel good to read it to him and sensed that the better everyone felt, the better it was for him, so he stifled his yawns and kept his leg from bouncing up and down impatiently. Occasionally, he'd ask her to read a passage again, and once in a while he'd nod. It was good enough to convince Lenny. In fact, Adam felt he was getting pretty good at faking it for everyone, everyone except Becky. Ever since she'd dropped the plates and stood looking into Adam's eyes, she'd stayed clear of him. At the time, Adam had seen only the vaguest connection between the accident and what he'd been thinking, but after his experiment during free-play yesterday, he was pretty sure he'd had something to do with it.

Adam surreptitiously glanced at his watch, then jumped up quickly and announced, "Free time!" He was out the door before Lenny even looked up. She sat watching the closing door with surprise; she'd been sure he was listening.

As Adam passed Molly's cage, he stopped and watched her, staring through the bars wistfully, wishing he could rush to her dark, warm body. Molly pressed herself tightly against the iron door, touching Adam's small, soft face with her outstretched fingers. Her eyes were yellow and hollow with a wrenching sadness. Most nights she found herself crying out from nightmares.

Adam kissed Molly's leathery fingers, then slipped out, climbing down the creaky stairs and walking through the dark, deserted factory to the bright, sunlit desert.

Adam strolled to the barbed-wire fence, turned back to the building to make sure no one was watching, then slid under, and began running down the dirt road.

Fifteen minutes later, he ducked behind a clump of brush and slithered toward Sheinberg's diner on his belly. Through the window, he saw a large man, hanging off his stool by almost a foot on each side, dunking a donut into steaming coffee. He was talking to Sheinberg between bites. Adam stared hard and tried to tune in.

Anderson pulled out his handkerchief, wiped his bullet head, then blew his nose. "Coffee on a hot day! Now, who the hell else but me would do such a dumb-ass thing?"

"A lot of people think it's better to drink something hot on a hot day. That way the air seems cool next to it."

"You don't say? Just shows there's more damn fools around than I would've thought." He laughed and struggled to get his meaty hand into a hip pocket already stretched to the limit by an equally meaty thigh.

"Forget it," said Sheinberg, waving Anderson's change away.

It was a ritual they went through every day, Anderson always answering, "Thanks. But we can't let this become a habit," then heaving himself up and barreling through the screen door, letting it bang shut behind him.

Sy drew himself an iced tea, walked over to the counter, and sat down, staring out into space, wiggling his aching feet.

Sally came out of the storeroom carrying a gallon jug of pickles. She pushed them into the refrigerator with a sigh that was meant to draw attention to the fact that she was a woman and not a packhorse, then slumped on the stool next to Sy. It had been a hard day, and neither of them had had a chance to sit down since breakfast.

Lillian pushed back a whole headful of stray, bleached hairs, shoving them into what at one time had been a bun. She drew herself a Coke and went to sit in the back booth. She pulled her uniform down over her bulging thighs and took out a compact and comb.

"Not at the tables," snapped Sally. "How many times I have to tell you that?"

Lillian grimaced and clicked the compact closed. She sat staring out of the window, slurping her Coke, shaking one of her large, smooth-shaven legs.

Sally watched Lillian but her mind was elsewhere. She turned back to Sy. "I wonder where she is. You know, Sy, I still wonder."

Sy shrugged. He didn't need anyone to tell him who "she" was and after a while he added, "Probably with some no-good who's keeping her barefoot and pregnant and loving the pants off of her."

Sally nodded, but in her head she saw Becky decomposing in a clump of bushes, and figured Sy felt pretty much the same way.

Sally kicked off her shoes and rubbed her feet. They were hot and swollen and even more covered with blisters than usual. All at once her body relaxed. She felt as if she were floating, like in those few moments just before sleep. She heard herself giggle and wondered what was so funny. Then she was standing up, and she realized she wasn't wearing the Sheinberg whites at all but a long chiffon gown she'd owned as a girl. Sy was in the corner, and he too was all dressed up, wearing a tuxedo that fit so beautifully it couldn't have been rented. Lillian was also standing and began dancing more gracefully than could have been expected. Sally could hear the music playing, and she hoped someone would ask her to dance. Sy came up to her, and Sally wondered how she knew his name and so much about him. He introduced himself and asked her to dance.

Sally held onto the hem of her skirt, whirling around the floor with Sy. She felt wonderful and whispered in his ear, laughing seductively.

Sy was beginning to sweat. It was hot on the dance floor, and the woman beside him was so lovely, and yet also so familiar. She seemed interested in him too. He wondered whether he'd be able to get a kiss from her. And always in his ear there was that voice saying, "Dance. Dance. Faster. Faster."

He quickened the pace and swung through the mobs of people on the dance floor. Everything began to spin, but still the voice said, "Dance. Dance." He took a deep breath and whirled even faster, sending the room spinning away into colorful streaks that bleached out the more quickly he moved, until he could see nothing at all, and found himself on the floor of the diner, clutching his heart and struggling for breath. Sally was on the ground next to him, and she too was gasping loudly.

Sy thought he heard childish laughter, but he could no longer tell what was real. Part of him said that he and Sally had just been dancing around the diner, but he knew that was impossible. Still, that was the second time he thought he'd been dancing. And Sally had told him about that dream, or had he imagined her telling him that too? Sy didn't get up; he just lay on the floor, his brittle chest heaving. Sally too remained where she was. Lillian stood, looking out the window, her eyes full of confusion.

"Only an earthquake," Sy said. He looked at Sally and she nodded, but he could tell she didn't believe it either.

Adam watched them a moment longer, then checked his watch. It was time to leave. He crawled away, careful to keep himself lower than the bushes, then scrambled up and ran back to the house, giggling to himself. He pictured how funny those people looked clomping around the diner. He loved his new doll-house, loved playing with his dolls, picking them up in his mind, spinning them madly around, then letting them drop. He couldn't wait until next free-play time, though he had to admit he was becoming a bit tired of watching them dance. He decided to think up something new and funny for tomorrow as he walked into the dark hole of the factory and ran down the stairs for dinner.

Becky's mother had called her "the witch." This was only partly because her long, auburn hair hung way below her shoulders, scraggly and uncombed for days on end. It was more the queer way she acted that caused Vanessa to call her the witch. As a baby, Becky seemed to know when her mother had something to say and turned her head in her direction in a way that gave Vanessa the creeps. Later, just at the moment when Van needed her most, Becky seemed to know and would pick that time to take off, usually to hide under the clapboard house they'd taken rooms in. In fact, Becky's mother believed so strongly in her power, she was sure that any ache or pain was a result of that eerie little girl who skulked around, listening at doors and pulling long faces. Often she wondered where Becky had gotten her queerness. Probably from her father, though who that was, she had no idea, since that month had been an especially active one for her.

For the most part, Becky tried not to listen to Van's ranting and raving. It was a strange, separate life she led in the dark, cold rooms her mother rented. Eating Rice Krispies and drinking milk, reading the words on the back of the box; hiding out until it was so late she had to come home and watch her mother entertaining her latest beau. Vanessa had never lifted a finger to Becky. What she'd done had been far worse. She'd ignored her.

Watching her mother splinter a chicken bone, sucking the marrow from it contentedly, Becky suddenly wished something would happen to her mother, something terrible. Just after that, Van began to choke and turn purple. She clawed at her throat making horrible, panicked sounds. Becky jumped up and banged her on the back, pleading with her not to die. With a loud cough, the bone dislodged and Vanessa turned terrified eyes on her daughter.

Becky left home that night. Never again did she try sending or reading thoughts; never again did she want such awful power in her hands. Still, strange dreams haunted her nights, and her days were spent trying to forget them. Only since Mark had the dreams withered away, and she was blessed with silence. With Mark's arms around her, her head on his chest, the terror receded.

But now, once again, her sleep was no longer peaceful. She awoke night after night, soaked in sweat, her mind flashing images of death and destruction, like strange aftershocks from an earthquake. Lately, the flashes had begun to happen during the day, and Becky found herself creeping around the house, cowering out of sight of everyone, especially Adam.

Adam had some kind of power. She could feel him probing her mind. She was reasonably sure that it had been he who'd sent the dishes crashing from her hands as a warning. If it were true, what would he be able to do when he'd learn to control all the power of his fabulous mind? Or had he already started to toy with her at night, when she was off guard? Maybe that was what those dreams meant.

Becky tried to put it out of her mind. She picked up a mop and a pail of soapy water and moved down the long corridor, looking like a washerwoman. She enjoyed making things clean and shiny. The rhythmic, mindless movement, the smell of pine cleaners, and the look of neatly ordered shelves gave her an animal satisfaction.

She moved to the back of the corridor and began mopping. Next door she could hear the hum of Gilda and Adam's small, piping voice as he worked with Cassidy. A shiver went through her as she thought of him sitting there, ruling over Gilda and Cassidy. Once again she wondered if she was the only one who knew it. She decided Cassidy did not, but the others sensed it. She had seen it in their faces. But discussing it with Mark was no longer possible. He, above all, was closer to the truth and therefore more adamant.

Becky felt her heart rate increasing and the strange but familiar slowing of her brain. Images, terrible and vibrant, burst through her mind: a young woman pitching down a flight of stairs, dark silhouettes digging a hole and throwing the lifeless body into the dirt. She wanted to scream out, but she couldn't; she was frozen, immobile, cold as death.

Adam was over twenty feet away, behind a closed door, but it had been him. She was sure of it. Panic seized her. She stood in the corridor, listening to the sounds in her head, trying to empty her mind but feeling the probing of another, searching her out.

If Adam could read her thoughts even from that distance, then he was already aware that she knew and he would punish her. He'd done it before; he'd do it again. She had to get out. There was no other choice.

Becky stood motionless, as if held in the grip of a force stronger than anything she'd ever known. Then suddenly she was released. She bolted, running down the long corridor, no longer thinking or feeling anything but the need for flight. She rushed through the steel door and began climbing the stairs, breath biting at her lungs.

She stopped midway, some semblance of calm returning as she clung to the hot, dry wall. Mark was in town, picking up supplies. If she could just wait for him, he'd take her in his tanned, muscular arms and eclipse all the pain and fear and confusion. He'd hold her in his warmth. Later they would take a walk together and she'd tell him everything she'd been thinking. He'd laugh at her or maybe not. All she knew was that she wouldn't be alone. All she had to do was walk back down the stairs and wait.

But behind these thoughts was another thought, transparent and distant, but there nonetheless, and she knew that everything she'd been thinking had come from another.

Her heart pitched violently, pumping blood in crazy hot flashes. Once again, Becky began running up the stairs, her legs shaking and weak, alarm making everything spin before her.

Just as she reached the top of the stairs, her foot caught on a loose board. As Becky fell backward down the stairs, there was an eternity of fleeting chimeras before reality caught up to her. She hit the floor and lay broken and bleeding, motionless before the steel door.

Molly jumped. Her body trembled and a black chill passed over the cage. She got up and began revolving around her cage, aimlessly picking up a bit of banana, rejecting it, taking one swing on her bar, then dropping to the ground. For once her mind wasn't on Adam. It was on darkness and moisture and soil. Memories of waxy green leaves played across her mind, and the smell of danger in the jungle came back to her. Great, black bull gorillas, displaying themselves, thrusting their genitals forward, beating their chests. Eyes, glittering yellow, the eyes of the panther. Her senses were filled with strange smells and dim shadows that danced in firelight.

After a while the feeling began to fade. The shadows receded and she sat down on the floor of her cage room. She remained there only for a moment, then once again she was up, rotating around her cage. Only through constant movement did she seem to get any kind of release, and that was only temporary, a distraction from something much more powerful.

There was a disturbance outside in the corridor. She stopped, listening to the sound of fear. She heard Adam's voice, then Cassidy's and Mark's, but it didn't calm the shaking or the agitation. Her body vibrated with a premonition of death. She knew something terrible had happened.

She sat down, facing the wall, signing, "Please tickle Molly. Please tickle." But even this had no power to calm her, and she was quickly up, scooting over to the bars of the cage, clutching them tightly and howling. The iron felt cold and dead under her leathery palms. She rattled at them but couldn't bring heat to the icy hard bars or to her body. She shook them even harder, crying out with terror.

It was over an hour before the door opened and Cassidy entered. He stood in the doorway watching Molly, bent, tired, his eyes moving restlessly, full of fear. It was like watching a reflection.

"What's the matter?" he signed.

Molly let go of the bars, grateful for the presence of another. "Molly feels funny." She stopped, her hands in midair. She couldn't explain how she felt.

"Pain?"

"No. Yes."

"Where?"

"Molly scared."

Cassidy looked around the cage room, his eyes flickering like dying light. "What is Molly scared of?"

"Molly doesn't know."

Molly sat down on the floor. Cassidy didn't walk into her cage or sit with her, but remained in the doorway, his eyes mirroring the fear Molly was feeling.

"Cassidy is worried about Molly," he signed. "It is better if Molly goes away for a while."

Molly's face stretched into horror. She howled, shattering the room with sound.

"Only for a short time."

She backed to the wall, hugging the cool hardness

as if seeking its protection. Her howl choked and became a terrible wail.

"Molly will come back soon."

Molly's breath began to come quickly, burning her
chest; her great hands clenched and unclenched. Every
muscle in her body stood out black and hard, and
from her mouth came the plaintive lamenting wail.

Cassidy watched the huge gorilla, her black body
gleaming, her muscles tightening and shifting under
her skin. The acrid smell of her seared his nostrils. It
confirmed his decision.

"Okay, Molly stays," he signed.

Molly regarded Cassidy suspiciously, reading the
lie in every movement of his body. As Cassidy turned
and walked out the door, Molly sank back into herself,
moaning softly, clutching her belly, just as she had
done when she was pregnant.

"Civilization dispenses with bodies efficiently. One
day they're there, then the next, they're shot full of
fluid and lowered away, neatly. And then there's
friends clustering around, carrying pots of chicken
stew and talking about overflowing toilets, est and
singles clubs after that. Everything making so much
noise, you can't even think."

Mark was cooking, circling the kitchen with jerky
but precise movements. Every once in a while he shivered as if from a terrible chill, but mostly he talked.
His voice droned on, toneless, incessant, but with a
dry, harsh edge to it that spoke of the emotion he was
trying to hide.

Lenny watched and listened but said nothing. She
had dealt with death before and knew there were no
rules.

"Yep, there's a lot to be said for civilization. In L.A. you don't have to bury your own mess. It all gets taken away so neatly and efficiently it's like the person was never there at all. And even more importantly there's no silence. Never any silence. And you never have to ask why." Then his voice collapsed into a painful knot. "Why? I don't understand."

Lenny stood up; her legs were shaky and she had to hold onto the table for support. "Let me get you a Valium."

Mark whirled around, his lips blue and rigid. "No! I want to feel this, Lenny. For Christ's sake, I want to feel one goddamn thing in my life."

Lenny shook her head. "I've been living in this house with the two of you for four years. You felt Becky."

"Not enough. I haven't even cried."

"There's such a thing as a grief beyond tears."

"She was scared and needed me. I wasn't there. I keep seeing her, her twisted body and that look of horror in her face. Oh God, that look. I'll never forget it. And then I see her sitting at the kitchen table, that day she moved in. Crumpled and scared. Just those two flashes, over and over, like I'm haunted."

"Stop, Mark. Stop!" Lenny moved toward him, tears in her eyes, her arms held out to comfort him. But he turned from them. Suddenly his eyes held the horror he had seen in Becky's frozen gaze. "There's something terrible going on. Becky told me, but I wouldn't listen. If only I'd listened."

"Mark, there's nothing terrible going on." Lenny's voice was shaking. "It's just what you've gone through."

Mark waved her away. "The worst has already happened. Adam helped us plant a tree next to her grave. Nice sentiment, don't you think? Oh boy! Lovely sentiment. We buried her like a goddamn bone. Not far off from BooBoo. If we're not careful we're going to have our very own boot hill out back."

"What do you mean by that?" Lenny's voice was sharp and full of anxiety.

"Where is he?"

Lenny was surprised and yet found herself trembling even more. "Who?"

Mark's voice was fierce. "You know exactly who."

"It's free-play time," announced Adam.

Lenny whirled around. Adam stood in the doorway, looking at the two of them with wide, innocent eyes. He didn't venture in, and his small shadow didn't even reach across to the two of them.

"Not today," Lenny answered after a while. Mark stood where he was, watching Adam. It was impossible to tell what he was thinking. Lenny wasn't sure what she herself was thinking.

"Why?" asked Adam, confused.

A tremor went through Lenny as she watched the little boy regarding her calmly. "Because of what just happened," she answered. "I explained all that to you earlier."

"Cassidy says women in India sometimes throw themselves on the funeral pyres of their husbands."

Lenny was frozen. Her lips were blue and pressed tightly together. She could barely get the words out. "Be back in time for dinner."

Adam smiled and ran to her with outspread arms. Lenny received him in her arms and he kissed her loudly on the stomach. It chilled her. She stood watching as he ran out the kitchen door and listened to his footsteps receding down the hall. She couldn't turn around for close to a minute and when she did, she saw Mark crying.

Adam sat outside of Sheinberg's diner in a clump of bushes. It was quiet and dark inside. Even the red pickup truck was gone. He could feel suspicion and fear still hanging in the air all around the diner, and for a moment he wondered if they'd gone forever. He decided they hadn't; everything looked exactly as it had before, and nothing seemed to be missing. He sat down to wait, stewing in a scratchy patch of dried weeds.

He'd had trouble enough getting out as it was. Everyone was making a big deal out of what had happened to Becky. When they had punished Adam nobody seemed to care half as much as they did about that strange girl who walked around saying practically nothing, and she wasn't a tenth as smart as Adam.

In the kitchen Lenny had seemed shocked, even repulsed by him. For a moment, he wondered if there was something he didn't understand, maybe something that was missing from him.

Adam pulled a blade of grass from the dry desert floor and began nibbling the end of it. Then he dug a small hole and pretended to be burying Becky. Cassidy and Mark had gotten a large canvas bag and a shovel and gone out in back of the house. Lenny hadn't let him watch, and when he'd asked what they were doing, she'd only shivered. But he'd known what they were doing anyway.

What did going out have to do with Becky dying? In truth, he wasn't even sorry that Becky had died. They could always get another Becky. It wasn't as if he'd liked her. And she didn't like him either. She'd wished him harm, and he hadn't done anything more than she had, except maybe succeed. And, as Vince Lombardi said, winning is everything. Of course, he was long gone too. Cassidy had told Adam that death comes to everything. He supposed that one day it would even come to him. But Cassidy had assured him that was a long way off. He was angered by the fuss that was being made about Becky's dying, and he wondered if there'd be as much made out of his own death. He pictured Mark and Cassidy digging a hole, and his own twisted, lifeless body being lowered into it. Everyone was crying and promising they'd never punish him again if he'd only come back. He tried to picture Cassidy throwing himself into the grave next to him, like those women in India, then got bored.

He glanced at his watch. It was 4:50. He'd wasted his whole free-play time, and now he'd have to rush back to the factory if he hoped to be on time.

Just then the red pickup truck bounced off the road, sending up clouds of dust as it pulled up to the diner. Sy, Sally, and Lillian got out, but Sy held them back, looking around cautiously before opening the door.

Sy led the way in and checked the back and even the bathrooms. He'd been right to suggest that they leave the diner in the late afternoon. Sally hadn't asked why he wanted to leave, but Sy could feel that she knew. Sy carefully closed all the doors and locked them, then went back into the kitchen area and switched on the grill, scraping back the blackened bits of hamburger and egg white with a spatula.

Adam remained crouched in the bushes nearby. If he hurried back now, he could make it to the dinner table on time. Still, he didn't move, his mind starting the sharp concentration that reached through the little lighted square of the window before him in sharp electric pulses. His eyes found Sy's face. Bright, vivid pictures flashed through his mind and across the dry, still desert air. He smiled as he felt the images catch hold. Then he felt a shiver at his thighs, as if he had to go to the bathroom. A hot sensation spread outward, effervescent, sparkling, pleasant, yet there was some pain in it too. He nodded solemnly, every inch the scientist. So that was what sex felt like.

He turned his concentration from Sy to Sally and then to the placid face of Lillian. She was staring out the window and for a second Adam felt she had seen him. But her eyes passed on, and Adam sharpened his mind into a funnel of energy.

Inside the little lighted square, Sy smiled. He looked over at Sally, and she too was smiling, a dimpled, knowing, impudent smile, a look from another time in her life, a time long forgotten. Sy felt the blood coursing through his body, his muscles tensed. He glanced over at Lillian, sitting in the back booth. Her leg was no longer swinging back and forth with boredom, and there was a smile on her face too.

"Undress," Adam whispered to them. "Get undressed."

There was neither embarrassment nor surprise in Sy's face, and the deathlike mask of ill health vanished as he watched the plump, white-skinned Lillian struggling with her uniform, pulling it over her head to reveal a push-up bra and panty hose. As she slid out of her nylons and threw them to the floor, her thighs, solid and marbled with delicate blue veins, came into view. When Sy turned around, he was surprised to see that Sally too was undressed, shivering and closed in upon herself like a shy little girl. Sy began to take his own clothes off slowly, holding to the moment. The women were watching him and he felt a mixture of embarrassment and excitement.

"Do it," Adam commanded, feeling a tingling between his thighs.

He sat breathless as the little animated figures in the window began to touch one another, a gentle stroking of soft flesh, vibrating under the touch, bodies encircling, cupping, entwining, until there was no way of telling where one began and the other ended. Sy began sinking to the ground with Lillian; Sally was following them with her hands, caressing hard muscle and soft, blue-veined flesh. The little figures clung together on the floor, shuddering in one another's arms. Sy moved to Lillian, glancing at her upturned face. Her eyes were closed and he closed his eyes in response. As Lillian's thighs spread under Sy's touch, Adam remembered the time. He stood up and quickly ran away. Sy felt a shock. A tumbling sensation sent him plunging downward into cold reality, and he was Sy again, shivering in his nakedness with the two women clinging to him on the floor. Sally and Lillian were also looking around startled. Suddenly they recoiled from one another. No one said a word as they grabbed for their clothes, pulling them over their heads with quickly beating hearts.

Sally walked to the cash register and began counting the money, though she'd counted it before they left for the afternoon. Lillian started to wipe down the tables. A terrified silence hung over them along with a dim image of a little boy with silver blond hair and innocent blue eyes.

*   *   *

By the time Adam came rushing in, his face flushed from running, everyone was seated at the table. Mark was staring straight ahead, robotlike, and Adam could see that Cassidy's body was a hard knot of tension. Adam slipped into his chair expecting to be scolded because of his lateness. Instead Lenny put food onto a plate and placed it in front of him. Adam noticed Becky's empty chair and suddenly remembered why everyone was acting so funny.

No one was speaking and Adam could hear the sound of Lenny and Cassidy chewing. Adam hated the sound and their silent, staring faces.

Finally Cassidy broke the quiet. "I think we should get rid of Molly."

Lenny started. "But why?"

"She's been acting funny lately."

"We've all been acting funny lately," answered Lenny.

"I can't trust her around Adam anymore. And there's no reason to keep her around now. She's just a lot of work."

"I don't understand you, Cassidy, I swear to Christ I don't." Lenny found herself crying, knowing that the tears were more for herself than Molly. "I thought you loved that ape."

"I do. I'm worried about her too."

"Bullshit. You don't love her at all. I doubt that you ever did."

"Oh boy," said Cassidy, "are we about to launch into a little parallel with you?"

Lenny's voice was soft and sad. "Maybe."

"Well, not tonight, okay? Now I say Molly goes. And she goes."

"No!" commanded Adam. "Molly stays." He was

sitting rigid in his chair, his face flushed with anger.

"Only for a little while," explained Cassidy.

"I love Molly and she stays."

Even Mark was roused out of his stupor by Adam's tone of voice. There was silence at the table, none of the adults looking at one another, intimidated by Adam's outburst and the power in it.

Adam's eyes scanned the table slowly.

"Molly stays," he said simply, his voice once again childish and soft, then he turned back to his meal as if nothing had happened.

Cassidy lay in bed, his body beyond tired but his mind alert. The total blackness of their windowless bedroom usually put him to sleep immediately. His problems normally began later, when anxiety grabbed at him and pulled him up with a jolt. But tonight neither the darkness nor the warmth of Lenny's curled body could help. Tonight, for the first time in months, he felt doubts. Opening his mind a chink to let them in produced a whole flood of fear, whirling and undulating in front of his eyes, appearing in no particular order, but feeding itself until Cassidy could be still no longer. He jumped out of bed.

Lenny turned over sleepily. "Is something wrong?"

"No. Just insomnia. Go back to sleep."

But Lenny rolled onto her back, and Cassidy could tell she was staring out into the blackness in his direction, though he couldn't see her.

"What's up?" she asked softly.

"I think I'll just take a walk. Maybe that'll help."

"So you saw it too." It was a statement, not a question.

"Saw what?" Cassidy asked, though he knew immediately what she meant.

"Cassidy, we have to stop this thing right now, while we can still handle him."

Cassidy laughed. "I wasn't thinking about Adam."

"Of course you were and so was I. That's all I've been able to think about since dinner. You saw the look on his face. More importantly, you saw what happened to us. How could you think about anything else?"

"If you're about to launch into the Adam-is-spoiled business again, why don't you put it on ice until morning?"

"It isn't that Adam is spoiled . . ." Her sentence drifted off.

Cassidy sighed. "All right, what is it, then?"

Lenny hesitated, chilled by her own thought. "He's evil."

Cassidy laughed again, but there was a tense, hysterical edge to it that made Lenny continue. "There's something going on inside him. It's something I don't understand, but I can feel that it's evil."

"You really are turning into some Catholic." Cassidy felt his way across the room toward the line of light coming from under the door. Lenny reached over and switched on the bedside lamp, catching Cassidy like a startled animal frozen in headlights.

"Not talking about it won't make it go away. There are things going on. You know it as well as I do."

Cassidy walked back to the bed. "Things? What things?"

Lenny's voice was soft but full of power. "Death."

"You don't think Adam had anything to do with Becky falling down the stairs? I was with him. The two of us were sitting in his bedroom."

"What was Becky so scared of?"

"Beats me. You said it yourself. Becky was a strange girl. But it wasn't Adam. He was in the bedroom with me."

"Why do you keep repeating that?"

"Because it proves Adam had nothing to do with it."

"No, it proves that you've thought of the possibility that he did. It also proves that you're avoiding the one real possibility—that he willed it."

Cassidy laughed. "Adam's good, but he isn't that good."

"Are you sure?"

"That Adam didn't mean to harm Becky? Absolutely." Cassidy relaxed. There were a lot of things he was unsure of, but this wasn't one of them. He was sure Adam had meant no harm. Cassidy pulled Lenny's covers up over her. "Now go to sleep. If you want, we can talk about this in the morning."

Lenny threw back the covers angrily. "No."

Cassidy nodded and sat down on the edge of the bed. "All right, let's look at this logically. You think Adam caused Becky to fall down the stairs, right?"

"I don't know if he meant it. But yes, in a sense he caused her death. He wanted it to happen."

"Okay, let's say he did. How?"

"Telepathy."

"He told her to fall and she did?"

"It could have been just a fleeting whim. All children have those kinds of thoughts."

Cassidy smiled. "But they don't do anything about them."

"Adam is different." Lenny's voice was strained.

Cassidy sat motionless on the edge of the bed. An unidentifiable current of energy seemed to be flowing through him; his heart was beating slowly, steadily, and he felt his whole body relax. He wasn't thinking about what Lenny said; he felt as if he were opening up like a flower.

Lenny watched Cassidy with a queer, frightened look on her face. "He was just here, wasn't he?"

Cassidy burst out laughing, and Lenny grabbed onto his arm, trying to ground him. "It's all true, isn't it?"

Cassidy touched Lenny's face softly. "Honey, what's going on with you?" Tenderly he pushed back a lock of hair that had strayed onto her forehead. "It's Becky, isn't it? We're all upset about Becky."

Lenny's voice was sharp. "Even Adam?"

Cassidy put his arms around Lenny, holding her tightly. At first she tried to pull away, then tears began to spill from her eyes and she succumbed to the warm, comforting arms that held her.

Standing in front of the bathroom mirror, Sy saw his old friend staring back at him, and once again he felt as if he were going to die. But this time he didn't clutch at his heart waiting for the specter to carry him away or plan out his final words. The death he felt had been much too real, and he immediately denied he had felt it at all. He laughed at the gray-white image staring at him, then quickened his pace into the diner.

But as Anderson sat slurping his midafternoon

snack of coffee and donuts, Sy could deny it no longer. He hung over the counter, putting his face close to Anderson's bald bullet head, whispering so that no one would hear them, though, in fact, they were totally alone.

"Ever find yourself doing something and not knowing the reason why?"

"All the time. Like eating this donut. I just started a diet this morning and here I am again." Anderson laughed, then allowed the soggy, sweet donut to melt into damp crumbs in his mouth.

"No. I mean like someone else was willing you to do something. And there was nothing you could do about it. Like you was being commanded."

Anderson looked at Sy as if he were an alien being. "I can't say as I've ever felt quite that way."

"Well, I have. And so has Sally and Lillian. Something queer's going on around here. And I got a feeling who's behind it all, too."

Anderson sighed and dipped his donut into the coffee. He popped the steaming morsel into his waiting mouth and burned the end of his tongue. "Damn it," he said through the rolling crumbs. "That's gonna give me a blister for sure."

"Listen to me, Anderson. This is important. Yesterday . . ." He stopped, embarrassed. "I don't want you telling no one else about this. Please. It's personal, and I don't want the whole town from the bowling alley down to the Picfair supermarket gabbing about it."

"Sure, Sy," answered Anderson. It occurred to him that perhaps it was his responsibility to bring Doc Keeler around for a little chat. Sally was too good-hearted a woman to know when her husband was going soft.

Sy leaned over the counter even farther and cupped his hand to Anderson's ear. "Yesterday I felt this thing taking me over, and next thing I knew, it was ten minutes later and . . . Well, I guess I better tell you everything. Me and Sally and Lillian, we was undressed and holding onto one another. We was touching one another, Anderson. You know what I mean?"

Anderson fought back a smile. "Now, Sy. Let's just start this thing at the beginning, okay? 'Cause you're saying some pretty startling things, and I just want to make sure I got this all straight." He pulled out his pad and pencil, licking the point with relish.

Adam sat cross-legged behind the bushes. Inside his dollhouse, Sy and Sally were writhing on the floor. Adam moved Lillian toward them, but he wasn't very interested in what he was doing, and Lillian stood over their nude bodies, staring into space. Finally, she sank to the ground.

Adam touched himself, trying to revive some of his earlier interest, but his mind started to wander. He had been playing with his dolls for only a short time, yet already he was bored, his mind wandering sluggishly. Already he could see his man doll begin to come back to himself.

Suddenly Sy stood up, naked and shivering. He rushed to the window and pounded on the pane. "I know you're out there," he yelled. "And I know who you are too!"

Sy ran back to Sally, grabbed her by the arm, and pulled her up angrily. Lillian remained lying on the

ground, curling into herself, sighing. Sy turned on
her and screamed, "Get dressed, damn you. Get
dressed and get out!" Lillian didn't move and Sy
kicked at her pale flabby body, yelling at her.

Adam watched, entranced. He loved the sound of
Sy screaming. He loved watching Sy's poor pitiful body
kicking out at Lillian. It was intensely exciting. He
sat forward, his eyes fixed on the lighted window and
the tiny nude figures inside. "Fight," he said softly.
"Keep fighting."

Sy whirled around, his eyes terrified points of light.
He ran back to the window and again pounded his
fist against the glass. "I hear you talking to me. I
know you're out there!"

Adam laughed merrily. "Fight," he repeated.

"No!" screamed Sy. "I won't do what you say. You
have no power over me."

Sy could feel a hot, rhythmic pounding in his tem-
ple. His body was trembling with the effort. But he
clutched tightly to himself, keeping out the intruder
who was trying to push into his body. There was one
thought in his mind. If he just kept to that thought,
maybe he had a chance. Over and over, he told himself that he was Sy Sheinberg. He was a man of little
money, power, and stature, but at least he was himself.

Adam tried to move in on the little naked man. He
was growing annoyed, as a child whose toys aren't
doing what he wants. "Kill each other," he insisted.
"I want you to kill each other."

Sy could feel his muscles twitching. His brain lay
open and raw. But he stuck where he was, pressed to
the diner window, fighting the impulses that surged
through his frail body.

Adam tightened his will, sending thought flashes flying at Sy. No one had ever fought him like this before,
and he was furious and thrilled.

Sy pressed to the window, looking out but seeing
nothing. Everything inside him was tightened into a
diamondlike rock, and neither anger nor fear nor any
other emotion could pierce it. Exhaustion came over
him in waves, and his thin, old muscles cramped and
clutched with a desperate need for movement. But Sy
knew if he moved, he was dead.

Adam too could feel the battle of wills. Between
him and the deathly white old man in the window
was a barrier, brittle but impenetrable. He concentrated on the barrier, feeling out its dimensions.

Sy held against the tide that weakened and strength-
ened, shifting back and forth as if he were arm
wrestling for his life. Then suddenly he realized that
in the end he would lose. Death was standing nearby,
peering with amusement over his bony, tensed shoulder. He wasn't at all like the shadowy specter Sy had
pictured, nor, he realized, was the kind of death he
was bringing. It was neither full of glory nor even
boring, as he'd feared. It was degrading and impure,
full of the stench of decay.

Adam felt it immediately. All at once there was no
barrier, only a naked old man and his plump wife and
a waitress shivering in the lighted window before him.
Immediately his mind pressed and slipped into Sy.

Sy turned from the window and walked out the door
into the steaming late afternoon. He stood looking out
at the bleached desert, his jaws clenched tightly together, then continued over to his pickup truck. In
the glove compartment was a brand-new revolver and

ammunition, bought only two days ago to protect them.

Sy loaded the gun awkwardly, then threw the catch. He hesitated, his eyes scanning the horizon. But they were sightless eyes, and almost immediately he broke off and walked back into the diner like a robot.

Lillian screamed. Sy watched impassively as she ran toward the bathroom. Sally grabbed his arm, tearing at him, her eyes pleading, but he threw her off and quickly followed Lillian. She was at the bathroom door, trying to tear it open with trembling fingers. Slowly Sy raised the gun, catching her large swollen right shoulder blade in the site.

Lillian screamed, "No!" clawing crazily at the locked door. The bullet shattered her spine, throwing her against the wood. She melted to the floor, her scream becoming a loud hiss as she crumpled into nothingness. Sy saw the red liquid welling from her back, running down the pale flabby skin of her naked body. He pulled off another shot, then turned to find Sally.

Sy glanced around the diner. She was nowhere to be seen. Perhaps she'd escaped while he was following Lillian. He started for the door, then suddenly knew she was under the table in the back booth.

Sy moved to the back of the diner, smiling to himself. "Come out," he said sharply.

Sally didn't move, pressed against the red plastic of the booth, but Sy could hear her whimpering like a dog. "Get out of there," he yelled.

Sally didn't come out. She clutched to the unyielding plastic, trying to press herself into safety.

Sy crouched down. Sally's thick legs were bent tightly against her belly. Her face was white and terrified, her mouth open, her teeth gleamed eerily in the shadows.

"Sy. Oh my God, Sy." Her voice was choked, full of the realization that her death was at hand. A tremor went through Sy; his hand began to shake. Sally stared at him, love and fear twisting her face. Then slowly, still on her hands and knees, she began to move toward him. Sy remained crouched, watching Sally crawl toward him.

Once again Sally opened her mouth to speak, but there were no more words. A bullet pierced her breast. She inhaled sharply and blood began to gush from her mouth. She choked violently, terror and death in her eyes. All at once she began a desperate crawl to the door, clawing the floor like a wounded animal. Sy watched her fighting her way to the door, coughing up her own blood. Just as she reached it, he fired again.

Time passed. Sy didn't know how long, but suddenly he looked around, no longer robotlike. There was blood all over the diner, and on the floor, two naked women's bodies. In one terrible flash, he remembered everything.

"Sally!" Sy screamed. He stood frozen in the middle of the room, then broke for the window, crying out in an agony of loss.

He banged on the glass. "You!" he shrieked. "You made me do it!"

But in his other hand he felt the coldness of the gun handle, and he knew that it didn't matter about the boy laughing outside; he had been the one to squeeze the trigger. Sy didn't turn back from the window. He knew what he had to do.

He lifted the gun slowly and turned it toward his chest and fired. He staggered backward, numbly pulling the trigger again. Then he fell to the floor, life hissing from him like a deflating tire.

Anderson had already checked his gun twice to make sure it was loaded, but he found himself checking it again as he stood outside the broken-down old factory, trying to look through a separation made by heat-curled boards. His face was twisted up, stiff and tortured. His eyes were red-rimmed and exhausted from a night of phone calls from frightened citizens and the shouting of Mayor Richards. But it was what he had seen the evening before that had affected him most deeply: the petrified, twisted bodies that only minutes before had been human, crumpled like marionettes. The image crushed his mind and made everything else seem faraway, muted, and unreal.

All the evidence indicated that Sy had gone crazy. In light of the story Sy had told him earlier that afternoon, this shouldn't have come as a total surprise. He supposed it had been coming on ever since Becky disappeared. Still, there was a thorny feeling that all was not as it seemed. While his deputy, Cason, was inside the diner with the coroner, Anderson had toured the grounds. He'd walked past the clump of bushes just outside the window where Sy had said he'd seen the face of a little boy, and found a small depression in the ground and scuff marks. They could have been from a little boy or a million other things. But even if they were made by a little boy, Anderson couldn't see what difference that would make.

Anderson pushed open the old door, then stood, shielding the light from his eyes, looking around the large, barnlike factory. He saw nothing but machinery and feathery cobwebs. He reached into his pocket for his handkerchief and began wiping his head, though for once he wasn't sweating. There was no question, here lived one pair of crazies. There was also no question that the strange horrors had started after those two boys came. Still, the reasonable explanation was that Sy had snapped, and all else was as a result of that. Perhaps Becky had seen it long ago and fled.

Still, Anderson couldn't bring himself to leave this place. He decided it was guilt. Sy had come to him for help repeatedly, and Anderson had not been there for him. As a human being, it had been disgraceful; as a sheriff, unforgivable. Sy was a man in distress, yet Anderson hadn't even seemed to notice or care about it. Worse, he'd laughed. Now Sy was dead, and Anderson knew he had to try to put things straight, even if it meant wasting a week of his time.

He walked back toward the creaky staircase, touching the handle of his gun as he started down, stopping once more to check it, then continuing. He was sweating now, and his fingers felt slippery and stiff.

When he got to the steel door, he rapped loudly. "This is Sheriff Anderson. Please open up."

There was the sound of shuffling feet, then, "What's the matter, sheriff?"

"I want to get in there," he said sharply. "Now please open up or I'll have to come back with a warrant."

"We wouldn't want you to have to do that." Cassidy opened the door, flashing his false smile but not stepping back to let Anderson in.

"I'd like to come in."

"It'd be better if you came back later. My partner and I are just doing an experiment."

"There's been some trouble up the road." Anderson tried to move inside, and Cassidy fell back, allowing him to enter.

Anderson looked around. "Where's your partner?"

"You want me to get him?"

Anderson nodded and Cassidy started down the long dark corridor toward the bedrooms. His heart was squeezed tightly in his chest, his hands were cold and clammy, though he couldn't imagine why. Trouble up the road meant nothing to him. Adam was in the back with Lenny. He'd warned them to stay there the moment he heard the knocking. There was no reason for panic; yet panic was there, squeezing his chest, clawing at his throat.

Anderson waited until Cassidy disappeared, then walked to the lead glass window and looked into the labs, searching for something, though he had no idea what it could be.

Cassidy was back with Mark quickly. The three of them walked to the kitchen, Mark offering him a cup of coffee and in general being less surly than Cassidy. The minute Anderson entered the kitchen, he began looking around, his eyes taking in everything but finding nothing out of the ordinary. Anderson went to sit on one of the chairs, and almost slid off the seat because of a phone book. He shook his head angrily. Stupid clumsy ass that he was, he couldn't even sit like a sheriff.

His anger at himself added power to his voice. "I want to know if you noticed anything funny."

"Today?" asked Mark.

"No. It'd be yesterday. Maybe it would be better if you went back several months. You been noticing any strange occurrences?" Anderson felt foolish asking this and turned his eyes from the two men, once again looking around the kitchen with its homey hat rack and paper flowers in bright-colored vases. He wondered if they were fairies.

"No. I haven't seen anything unusual at all," answered Mark. "In fact, I was beginning to think nothing ever happened here."

Anderson nodded; he wished that were true. He turned to Cassidy. "How about you?" But Cassidy just shrugged and shook that hairy head of his.

"You haven't told us what happened," said Mark.

"No, I haven't. And I won't. Not that it hasn't probably run all up and down town by now. But if I was you, I wouldn't go round hanging on them stories. It was something pretty damn terrible, take my word."

"A robbery?" asked Mark, glancing quickly at Cassidy.

"Murder," answered Anderson. "Lots of it. Three in all. Something the likes of which no one in this town has ever known."

"Until we came?"

Cassidy stared at Anderson, a cynical sneer on his face. Anderson wanted to rip it off. His fists clenched in response. "I didn't say that, did I?"

Mark shot Cassidy a look, telling him to be cool. "I wish we could help you," he said.

"I don't know about that. But I can tell your friend over there don't exactly feel the same way."

"That's just how he acts."

"It'll get him into a heap of trouble one of these days."

Mark smiled at Anderson pleasantly. "I wouldn't be surprised."

Anderson just shook his head at both of them. "I

only got one more question. Either of you two know anything about a little boy? Blond. About four or five years old."

Everything collapsed inside of Mark. A violent tremor passed through his body and he had to hold onto the wall behind him to keep himself standing. He didn't know if anyone was watching him or not; he couldn't see anything.

"What would a kid have to do with it?" Cassidy's voice was calm and slightly mocking. It was only later, when Mark replayed the scene in his mind, that he came to the conclusion that Cassidy had made no connection at all. It was a startling conclusion, one almost impossible to believe, except for a man like Cassidy.

Anderson heaved himself up. "Never mind what he had to do with it. I asked if you seen one around here."

"No. I haven't. How about you, Mark?"

Mark heard himself say no, but he wasn't really aware of what he was doing. His chest was on fire, as if his ribs had been shattered and his skin was bruised and bloodied. He was vaguely aware of Anderson leaving and Cassidy walking into the laboratory again. He didn't know how long after that he let out a loud horrified scream.

The sun was high and hot, glazing the desert floor with shimmering light. High above, a large bird circled the flats looking for field mice.

Anderson got into his car and screeched away from the factory. He felt like a turkey in a pressure cooker. Sweat started to roll off him, making huge dark patches on his clothes.

As he turned onto the highway, he switched on the air conditioner and got a blast of hot air in his face. He left the air conditioner on; perhaps eventually it would be able to overcome the intense heat. But he had little hope; from June through October there was no beating the desert. You could only conform to it.

Anderson switched on the radio and tried to reach Cason. There was no answer, which meant one of two things: either Cason was onto something, or, more probably, onto some slut. Anderson shut off the radio and yawned, looking out at the long, straight highway that stretched endlessly before him and the flat, featureless land on either side.

He felt uneasy, as if there was something urgent in the back of his mind, something he'd forgotten. On the surface, his visit to the factory had been unrewarding. Or had it? He had the feeling that he'd seen something while he was there, but he couldn't remember anything out of the ordinary. In his mind Anderson retraced his route through the factory and down into the basement. Cassidy opening the door, walking down the long corridor, coming back with Mark.

Mentally, he entered the kitchen. He looked around at the neatly stacked plates and cups, the dining room table and its five chairs. Then he remembered the phone book. Sometimes people used phone books for little children. His mind drifted over to the hat rack. There had been a squashed old ten-gallon hat on it. Of course, the hat could have belonged to one of the men, but it was very beaten up, hardly the kind a city boy would wear. Becky had always worn a hat like that, but so did a million other people. He had one at home himself. As far as evidence went, one ten-gallon hat and a phone book could hardly qualify as conclusive.

Still, Anderson pulled over to the shoulder of the road and turned on the radio. This time he got Cason's tired voice in response.

"I'm on my way back to the factory."

"The hippies, huh?" answered Cason. "You got some kind of evidence against them?"

"A phone book." Anderson switched off the microphone before Cason got a chance to make a sarcastic comment, then made a screeching U turn and started back.

The sun was beating so hard against the windshield it was a wonder that the glass didn't melt. Anderson's old air conditioner whined and moaned but did little good, and the breeze that rushed through the car window was like a hot sledgehammer.

The highway was almost completely empty, only a souped-up Ford ahead and a truck carrying bottled water coming from the opposite direction. Again Anderson yawned. Now that he was on his way back, he wondered what the hell he was going to say or do that would be any different than before.

Once again, mentally, he retraveled the long dark corridor to the kitchen. He didn't enter. His mind seemed stuck in the corridor, which was no longer in a house at all. It had become a dark, gray rut that seemed to belong to him.

A boy. What could a little boy have to do with a murder-suicide? A small face with blond curly hair and wide innocent eyes flashed into his mind. Anderson tried to laugh at the power of Sy's suggestion, but the boy seemed to be talking, and he found himself struggling to hear what he was saying.

"Anderson, go to sleep." It was a childish voice. Anderson tried to laugh at it, but his eyes started to close. He shook his head, but still his lids dropped lower and lower. It was overpowering. "No!" he screamed, riveting his gaze on the windshield.

"Sleep," the childish voice said again, but Anderson didn't hear it. Already he'd begun to drift in the warm half-world before sleep.

Jason Roberts saw the police car slip over the yellow line and careen directly toward him. He slammed on the brakes, knowing instantly that it would do little good. "It was like a ghost car," he would tell everyone during his long convalescence at Mercy General. "All I could see was this car, and then it hit. I could hear all my water bottles crashing to the ground, shattering glass all over the road. And Jesus Christ, you know that I thought? Son of a bitch, I gotta pay for them bottles."

Mark took Lenny by the arm and guided her through the steel door and toward the stairs. His face was white and haggard. He could have been fifty years old.

Lenny took one look at that face, the tense worry lines, the eyes full of pain and sorrow, and followed. Once she opened her mouth to speak, but Mark shook his head, and his eyes seemed more frightened than sad.

Mark led Lenny through the terrible midday heat to his car. He opened the door for her and helped her in. It was a gentlemanly act that so contrasted with the look on his face that once again Lenny asked what was going on.

The hunted look tore at Mark's face. "He'll hear us," was all he said.

They drove down the long rutted dirt road and out onto the highway in silence. Mark was clutching at the wheel, his eyes on the windshield. Up ahead, there was a huge pileup of traffic. A knot of men stood beside a large jackknifed truck. It wasn't until they got closer that Lenny saw the shattered remains of a police car and, lying on the ground, under a sheet, the outline of a man.

As Mark drove on the shoulder to avoid the broken glass and twisted steel, his hands were shaking and cold sweat made his body shiver. "Him," he said under his breath. It was like a curse.

He clutched at the wheel, his knuckles white, his hands slipping from moisture. Finally he turned to Lenny. "I don't think he can hear us now. You can tell when he's listening, you know. You can feel him inside you."

"What are you talking about?"

Mark's laugh was dry and tinged with hysteria. "Don't you know?"

"This is crazy."

"Yeah, isn't it though? It's the most goddamn crazy thing in the world. And yet I know it's true."

"What's true?" Lenny's voice was impatient. But behind the impatience was fear, and she knew what was coming as surely as if she'd lived it before. All that was missing were the details.

"Adam is evil," Mark answered. "Becky said it once, but none of us listened. I think he's killed."

Lenny didn't answer. She sighed deeply and looked out the window at the vast emptiness.

"That police car back there, that was Adam, too.

Anderson was at the factory less than an hour ago, questioning Cassidy and me about the murders at the diner. He wanted to know if we had seen a little boy."

Lenny turned back to Mark. Her voice was so flat and expressionless, it surprised even herself. "And Becky?" she asked.

"Somehow I get the feeling that Becky was different. I think she knew what Adam was capable of and panicked. Perhaps it was her death that taught him what he could do. I just don't know."

"It doesn't make much difference. The other is enough."

"You believe me?" Mark had expected his entire shaky mental history to be thrown in his face. He had expected an argument or at least questions as to how a little boy could be a murderer. Instead Lenny seemed to accept what he was saying as true. Relief swept over him. At least he wasn't completely alone.

"We've all known it for some time." Lenny was staring at Mark. Once again her voice was flat and expressionless but her face was ravaged.

Mark turned from her and pounded his fist against the steering wheel. It was true. They'd all known and refused to believe it. They'd all gone along, blocking out certain thoughts, ignoring certain happenings, relinquishing responsibility to Cassidy. They'd known everything and done nothing.

"He does it through telepathy," said Mark.

"Yes."

"He can read minds."

"Yes."

"I think with some people he can take over their minds and make them do things."

Lenny nodded solemnly. "That's the way I see it too."

Mark looked over at Lenny's determined little face. If he had to go searching for allies, here was one he would choose immediately. He remembered her brisk, cheerful manner the day she moved in and was comforted by it but also saddened. How much they had changed since then.

"The thing I don't understand," continued Lenny, "is why he hasn't done it to us." Suddenly her eyes became filled with fear.

Mark touched her arm reassuringly. "Don't worry. He hasn't done it to me."

Lenny relaxed. "Then why?"

"The way I figure it is you and I and Cassidy are too complex. He can get into our minds. I've felt him there, probing, but as far as pushing us into a direction we don't want to go, he hasn't got the power." Mark hesitated, looking down the sunlit highway. A dead animal was decaying on the road. He shivered. "Becky was a simple girl. That's what I loved in her."

"So you believe he isn't strong enough to get to us yet." The flat emptiness was back in Lenny's voice.

"There's another alternative. Maybe he doesn't do it because he loves us and doesn't want to hurt us."

"You believe that?" asked Lenny.

"No. But I was hoping you would tell me I'm wrong."

"There's a third alternative."

Mark nodded. "You mean that so far he's had no reason to push us, but if he did, he could?"

"And would."

"I think for purposes of sanity, we better forget that alternative."

The two of them fell silent, looking out the window, seeing nothing but their own reflections.

"Where are we going?" Lenny asked after a while.

"I haven't a clue." Mark slowed the car down and pulled over to the side of the road. Just ahead, the San Bernardino mountains rose like blue, hazy pyramids, the road making a long line into the heart of them.

"We can't just leave Cassidy," Lenny said after a while.

"He'll never believe us."

"Oh, he'll believe us all right." Lenny's voice was hollow. "The problem is, will he want to?"

Mark shook his head. "I don't think he knows."

"All the more reason for us to go back. We have to tell Cassidy."

Mark rubbed his hands across his face. He felt like he was burning up with fever, yet there were chills running through his body. "And what if Adam stops us?"

"You yourself said we have to believe he still doesn't have the power over us."

Mark shook his head. "We can't risk it."

"Please," pleaded Lenny. "We have to try to save Cassidy." She started to cry. "Why am I so crazy in love with him? Will you just answer me that one?"

"For the same reason I am. Because whatever he's done, whatever evil he's created, he dared. Totally. Completely. All the way to death and damnation. And there are very few men who can say that about themselves. He was one of the few who stood up and cried out to God, 'If you gave me this fabulous brain, how could you not allow me to use it?' "

Lenny nodded. "And what was God's answer?"

Mark started the car and turned back onto the road to the factory. "That's just it. I don't think there was an answer. I think there was just silence."

Adam was bouncing a ball against the side of the building when Mark and Lenny pulled up. "Onesies, twosies, threesies, foursies," he chanted, clapping his hands before catching the ball. It was a game Lenny remembered from her own childhood. Seeing Adam's concentrated pout, hearing his childish voice, made Lenny begin to doubt everything. She looked over at Mark and could see he was thinking the same thing.

"It's true," he said softly. "It's all true."

Lenny nodded. "Let's go find Cassidy."

As Mark and Lenny walked into the factory, Adam watched them from the corner of his eye, never once interrupting his game.

They found Cassidy in the inner laboratory, hunched over a petri dish, his burrlike head flopping back and forth as he jabbered happily to himself. He spoke without looking up. "For Christ's sake, Mark, you know better than to come in here without a lab gown. Luckily these epithelial cells are hearty little bastards."

Mark started. "What are you doing?"

"Adam wants to know where he came from, so I'm showing him."

Lenny was shocked. "You're not doing that experiment again?"

"No. I'm just showing him," Cassidy laughed fondly. "All we need is another Adam. He keeps us running all by himself."

Lenny and Mark looked at one another. It was as if Cassidy were from another planet.

"How far are you planning on taking this experiment?" asked Lenny.

"I told you, I'm just showing Adam where he came from."

"How far?" Mark insisted.

Cassidy shrugged and placed the petri dish into the incubator. There were twenty petri dishes there, each filled with gleaming liquid. Cassidy pulled off his rubber gloves and threw them into a dispenser. "As far as I need to. Only this time I'm using his cells. Can you imagine? I'm doing the experiment with his cells. It's almost impossible to think of engineering them. I mean, how do you perfect perfection?" He looked up. "So, what's the big problem? You two look like you just got the death sentence." He laughed. Neither Mark nor Lenny spoke. Cassidy looked from one to the other impatiently. "Well?"

"We want to talk to you about Adam," Mark said finally.

"Sure. Shoot."

Lenny's voice was chilling. "Not here!"

"Fine. You want to go to our bedroom?"

"We have to go far away. We can't talk here." She leaned toward Cassidy. "He can hear us."

Cassidy started to laugh. It came over him in huge waves, great gales of his horse laugh filling the room.

"You know what we're saying, Cassidy," said Mark. "Don't pretend."

"Wrong. I haven't the foggiest. But I'll tell you one thing. We can't just go off and leave Adam in this house alone. Something could happen to him."

"God willing," Lenny whispered.

Mark touched Cassidy's arm. "It's gone too far now. We have to stop here."

"Stop what?"

"Him." Again Lenny's chilling voice cut through the room.

"Stop?" Cassidy backed to a chair and sat down, stunned. "You're talking about killing Adam, aren't you?"

Lenny clutched Cassidy's arm. "Please. We have to do something before he gets too powerful."

"I am already."

Lenny screamed. Standing in the darkroom door was Adam. He slid the cylinder closed behind him and entered the inner laboratory, his face puckered with childish irritation.

Mark looked around wildly. His eyes caught hold of a shelf of chemicals. He backed to it, sliding the glass panel open. Adam's eyes seemed to be on Lenny, but Mark couldn't be sure. There was nothing he could be sure of anymore. He grabbed a bottle of sulfuric acid. Still Adam didn't move. Quickly Mark removed the stopper and turned to him, holding the bottle of acid in front of him.

Adam laughed innocently. He stayed where he was, watching Mark. But behind the smiling little face was his will, as tight as a fist, and Mark could feel the power of it.

Mark stood, motionless. If he threw the bottle of acid, there was a chance it might splash on Lenny or Cassidy. He looked over at the two of them, but they too stood immobilized, suspended.

Mark's arm tensed. Slowly it began to move forward. He was horrified. He wasn't guiding it; his arm was moving without him. Mark tried to push against the force, but it was his own arm and his own force that was moving it, and he couldn't fight against that. His whole body tightened into a knot, but the bottle kept moving forward, slowly, tauntingly, until it was in front of him. The bottle began to tilt. As drops of acid spilled onto the floor just in front of him, the stench of burning floor bit the air. There was a terrible hiss. It was the only noise in the room. Then the bottle began to move toward him, propelled by his own hand, scorching a black track that moved closer to him, up to his feet.

Mark watched with horror as Adam guided the bottle along the toe of his shoe. Burning warmth spread across his foot without actually touching it. An acrid stench filled the room. Mark watched the bottle, unable to let go of it, unable to move at all. Then suddenly his hand stopped. The bottle tilted back and the drops of acid slowed.

"What were you saying about me?" Adam's voice was reasonable and calm as he walked into the center of the lab and stood waiting for an answer.

No one said a word. Cassidy watched the little boy with the soft blond curls and large blue eyes, his face ashen and twisted.

"Come on now, I want to know." Adam's voice was full of contempt. "Sticks and stones can break my bones, but names can never hurt me."

Still there was no answer, and Adam looked around at them petulantly. "All right then, I'll tell you what was going on. You were trying to decide what to do about me. Isn't that right?"

Adam was smiling at them, but inside he was filled with smoldering anger that burned like an ulcer in the heart of him. Feeding it always was the power, unlimited, unequivocal, making the anger more intense with every attempt to satiate it. For a moment Adam wondered when everything had started to change, then decided it didn't matter anymore. He had changed; they had changed. Everything was different now. And the warmth and softness he had felt before was no more.

"Well?" he demanded again. "Isn't that what was going on?"

This time the three of them found their heads nodding up and down, like marionettes.

"See, I knew it," Adam cried delightedly. "But don't you see, there's nothing for you to decide. I'm in control. I've been in control for some time."

Chapter 11

Mark had learned all the rest periods. During the night there were at least six hours. Then there were the times when Adam was in the lab, though Mark could rarely be sure he was in there, and even if he was, that he was concentrating totally on what he was doing. Lately Mark had begun to suspect that bad weather could disturb thought transmission. Things like big winds or rain seemed to keep Adam's mind at a distance. But he couldn't be sure of that either. And even if it were true, bad weather happened only occasionally in the desert.

When Mark listed off all these times to himself, it sounded like a lot, but in fact it was very little time. He too had to sleep.

Mark rolled over and checked his watch. It was four o'clock in the morning. He could pretty much bank on Adam being asleep for another two hours, but to be on the safe side, he only allowed himself another half hour of thinking.

He tried to reconstruct his meeting with Cassidy in the corridor. It was hard to tell if he'd read it right. It had always been hard to tell what Cassidy was thinking, and now, with Adam in control, keeping the three of them apart and like prisoners, it was almost impossible to tell what he himself felt, let alone Cassidy.

Mark had seen Lenny the day before yesterday. It was only for a brief moment and neither of them had been allowed to speak. Mark had felt overwhelmed by the stab of emotion as memories of Becky came flooding back. But he stopped them quickly. Adam didn't like him thinking about Becky. It got him angry.

Lenny had smiled at him. She seemed to be holding up all right. The silence Mark had been living in for the past two months had taught him to understand what was going on without words. He was beginning to be able to sense things just by feeling the air. Mark could feel it if Adam's small feet tripped down the corridor or if Cassidy were nearby. He could almost smell Molly as she followed Adam around.

Mark thought about Molly. He didn't doubt that she would kill any of them if Adam wished it. He had once wondered if Molly could feel love. Now he had his answer; she could love, with all the brutal intensity of a human being.

Mark's mind flitted back to Cassidy and his stooped shoulders and haunted eyes. Had his eyes truly reached out to Mark in the corridor yesterday, or had it been his imagination? And even if they had, what difference did that make? How could they possibly plan their escape together when they couldn't even think without Adam monitoring them? And then there was the problem of Lenny. She, more than any of them, was being kept apart. How could they reach her?

Mark's mind speeded up, covering the day ahead, the hours spent in his locked, windowless room where he was only able to guess at what went on outside. He knew that Adam and Cassidy were spending a great deal of time in the laboratory and assumed that meant that they were doing the experiment.

Mark felt that Lenny had been relegated to housekeeping. Three times a day, he was taken to the kitchen where a hot meal was laid out on the table. The dishes were always done, the kitchen clean and neat. Since it was highly unlikely that Adam or Cassidy were scrubbing floors, it had to be Lenny. This left Mark with only one unanswered question. Everyone had a job but Mark. Why was Adam keeping him around? Certainly he was needed to sign correspondence, arrange for monies to be transferred, write checks, but that could be arranged in some other way. And in the end there was the feeling that Adam was keeping him around for something else. Amusement was the word that most often came into his mind. He felt as if he were being fed and groomed like a gamecock.

A shiver passed through Mark and he quickly turned his mind back to escape. His room had no windows, his door was locked. As far as he knew, Adam had the only key, and he never forgot to use it either. Escape during the night was impossible, and the chances of escape during the day seemed little better.

Unless there was a thunderstorm. There had been one last month; it was possible there might be one again soon. It seemed typical of his whole life. Mark's chances always seemed to rest on improbabilities like thunderstorms in the desert. To make matters worse, he wasn't even sure his theory was correct. Last month he had felt Adam's brain fading as the wind raged and the lightning cracked the sky, but that might just have been coincidence.

Mark jerked off his covers and sat up quickly. He didn't want to think about that.

"What don't you want to think about?"

Mark felt his muscles relax, his brain seemed to slow, as did his heart. It was Adam. Mark quickly voided his mind and began to stare at the walls of his bedroom. He'd learned better than to try and fight Adam. His only way around was emptiness.

Adam laughed, but Mark shut out the sound. He didn't know if Adam had heard what he'd been thinking before. All he knew was he couldn't think about it.

Lenny moved through the kitchen mechanically, cracking eggs against the side of a bowl, stirring them with a fork. Her mind too was virtually empty—all that occupied it was the quickly disappearing individuality of yolk and white. She separated the bacon, put it into a pan, and turned on the flame. Her movements were numb and lifeless. There was no joy in cooking when you couldn't see people eating what you had prepared. She stopped, coming closer to a laugh than she had in a long time. It was amazing that, under the circumstances, the possibility of joy even occurred to her. But people were strange, hearty beings. Joy was a possibility.

Lenny took several oranges out of the refrigerator and squeezed them. Adam liked fresh, squeezed juice. Yesterday she'd gotten the feeling that it was Cassidy who had his breakfast first. She hadn't spoken to Cassidy in over two months and had only seen him when their paths crossed in the corridor. His eyes were hidden and tortured. But she couldn't think about that. She concentrated on pouring the juice into four glasses and putting them in the refrigerator. She stopped, staring into space. It was impossible to believe they could go on like this forever. It was impossible to believe they'd be able to get away.

"You can't get away." Lenny heard Adam's voice inside her head, as clearly as if he were standing beside her.

"That's what you think," she said out loud. She heard Adam laugh, and said angrily, "Things will change. I'll make them change."

Again Adam laughed. "I shouldn't allow you to talk to me that way."

"Then kill me."

"I need you."

"Why?" Lenny's voice was hushed and filled with horror.

"I wouldn't let any of the others talk to me the way you do. If they did, I'd hurt them."

"What do you want from me?"

But Adam's only answer was his laugh. "I think Mark is planning an escape," he said after a while.

"I hope he makes it."

"Continue making breakfast. I'm hungry. Don't you want to know how I figured out that Mark is about to make an escape?"

Lenny didn't answer. She put butter in a frying pan, swirled it around, then poured in the eggs and began scrambling them.

"The way I know is, Mark's mind is becoming too

blank. He's afraid I'll read that he's thinking about escape and is blocking out all thoughts. Pretty clever of me, huh?"

"You're a fool," muttered Lenny.

Adam chuckled. "I know you don't mean that. Are my eggs almost finished? I'm about to go into the bathroom and brush my teeth. I'll be ready to eat in two minutes."

"Cassidy eats first."

"What makes you think that?" Adam seemed concerned. "I don't want you sneaking around, trying to talk to Cassidy. I'll punish you if you do."

"The hell with you!" Lenny pulled the eggs off the fire and emptied them into a deep bowl. She covered it with a lid.

"I want you at the laboratory at ten o'clock."

"Why?"

"Why, why, why, all you do is ask questions. I'm really getting tired of you."

"Then kill me." This time Lenny sounded as if she meant it. Adam started to laugh. Lenny stood in the middle of the kitchen, covering her ears, but still the sound of Adam's laughter rang in her head. "Leave me alone," she cried out. "For God's sake, leave me alone!"

But all she could hear was the laughter.

Cassidy shuffled from the centrifuge to the lab bench. His shuffling and downcast gaze amazed Adam. Cassidy had only been what Adam supposed could be called a prisoner for a little over two months, yet all the marks of the prisoner were there, as if a man's spirit broke long before his body.

Cassidy set the centrifuge, then placed the cultured

cells into their holders and started them whirling. Adam turned away and ran his thin, baby fingernails along the grain of the wooden drawers. So much of lab work was boring and repetitive. He couldn't imagine what Cassidy loved about it. But Adam could read the enjoyment in Cassidy's face. Even as things were, he knew that Cassidy was enjoying doing the experiment again.

"How long will it take before the cell is ready for implantation?" Adam asked, stifling a yawn.

"That depends on how many more times you want to strengthen the cell by culturing."

Adam raised his eyebrows. "You don't approve, Cassidy?"

Cassidy shrugged and turned back to the centrifuge. "At any rate, we should start hormones on Molly today."

Adam walked over to the log that recorded his own birth and flipped through the pages. "You have terrible penmanship," he said.

"Adam, did you hear me? What I'm saying is important. We have to start the hormones today if we want everything to work."

"No hormones."

Cassidy stood totally still. The whirring of the centrifuge seemed to become louder and louder, until it filled his head.

"You'll kill it," Cassidy said after a pause. Adam laughed and Cassidy turned to him, angry. "What's so funny?"

"You are." Adam's face was amused.

Cassidy heard the centrifuge shut off and the samples slowing down, but the whirring remained in his head. He recognized it as an idea, a feeling that he couldn't really understand, let alone put into words. But there was the sense that should he be able to get hold of the idea, it would blast him into a million pieces.

"The centrifuge has stopped," said Adam, looking up from the logs.

Cassidy hesitated. If he pushed forward now, he could probably grasp the idea. It seemed to be his last chance, not only at the idea but almost at humanity. It was right in front of him, and if he reached out now, he could take hold of it and know everything. Cassidy collapsed into himself, moving so close he could feel the idea brushing his fingertips. But just as he drew up to it, he stopped, suddenly recoiling as if the light of a great explosion had driven him back.

Cassidy shut his mind, but the idea remained. Everything was a game. He turned back to the centrifuge and removed the test tubes, shaking them, holding them to the light. A game.

Mark was allowed to go to the bathroom three times a day, at six o'clock in the morning, at noon, then again at five in the afternoon. His body was telling him that it was almost five o'clock. It was strange how quickly the body adjusted to routine, even a hated one.

At five o'clock Mark often caught a glimpse of Cassidy. He suspected he was on his way to the kitchen for dinner, though he knew no one's schedule but his own. Mark closed down his mind. He didn't want to think about seeing Cassidy tonight. But if he did, he knew what he would do.

Mark saw the lock on his door turn. There was a

quiet knock but still the door didn't open. Adam's politeness no longer amused Mark. He was beginning to feel it was all part of the game, whatever that might be.

Mark walked to the door and opened it. Adam was standing there and behind him was the shadow of Molly, like some hirsute bodyguard. Mark wished to God that humor had been a possibility. There was so much to laugh at. Perhaps one day he'd be able to laugh, indeed, to guffaw, giggle, titter, chuckle, piss in his pants about it. He saw an ironical expression cross Adam's face and quickly shut himself down again.

Mark followed Adam into the hallway and started toward the bathroom. He pushed his mind away from danger and into the safety of baseball, then began to laugh as he remembered it was the same device he'd used to hold back orgasm. His laugh surprised him. He had been wrong before. Of course he could still laugh, just like he could still go to the bathroom and eat and sleep. What was so puzzling was not the horror but the normalcy. You just didn't think of peeing in the face of tragedy. And yet it was exactly like that. Mark quickly closed his mind to this thought, then allowed it to open. By this time Adam was used to his mental carping.

Beyond the huge silhouette of Molly and the small figure of Adam, he saw someone else enter the hallway. Mark tried to stop his heart from pounding. It was Cassidy.

The '76 World Series had been one of the dullest Mark could remember. The Reds had won it in four. It seemed like a good place to start. Cassidy was moving slowly toward him. He tried not to measure the distance between them in his mind, but he couldn't help calculating that if they both continued at the same pace, Mark would reach the bathroom before he and Cassidy passed one another.

Mark slowed, scratching his leg, imagining an itch that soon became real. He glanced up. Cassidy seemed to be quickening his pace.

"What's the matter?" asked Adam, glancing back at Mark.

"Mosquito bite." Mark finished tearing at his leg with his nails and started to walk again. He kept his eyes to the ground, glancing up occasionally to keep Cassidy in his line of sight. He wanted to see Cassidy's eyes; if he could just see his eyes, then he'd know.

Old Johnny Bench was up to bat. It was the fourth game of the World Series, and a nice cool breeze drifted through Yankee Stadium. Two men were on base. Or was it three? Perez and Driessen had walked. Mark couldn't remember if there was anyone else.

Cassidy was only a few feet ahead, his eyes riveted to the ground. Mark imagined Bench, Mr. Clean-Cut, all-American boy, about to enter into the marriage of the year, only to quickly become party to the divorce of the year. He wondered if Johnny and his wife had ever sworn at one another, or if they'd just said "Golly gee" and "My my." He wondered what they were like when they fucked. Still, Bench was one hell of a hitter. He imagined the snarling New York crowd up on their feet, cursing the hell out of the all-American.

Cassidy was close. Mark felt himself wavering. But then there was the crack of the bat and the ball burst into the air, Going, going, gone!

Suddenly Cassidy was there. Mark glanced up, holding Cassidy's eyes for barely a second. His lips mouthed only one word, *escape*. Cassidy's eyes widened momentarily, then he looked away. There had been so little time, but eye contact had been made, and in that quick glance Mark had received his answer. It was yes.

That night, the pictures started for Mark. It was not as a result of conscious trying, though Mark suspected that somewhere inside himself he had been trying. Nor was it merely the result of the silence, though he suspected the silence had a part in it. It came at a moment of total relaxation, the first he'd had in months. He supposed the relaxation had been due to what he'd read in Cassidy's eyes.

It had been close to midnight, and sleep was just beginning to overtake him. In fact, at first that was all he thought was happening. The pictures were scattered and seemingly random. If it hadn't been for the weakness of them, Mark would have assumed it was only Adam. Actually that was what he suspected at first.

The flashes gained strength; there was Cassidy's room, Lenny smiling, the pulsing tiny point of mother-of-pearl matter that had started everything. With a jolt, he realized that was something Adam couldn't really know yet. Then he saw his own face; there was a clarity in the picture of himself that only another person separate from him could have. Nor could it be Adam's view of him. Adam's view of Mark was less biased, both pro and con; it was a clinical view. Not long after that, Mark recognized the mind pictures as Cassidy's. Mark hadn't waited to try to send his message back to Cassidy. Pictures had tumbled out of his mind in quick, sharp confusion. But he felt his failure almost immediately. And when he'd tried to relax again and receive from Cassidy, there had been nothing.

It had been agony for Mark to conceal his excitement the whole day. The thought that he was no longer alone was so throbbingly joyous it was painful, and his body cried out for release.

Mark fell back on his bed, though he hadn't even had dinner yet. He closed his eyes and tried to relax every muscle in his body. It was useless to expect Cassidy before night, and yet he emptied his mind, waiting.

Fifteen minutes later, it happened once again; he saw his own face, then Cassidy's room and, quickly following, the night sky. Was Cassidy trying to tell him to wait until Adam was asleep before they chanced reaching out to one another? Mark didn't want to think about what those pictures meant. It would be so easy for Adam to intercept them. Or was that all it was? Was it after all Adam himself who was sending the messages?

Mark sat up, feeling danger nearby. Almost immediately, there was a knock at his door. He listened to his lock being turned, his heart pounding, waiting for Adam to walk in and tell him he'd heard everything. There was a long delay and finally Adam opened the door. Mark could see the dark shadow of Molly behind Adam as he walked into the room and looked around. Mark stayed on the bed, his heart jumping crazily in his chest.

"Why didn't you open the door?" asked Adam impatiently.

"I was dozing."

Adam raised his eyebrows ironically, but Mark felt quite clearly the confusion in Adam's question. If he had heard anything, he hadn't understood it, or at least he wasn't sure he'd understood.

"It's time for dinner." Adam waited for Mark to climb off the bed and follow him down the long corridor to his solitary, cold meal. Mark could tell he was low man on the totem pole by the temperature of his food.

Mark went to the closet and found his slippers. Adam shook his head. "From now on no slippers." Mark nodded and reached for his robe. "No robe either. From now on, no clothes at all."

Again Mark nodded, but he glanced over at Adam, terrified. Adam's face was suspicious, but only mildly so. It had been Adam's expression for some time now. Mark could see nothing out of the ordinary. And yet the dictum of no clothes could mean nothing else. Unless Adam had only just thought of it.

"Don't you blame me for being suspicious?" Adam answered Mark's unspoken thought.

Mark glanced once more at Adam, but saw nothing he hadn't seen yesterday and the day before. He took hold of his mind and emptied it. He would try to figure it all out later, when Adam was finally asleep.

Mark closed the door behind himself and followed Adam and Molly down the long, dark corridor toward the smell of garlic and butter. His mouth began to water, and once again he was struck with his own banality. But the thought seemed less poisonous now. Then he realized his sudden lack of anger could be dangerous too. Everything that crossed his mind held

too many clues. Mark shut down his mind completely
as he turned into the kitchen he used to love.

As Adam cuddled into the warm, animal smell of
Molly, he got a flash of how he'd felt several months
back. It was painful to remember. Then everything
had seemed to glitter with newness and wonder. He'd
wanted to cry out at each new experience, dance at
each new taste and sound. Cassidy and Mark had been
two tall trees, there only to love and feed him. Not
long ago, he'd imagined love as something pure and
unselfish. But now he knew better. Adam hated his
life now, the boredom, the loss of what at one time
had felt like unending love. And yet that past was
lost to him forever.

Now there was only Molly. Molly loved Adam pure-
ly, as if he were her own body. It was the only thing
in his life that hadn't diminished or changed. Adam
felt the need for Molly's unquestioning love with a
craving he couldn't understand, and he grasped at
it greedily, like a baby for a bottle. Terror only
came to him when he thought of losing her love. It
had been coming to him more often recently. And
he buried himself deeper into the dark smells of her
body, blocking out the thought.

Molly started to rock Adam back and forth in her
arms, feeling his little body succumb to the rhythmic
motion of her arms. Suddenly she felt Adam's body
tense, and she released him reluctantly, placing him
carefully down on the ground next to her. Adam's
face was disturbed and sad. Molly tried to remember
what she'd done wrong but couldn't. She waited,
watching Adam's face, searching it for signs.

"If Adam has a brother who looks just like him, who will you love?"

Molly watched Adam's hand signals, confused by the complex blending of possibles and probables. Finally she answered, "Molly loves Adam."

"But what if another Adam comes to stay here?"

"Molly loves Adam." She reached her dark warm arms down to Adam but he shook his head. "Does Adam want to look at picture book?" Molly got up and scooted over to her toy box. She lifted the lid and looked inside.

Adam got up and grabbed her arm, pulling at her. "I am talking to you," he signed angrily.

Molly stopped, confused and saddened. "Molly is bad?"

"Molly doesn't listen."

"Molly try." She sat down on the floor, watching Adam carefully, forcing her dimly lit mind to understand what was expected of her.

Almost immediately Adam's anger disintegrated and turned inward. While his reaction was the kind he would have expected from Mark or Cassidy, it was not one he expected of himself. He hated the fact that he could be vulnerable to things like anger, fear, jealousy. Yet time and again he found himself beset with emotions so strong he wanted to run from them.

It was the same with this whole idea he had of wanting a brother. It had been his first thought the moment he began to gain control. But he hadn't realized until recently how closely that connected him to the rest of the universe. As the biologist François Jacob had said, "The dream of a bacterium is to become two bacteria." Everything wants to duplicate, regenerate, perpetuate. After all, what was cancer but a crazed bunch of oversexed cells? And he was no different. The kinship between everything staggered him. It made him wonder if there wasn't something more powerful than even he.

The emotions he felt were also a part of that. As much as Adam considered himself outside the rules, he was still a human being. He was connected by his needs; he was connected by his weaknesses. The idea of feeling sibling rivalry for what would be, in effect, a clone, might be ridiculous, but he had been feeling it. Adam smiled ironically at the thought, looking more like Mark than he ever had before.

Molly caught the smile. "Adam is happy?" she signed.

"Yes," answered Adam. "Does Molly love Adam?"

Molly clapped her leathery hands together in delight. "Molly loves Adam." Molly opened her arms to Adam and sighed deeply as he crawled onto her lap. Never before had she been as happy as she had recently. Yet all around her, shadowy creatures seemed to creep forward under the dark green leaves, showering moisture onto the blackened earth.

Mark lay in bed, breathless, waiting for a signal that might never come or that might so easily be intercepted. Mark didn't even dare to glance at his watch but he guessed it had to be close to eleven o'clock.

Mark knew it was much too risky a time, and if Cassidy tried to contact him at all, it wouldn't be now. But still he waited, fighting off sleep, fighting his thoughts. He felt like a man in suspended animation. And yet the beating of his heart told him he was very much alive.

The flashes started a few minutes later, slow and weak, but there nonetheless. Mark forced himself to relax and allow the pictures to wash over his body. Once again the sequence: his own face, Cassidy's room. It was like call signals on a radio. Then suddenly he saw a thunderstorm. Lightning cracked across the sky, a low rumble of thunder shook the parched desert.

Mark had to hold himself back from crying out. So Cassidy had noticed it, too. This was proof that the images weren't coming from Adam. It also made his theory that weather disrupted Adam's power seem a lot more plausible. He had never stopped trusting Cassidy's brain.

Mark concentrated on sending back an image of a thunderstorm. He wanted Cassidy to know he understood and agreed. They would wait for bad weather, then they would try to escape.

He waited, but in return there was nothing, no images flashing back at Mark, nothing but emptiness. Mark stopped sending, feeling that Cassidy was no longer with him, terrified that Adam had intercepted their messages, or, even worse, that everything had been in Mark's mind and Cassidy had never been there at all.

He waited, staring out into the black room, his whole body tightened into a painful knot. Then, once again, Mark saw his own face and the room he recognized as Cassidy's. It occurred to Mark that Cassidy had been checking to make sure that Adam wasn't silently listening, dreaming up a plot of his own, and once again Mark felt all the delight and wonder that he used to with Cassidy.

Cassidy was sending a picture of the darkened

corridor. Mark knew he meant nighttime and wondered how Cassidy would be able to get the key to his room. But in his head he saw Cassidy opening his door, stopping to listen outside of Adam's room, then waving him on to follow. He opened another door, and Mark saw Lenny's smiling face, just as she had been when they'd all sat around the kitchen table, bickering and teasing one another. Cassidy stopped sending, and Mark realized that Cassidy was asking him whether they should take Lenny. Mark's answer was immediate. Lenny's smiling face lit his brain.

All at once, Mark had an image of a hand reaching out to him. It was Cassidy's hand, trembling, needy, trusting. In his mind Mark took Cassidy's hand in his and held tightly to it. He didn't let go. And when sleep overtook him, Cassidy's trembling hand was still in his.

Chapter 12

A low-pressure system had moved up the coast and stalled ten miles out to sea, dumping rain into one of the few places in that vicinity that never needed it. Muggy air hung over the desert, surrounding it like a veil, making the days even more oppressively hot than usual.

Mark crept along the side of the factory, unused to the freedom of being outside. And though Molly's silent black eyes watched his every move, he still felt freer than he had in a long while. Adam had instituted these exercise periods for Mark around the same time he'd begun the new rule of nudity. More importantly, both had occurred at the moment when he and Cassidy had started to communicate. There could be no question that Adam was aware something was going on, though from his reaction, Mark suspected he didn't know exactly what it was.

As Mark rounded the outhouse, he caught sight of the bumper of his car. He hadn't seen his car in over two months, and he stopped, looking at it as if it were a memento from his childhood. The car was covered with desert dust and there was a large dent in the side. Whoever was driving it to pick up supplies had also knocked off a good chunk of bumper and scratched the hood. Mark was amazed at his annoyance. He walked closer to the car, touching it fondly, as if it were a real person. Quickly he turned and walked away, bombarded with memories of himself.

He walked back to the factory walls, looking for a bit of shade. Finding some, he sat down on the hot ground. The sky was a hazy, low-lying lid. Mark strained to find a hint of a cloud, but could find none.

Several feet off, the door to the factory opened, and Lenny walked out, blinking in the bright sunlight. She stood totally still, like a startled desert animal, shielding her eyes. Mark hadn't thought much about his own nudity, but seeing Lenny so pale and vulnerable, like a frightened animal, he wanted to cry out in anger.

Lenny spotted Mark and broke into a smile. Mark smiled back, but he didn't move toward her, nor did she move to him. The two of them remained in their own territory, unable to imagine taking the few steps necessary to reach one another, not even daring to want to.

Once again the door opened. This time it was Cassidy. He too was naked and came out blinking against the sunlight. His reaction was exactly the same as Lenny's and Mark's. Mark was astounded by the similarity between them.

Mark looked around, wondering where Adam was and, more to the point, what he was up to. Perhaps this was the end. Adam would have known about the low front too, and if he knew that they were waiting for it to shift and move toward the desert, he might want to get rid of them before they had a chance to escape. But he couldn't think about that.

Lenny was watching Cassidy, and even ten yards away, Mark could read the love in her eyes. Memories of Becky came flooding back: a startled laugh, a fluid gesture, her trusting eyes. They were overpowering, sad, unbearably sweet flashes.

Lenny broke from her immobility and walked over to Cassidy. Mark waited for Adam's reaction. He looked back at the factory, expecting the door to open at any moment. He glanced over at Molly, but she too remained where she was. Lenny and Cassidy embraced, touching one another's faces softly as if they were blind.

Again Mark turned back to the factory. There was no sign of life in the old building, no sound or movement from inside, yet Mark could feel Adam's presence and knew that this too was planned, as was everything else in that house.

Mark tried to make some kind of sense out of what was happening, no longer even caring if Adam was listening in. He wondered if Adam were trying to placate them by allowing them this meeting, or if he were trying to give the impression of carelessness to trick them into letting down their own guards. He even considered the possibility that in some way Adam still loved them and was beginning to feel badly about what he was making them do. He doubted that any of the possibilities were true, particularly the last. When Adam merged his mind with Mark, he could feel the bitterness and impassivity, the greed and ruthlessness. He had felt it all and been staggered by the strength and power. No, Adam did not love them.

Mark looked up and saw Lenny and Cassidy smiling at him. He hesitated for only a moment longer, then went running to the two of them. He threw his arms around Lenny and Cassidy, breathing in their humanity, touching his forehead to theirs.

Far off on the horizon, Mark caught sight of a thin silver line, cutting the distant sky like a thread. He froze, hoping for a barely perceptible rumble to follow, a small sound that would announce that the rain was over the mountains, and that it might be moving toward them. It came. Mark's eyes caught Cassidy's for just one moment, then Adam appeared at the door of the factory.

"Mark, I think we should give Cassidy and Lenny some time alone, don't you?" The little boy leered, then announced, "We'll all have dinner together tonight." He turned back into the factory. "Coming, Mark?"

Mark walked back to the factory, leaving Cassidy and Lenny. He tried to empty his mind of everything, but a rumble of distant thunder reverberated in his soul.

Wilt Cason was wrestling with his soul as well as his desk drawer, which had swelled with the heat. With the aid of a screwdriver, he managed to conquer the drawer. He had less success with his soul.

He pulled a pad and pencil out of the drawer and began writing down the facts, starting at the very beginning. The girl, Becky, had disappeared. According to Anderson, Sy felt she'd been seeing one of the boys at the factory. Sy next told Anderson that a little boy was making them do things; he connected it with the factory. Up until this point, it was clear that

Anderson felt Sy was going nuts. But next came the deaths at the diner. Anderson's reaction had gone beyond horror. Cason suspected Anderson felt some kind of responsibility for it. The last fact, and this he underlined, was that Anderson went back to the factory with that strange message about a phone book. He never arrived at his destination.

Cason leaned back in his chair and stared at the list. There wasn't a thing on it that could link all these deaths and disappearances with those two deadbeats at the factory. He shoved the list in his drawer and slammed it shut, realizing too late that it had probably jammed again. "I got enough problems of my own," he grunted.

Immediately his mind sped to those problems: one slightly pregnant girl who was threatening exposure; one neat, dapper, but very angry mayor breathing fire about the number of people who had been turning up dead recently. Cason certainly had enough problems as it was without the memory of that bloodied, battered body lying under the coroner's sheet haunting him.

Anderson's eyes had been open, ga-ga with terror. Well, of course he was terrified. Who wouldn't be, seeing two tons of water and glass crashing down on him?

Cason reached for the drawer and tried to open it again. He'd been right; it was jammed. Instinctively his hand went to his badge. It was about the only cold thing he'd touched since he left home that morning. That badge meant a lot to Cason. From the minute he'd pinned it on he'd been a changed man. No more humping in the police car, no more stopping off for a quick beer or catching forty winks parked behind a clump of bushes. Suddenly Cason was the picture of probity. He suspected all the deaths had something to do with his change also.

The strange thing was, with all the hoopla about the diner deaths and then Anderson's accident, no one had even suggested going up to the factory to take a look around. It was almost as if there had been a vow of silence about it, unspoken, but strong and rigid. The whole subject of the factory and the two weirdos who lived there never came up in conversation anymore, although before the town talked of little else. Cason suspected it wasn't because they felt there was no connection between it and the terrible happenings, but because they felt there was.

Cason got up from the desk and went to the basin, drawing a sinkful of cold water and dunking his head into it. He came up, shaking like a dog, and caught sight of himself in the cracked mirror. Anderson had been a big, burly man, a man who was every inch the sheriff. Cason was slim. As a kid, he'd even written away for those Charles Atlas manuals, which he'd kept hidden under his mattress. Anderson had experience, a good fifteen years in police work of some kind, and Cason was young, with a handsome, little boy face that was helpful with the chicks but a definite disadvantage when confronting trouble.

He turned from the mirror. Was that the reason he hadn't gone up to the factory and confronted those hippies? He shook his head violently, scattering water across the room. No. He hadn't gone up there because there was no reason to suspect a connection. But then why hadn't he told anyone about Anderson's last message?

Cason walked back to his desk and slumped in his

chair. Anderson was a man who had filled that ripped old swivel chair amply. Cason could see him sitting in it, his big muddy boots on the desk, mopping that bullet head of his with a handkerchief the size of a bath towel. What would Anderson have done in a situation like this? But he had gotten his answer already, in Anderson's last message to him on the car radio. Cason reached over and picked up the phone, dialing the mayor's office with trembling fingers.

"Sleep well," said Adam as he closed Mark's door. "See you in the morning."

Mark listened as the lock clicked, wondering if the irony he heard in Adam's voice was truly there or if it was only his imagination. The click of the lock seemed to echo in his mind. Cassidy had sent Mark a picture of himself opening the door with a key, but how had he gotten it? Mark was completely dependent on Cassidy, his being able to get the key, unlock the door, and lead them to safety.

Mark walked to his bed and slid under the cool covers. He lay still. Up above there was a faint trace of a rumble. Mark's body stiffened, but he didn't betray himself. He rubbed his legs against the cool sheets, burying his head deep into his pillow. Another rumble, louder, sharper. Even in the air-conditioned room Mark could sense the storm was about to begin.

He waited, not even daring to check his watch. Adam would be extra cautious tonight and any movement could betray them. He wondered as he lay isolated in the blackness what time it was, decided it couldn't be more than midnight, then distrusted his decision. He had no perception of time, just as he had no perception of direction. He would be dependent on

Cassidy for even that. When Cassidy was ready, he'd come, and Mark just had to hope he was right.

A sound outside his door. Mark fought the impulse to sit up. He waited, listening to the silence. But it had been nothing.

Again a sound. Mark lay rigid, trying to stop his mind from betrayng the fear and excitement that ravaged his body. But again there was only silence. Then quickly following, he saw his own face, and he knew Cassidy was nearby. Emptiness followed, but this time Mark understood that Cassidy was just pausing to make sure Adam wasn't listening.

A crash of thunder and once more the picture of Cassidy, then Mark, shading his eyes against a sun he had until recently taken for granted. All at once he heard the lock click free and his door quietly opening. Dim light filled the room for only a second, then there was darkness again. Mark lay staring out into the blackness, feeling the presence of Cassidy in his room, the heat of his body reaching out across the room and touching him. Mark slid out of bed quietly and walked toward the heat of Cassidy. Their hands met in a clasp, then Cassidy handed him a soft bundle. Mark recognized it as clothes.

Cassidy waited as Mark dressed quickly, then opened the door and the two of them slipped out. No longer in darkness, Cassidy's body stood out against the gray light like a black, hunched shadow. He stopped at Adam's door, leaning toward it, listening, then they continued to Lenny's door. Cassidy slipped a key into the lock and opened the door.

Lenny came out quickly and Mark could feel her fear through the darkness as she dressed, then stood in the hallway next to the two men.

They paused, unable to move forward and break the spell. If Adam were going to stop them, now would be the time. Once they'd made it back past his door, the chances of escape went way up. Still, they didn't move. The possibility of failure immobilized them. It almost seemed better to be suspended there, captive but still with hope, than to learn the truth.

Finally Cassidy turned and led the way to Adam's door. He stopped, leaning to the door. A tremor passed through his body. He had heard something.

Mark strained to listen and thought he could hear a soft rustle come from inside the room. But he could no longer tell what he was hearing and what he was imagining.

There was another rustling sound. Lenny leaned back, her eyes glittering with terror. It was only a hint of a gesture, but Mark read it immediately. He reached out and touched Lenny's arm, keeping her close beside him. If any of them panicked, there would be no chance of calming down again. Lenny tried for a smile, brave, controlled, and Mark realized that panic wasn't a possibility for Lenny. The only one of them that could panic would be he. On the other hand, he'd had several major opportunities for panic and hadn't succumbed once. In fact, he'd been reasonably strong and controlled. But given any chance to run himself down, he'd jump, just as always. He vowed that once on the outside, he'd hightail it to the nearest shrink and sign up for a ten-year course of daily sessions. He was beginning to feel well enough to consider the possibility that he could use help.

Cassidy leaned to the door for a while longer, then nodded back to them. Mark felt himself release breath he didn't even know he was holding. Obviously the rustling had just been Adam stirring in his sleep.

They started down the corridor again. A creaking noise was coming from Molly's cage room as she swung back and forth on her bar, trying to make the long night pass. It was a stroke of luck that Molly was awake. The noise she was making would probably help block out any sounds they made. For the first time, Mark allowed himself to feel a little optimism. Things seemed to be going in their favor in a way that made him wonder if a force for good wasn't intervening.

As they reached the steel door, Cassidy pulled a key out of his pocket and unlocked it, then slowly, carefully, he opened the door, pausing every inch. It took close to two minutes before he'd opened it enough for the three of them to pass through. Mark was astounded by Cassidy's patience as he worked at the door.

Watching the frizzy-haired, stoop-shouldered Cassidy working with such concentration, all the insanity of the past disappeared, and he appeared before Mark as the young, eager man he had known since college.

Cassidy held the door open until Mark and Lenny had passed through, then with the same patience as before, he slowly closed it. Lenny and Mark started up the stairs but paused midway, waiting for Cassidy, as if even a few feet between them were painful. When Cassidy finally finished, he looked up and saw them waiting. He smiled, his face full of life and hope. Lenny reluctantly turned from it and continued up the steps, Mark just behind her, and Cassidy at the rear.

Lenny stopped at the top of the stairs. Ahead was the factory. Shadowy, black, a large expanse of creaking boards they would have to cross before they reached the front door. They would have to pass directly over Adam's bedroom, and every step would give them away.

The three of them held tightly to the landing, looking across the black hole of the factory. Suddenly a flash of lightning lit up the darkness in electric stripes of light. It was quickly followed by a rumble of thunder that built until Mark could feel it running through his body, majestic and stately, yet primitively frightening.

"If we time it right, the storm'll cover any noise." Cassidy's face was ablaze with the electric light, but his voice was weak and tremulous. As darkness once again closed around them, Mark was struck by how much they had changed from the two men who had walked into that factory the first time and wrestled joyfully on the bedroom floor.

A flash of lightning cut the blackness and Cassidy started across the floor, walking slowly, breaking each step into several cautious movements. Thunder reverberated, everything seeming to shake from its power. Then, suddenly, silence and darkness. Cassidy stopped, his head tilted, as if listening to noises so subtle that only he could hear them.

They waited, veiled in quiet, looking at one another from out of the shadowy darkness. There was a rumble of thunder, distant and weak, but it ended almost as soon as it started. And once again there was silence. Mark felt like he was going to vomit. Caught in the middle of the factory, blackness all around him, Mark was a man hanging from a lifeline that could break at any moment. The storm was ending. Mark felt all the power ebb from him.

Then the rain began. Cool, damp air rushed through the gaps in the boards, and they could smell

the water and freshness in it. The wind brushed
against their faces, making them feel closer to freedom
than they had in months. It was hard for Mark to hold
himself back from running to the door, throwing it
open, and rushing into the cooling rain. But the three
of them started cautiously forward, pausing every few
feet, and when they got to the door, Cassidy opened it
carefully, taking even longer than he had with the
steel door.

As the door opened, rain sprayed in with the gusting
wind and there was the smell of damp earth and desert
flowers. Mark passed through; rain slapped his face,
reviving him. The damp air tugged at his body,
rustling his hair, and Mark moved into the dark night,
opening his mouth to the rain, allowing it to run,
cool and clean, into his throat.

"Oh God," whispered Lenny. "We're going to make
it, aren't we?"

She was standing next to Mark and he could hear
the tears in her voice; he could feel her body shaking.
He wanted to take her in his arms and hold her. He
wanted to feel the joy in her tears and taste their
salt. He looked over at Cassidy, but he seemed stoical,
staring out into the turbulent night with preoccupied,
pensive eyes.

Cassidy motioned for Lenny to be quiet. "It's still
possible that Adam's just playing with us," he whispered.

A shock of fear went through Mark. "He wouldn't
let us get so near the car if it was just a game."

Cassidy took in breath, then whispered, "There's no
coil wire." He looked away quickly. Mark saw it all.
Adam probably never left the car without the coil

wire in his hot little hand. "I tried but couldn't get it," Cassidy added.

Lenny's joy had evaporated and in its place was an iron control just barely concealing the terror. "So what do we do?" she asked.

"God gave us feet," answered Cassidy. "Good time to test them out."

"Never thought I'd hear God out of your mouth." Lenny smiled, thinking how only hours before, when she and Cassidy made love after so many months, she feared it would be the last time they'd be together.

Cassidy didn't see Lenny's smile. His mind was, as always, on the future. He put his arm on Mark's shoulder. "You go first, then Lenny, then me."

Mark nodded. "Good luck," he said as he turned to the dirt path and started to run.

He thought he heard Cassidy answer, "Luck has nothing to do with it." But then all sounds were drowned out by his own breath ringing in his ears.

There were three cars at the fork where the road from the old factory met the highway. Ten men sat hunched in the cars, lights out, eyes riveted to the windows. Cason moved from car to car, soaked with rain despite the official oilskin cloak and hat that covered him. His feet were squishing in his shoes, sending great gushes of water over the sides with every step he took.

Had anyone asked Cason what he hoped to find out there, he wouldn't have had an answer. But the strange part was, no one had asked. Not even the bantam-cock Mayor Richards, who questioned everything, including the amount of paper clips used when a stapler had just recently been purchased. Once again Cason was struck with the feeling that they all knew something was going on. It was the same kind of feeling he got when some turkey walked into a room and he knew right off he'd be trouble. There'd be something in the air, some kind of electricity that told you things. He guessed most people had it. The problem was they didn't want to use it until it was too late.

It had been Cason's idea to set out tonight, reasoning that whatever was going on up at the factory would more likely be exposed and open. Even if those men hadn't relaxed and become less cautious with the two-month delay in action, they'd hardly expect anything tonight. Cason still guessed he was right, though standing, dripping like a sewer rat, trying to keep a motley crew of ten men in some semblance of order, he questioned his decision with every watery step.

Cason moved up to the front car where his deputy, Murray, a thin pimply boy fresh out of puberty, sat with Mayor Richards. Cason hung in the window, splattering the mayor's raincoat with drops of rain. "I think we should fan out and surround the place."

Richards didn't answer. He was staring out of the rain-streaked windshield, frozen like a scared rabbit. Finally he pointed a manicured finger toward the factory. "Look!" His voice trembled.

Cason squinted through the rain. He saw nothing.

"A shadow," whispered Richards. "I think I saw a shadow out there!"

Cason glanced at Murray, but he too was riveted to the dark night. "Probably just a rabbit," he answered calmly.

"The size of a man?"

Cason shielded his eyes against the rain, watching the hunched, black outline of the factory for close to a minute. All he saw was wasteland interrupted only occasionally by some scrub or a Joshua tree. Still, he didn't blame Richards for getting the spooks. He was getting them himself. It was eerier than hell out there.

Cason turned back to the car. "Don't see nothing. But I guess we better find out."

"No!" Richards's voice was urgent.

"That's what we're here for, ain't it?"

Richards didn't answer, and when Cason followed his eyes, he felt a dark shadow of terror cross over him. Though he saw nothing living out there, he too felt the presence of something or someone.

Cason climbed back into the driver's seat, locking the door. "We'll wait here until the rain breaks, then we'll close in," he said sheepishly.

But Richards didn't notice his tone of voice; he was looking out at the dark deserted factory and feeling a chill of unknown danger.

Mark saw the outline of the cars from way off. He stopped, waiting for Cassidy and Lenny to catch up, then pointed. "Looks like help is closer than we thought."

"What makes you think it's help?" answered Cassidy darkly.

"Well, it's hardly a Sioux raiding party. It's probably just some of the townies. Maybe we've been furnishing a lover's lane for the town without even knowing it. Just think, all those little bare asses humping away only yards from our door." Mark felt exuberant.

Cassidy looked disturbed. "There are a lot of cars. I always wondered why they never came up after Anderson died."

"You think that's why they're here?"

Cassidy wasn't listening and it took a moment for him to play back the question. "Yeah. You bet. Probably tanked up and ugly as hell, too."

"Cassidy, it's a perfect opportunity," Mark's voice was getting desperate and he looked away so that no one would notice the anxiety in his eyes. "We were planning on going into town anyway."

"It's one thing going into town, another thing being brought there by them."

"You honestly think they'd hurt us?"

"It hardly seems worth trying it out. I say we cut across and head to town on our own steam."

Mark nodded, though he wasn't convinced. So far Cassidy's hunches had paid off. It didn't make much sense to start questioning them now. Still, the feeling that Cassidy's paranoia could ruin everything disturbed Mark's recent hopefulness. And when he turned and headed across the hard desert floor, the cool rain and howling wind seemed sinister.

Richards leaned forward over the seat and pointed his finger into the black night. "Over there! Goddamn you. Over there!"

This time Cason thought he saw something. He started up the car. Headlights flashed on, illuminating the darkness. For a brief moment, caught in brilliant white lights, there seemed to be the shadow of a man. The other two cars must have seen it too, because lights went on all over the place, and the roar of starting engines filled Cason's ears.

But the shadow disappeared almost at once, and Cason wondered if it had ever been there at all.

"It's gone!" Richards's voice was panicky.

Cason pulled his revolver, staring out at the dark highway, unsure whether to go into the factory or follow the shadow. Richards and Murray were breathing short and scared. They were no help. Finally he rolled down the window and called back to the other cars, "Follow me."

Cason threw his car into gear and screeched onto the highway. One of his hands was on the steering wheel, the other clutching to the handle of his gun like a claw, as his eyes scanned the darkness.

The other cars pulled out behind him. Headlights swooped along the blackness, illuminating Joshua trees and boulders. The cars moved forward slowly through the night, while inside each man held tightly to his gun, looking for his own special terror.

Mark was pressed to a clump of dried brush. The headlights had cut into his heart. The voices, scared and high-pitched, the thundering engines of the cars, and the brutal lights slicing the night immobilized him, and he knew Cassidy had been right.

Mark didn't move until the lights and the noise had begun to recede into the night. Then he turned back and scanned the landscape for Cassidy and Lenny. He saw nothing. Even though he reasoned that they too had hidden themselves, the fear of being alone began to take him over. A picture of Adam flashed through his mind. He was laughing.

He wanted to cry out; he could neither go forward nor backward, yet staying where he was was an impossibility. He felt devastatingly alone, cut off in an island of blackness. He looked out at the terrible lights disappearing down the highway; their shining in the darkness was like rising smoke.

He started forward, keeping close to the ground. Almost immediately he stopped, looking back for Cassidy and Lenny. But they were nowhere in sight. Once again he moved through the storm, shivering like a hunted rabbit.

Suddenly the car lights swung around, flashing across the gloom. Mark hit the ground, pressing himself tightly to it. All at once, the sound of bullets cut through the night, echoing all around him. At first he thought Cassidy and Lenny had been spotted, but he looked all around him and saw nothing.

The lights sped past, plunging him once again into darkness. The men had been firing blindly.

He remained where he was, hugging the ground for a long time, then slowly got up. Behind him in the darkness he saw the shadows of two people.

"Don't stop! Keep going!" It was Cassidy's voice resounding through the rain-soaked night.

Mark started to run, splashing through the pools of water. The ground was thick, oozing mud, and he slid several times, catching himself, then continuing on.

The sky was a heavy dome over his head, the rain closed him off. Every once in a while a huge jagged bolt of lightning lit the sky, and the flat desert with its Joshua trees stood out eerie, blue-black, and endless.

Again the face of Adam flashed into his mind, but he couldn't tell if it was really Adam or his fear pulling at him. Mark slipped under the barbed wire fence, breath resounding in his ears, then glanced back. Cassidy and Lenny were nowhere in sight.

He stopped. For a moment it occurred to him that everything that had been happening was in his mind. But he knew it was real. Everything was much too crazy to be anything else.

Mark called out, "Cassidy! Lenny!" But his voice was eaten up by the wind and rain.

Lightning stripped the sky; the landscape stood out for a second, gnarled and rocky, then was plunged into darkness. Mark called out again, hearing the sound come back at him, deadened, damp and flat, fading almost immediately into the pounding rain.

The feeling of another presence returned. Mark looked inward, trying to tell if it was Cassidy or Adam. The presence just sat there, quietly listening, betraying nothing about itself. And Mark knew that it could be no one but Adam.

He froze, standing in the black hole of the desert with the knowledge that Adam was nearby and he was only seconds from death. He screamed. Suddenly a hand grabbed him. Mark tried to pull away; he was crying out blindly. But the hand held him tightly in its grip.

"Mark! For God's sake, it's me. Cassidy!"

Mark could hear nothing but his own fear howling through his head, and he struggled even harder against the hand that held him.

"Stop, Mark! Stop!" Cassidy dug his nails deep into Mark's arm. His voice pierced through the panic and reached the man.

"Cassidy. Thank God it's you." Mark put his arms around Cassidy and held him close. The fear of being

alone had been greater than any fear he'd ever felt,
even death, and he clung tightly to Cassidy with needy,
desperate arms.

Cassidy tensed and slipped from Mark's arms. "We
better get moving."

For the first time, Mark noticed Cassidy was alone.
"Where's Lenny?"

"She twisted her ankle. We have to leave her."

Mark looked around at the black emptiness, shocked.
"We can't leave Lenny. We'll carry her. I'll carry
her."

Cassidy shook his head. "Too dangerous. Don't
worry. I hid her away where no one will find her.
Tomorrow, when we get all this straightened out,
we'll come back for her. It's better this way."

The rain had slowed down, but still the wind beat
at the black, shadowy landscape. "And what if Adam
finds her first?"

Cassidy laughed. "Adam won't find her."

Mark was chilled by Cassidy's laugh. "Of course
he will. I felt him just a moment ago. And now the
rain is stopping . . ."

Cassidy laughed again. "Adam is a little boy. Sure
he's got incredible powers, but he's still only a
child. Don't you see, it was us who made it work?
Without us, he's nothing."

And suddenly Mark saw what he had forgotten for
months. Adam was a little boy; he barely reached
Mark's waist.

"Adam is just a little boy!" Mark said feeling
laughter building inside himself. "Oh Jesus, Cassidy, Adam's a fucking kid. He still wets his goddamn bed." Mark's laughter mixed with tears and
echoed through his whole body.

Cassidy touched Mark's arm and turned him around. "Come on, let's get some help. Town's this way."

Mark paused, confused in the darkness, then followed the hunched shadow of Cassidy as he moved through the moonless night. The wind was still strong, spraying them with chilling rain. He tried to see the highway but couldn't. Mark had never experienced such darkness. He turned back, looking for the terrifying headlights, but all was blackness.

Cassidy saw Mark's hesitation and caught up to him. "It's okay. They gave up and went back to town."

"Who?"

"Those clowns who were shooting at us."

"Are you sure?" Mark wondered how Cassidy could hope to predict what those men had done, then remembered how right he'd been before. He tried to calm himself down. Lenny's absence was leaving an emptiness inside of him that was feeding his fear.

Finally Mark said, "I'm sorry about before. If you'd listened to me, we'd probably be dead in some ditch and Adam would be cooing innocently at some police station, charming everyone until he was adopted by some nice unsuspecting family." Mark shivered.

"Yeah, I can just see him crying out for Mommy."

"With a lisp," Mark added. "He wouldn't forget some nice touch like a lisp. He'd open his little arms wide and say 'I love you.' "

Cassidy stopped and said sadly, "I think he did love us."

Mark quickly touched Cassidy's arm. "It doesn't matter anymore. Come on."

Cassidy began walking again, his shoulders even more hunched than before, his head bent toward the ground.

"Do you think they'll kill him?" Cassidy's voice was pleading.

"No. They won't do that. But he'll be watched. He has to be watched. You can see that now, can't you?"

Cassidy nodded and whispered, "Yes. He has to be watched."

They continued in silence. Mark glanced at Cassidy but could see that his mind was back at the factory with Adam. "How much farther to town?" he asked.

"Not far." Cassidy's voice was faraway.

"We're doing the right thing," Mark said.

"And us? What do you think they'll do to us?" He turned to Mark, his eyes sparkling with terror. "I killed Schaftner."

Mark started to tremble. And yet, once again, he felt he was hearing something that he already knew.

"Don't you have anything to say about that?" Cassidy's voice was sharp.

Mark sighed. "No one will ever have to know."

Cassidy looked at Mark, relieved and hopeful. "You really think everything's going to be okay?"

Mark nodded. He too felt relieved. "You know, there was a time when I was worried that you were totally under Adam's control."

Cassidy interrupted. "He never had total control over me." He looked at Mark, needing his agreement.

Mark nodded. "Now I know that. But then you were working with him in the laboratory all the time." Mark paused, then decided not to continue. "You don't think when we were talking back there we turned the wrong way?"

Cassidy laughed. "You've got a lousy sense of direction."

Mark continued walking. He hated the fact that

he had a bad sense of direction. It made him feel like a blind man.

The rain stopped, and the silver disk of the moon appeared fleetingly between the clouds, casting light across the desert, making it glitter like a field of diamonds. Mark looked around, able to see for the first time. Up ahead he saw nothing but desert.

"We should be able to see the lights of town by now."

"Relax. There's a slope just before it. Remember?"

Mark shrugged. He'd never paid much attention. Then slowly, like a dark shadow, the presence fell over him. It sat deep inside him, listening and laughing, and with the presence came a question. "What were you and Adam doing in the laboratory?" Mark's voice sounded strange and choked off.

"We were continuing the experiment."

Mark trembled. "How far did you go?"

"Blastula stage."

"In other words, ready for implantation."

Cassidy smiled. "So I did teach you something."

Mark stopped, dread spreading through his body. "And did you implant?"

"Two weeks ago. The urine test was positive. But you know that doesn't mean anything." Cassidy's voice was flat and scientific but he was smiling.

Mark's whole body crumpled. Suddenly he saw it all. He grabbed Cassidy's arm and pulled him around. "Your eyes," he breathed. "Oh God, look at your eyes. He's here, isn't he?"

"He's everywhere."

Mark clutched tightly to Cassidy's arm, hoping there was some possibility of reaching him. "Not without you, he isn't."

"He's God."

"Those cars."

"The sheriff and a few men. They're gone."

"But they'll be back."

"Not before Adam and I have left."

Mark sighed deeply, all hope escaping with his breath. "The town's the other way, isn't it?"

"We circled around. The fork's just over there." He pointed several hundred yards ahead.

"But why all the trouble of escape? You didn't need to test whether I'd do it. You knew I would."

But inside Mark's head, Adam was laughing gaily, clapping his hands together in amusement and Mark knew the answer. Everything was a game.

"Oh God!" Mark broke down. Tears came from deep inside him, and he could feel sickness move toward his throat.

Cassidy reached into his pocket. "I brought two knives." He clicked the button, opening one of the switchblades with a whooshing sound. "They're both the same." He held the open knife out to Mark.

Suddenly everything seemed unreal, a dream. Mark shook his head. His voice was lifeless and detached. "There's no use fighting. He wouldn't let you die. He needs you."

Cassidy smiled. "True. But even if there's a little chance, one in a thousand, you'll take it. I would."

Mark remembered Cassidy standing at the door of Sol's mansion, telling Mark he'd do the experiment, even if his chance of success was only one in a thousand. "What a terrible waste," he shuddered.

Cassidy smiled coldly. "Don't brag."

"I wasn't talking about me. No, the world will waffle on without me. I was talking about you.

You could have been the greatest scientist that ever lived."

"I am."

"No. Cassidy. You lost all chance at greatness when you started pursuing it."

"I would have lost it if I hadn't, too." Cassidy looked off into the distance, and he also seemed to be living a dream.

"Probably," answered Mark. He no longer knew the answer. He no longer even cared.

Cassidy nudged the knife into Mark's hand. Mark felt himself take it, but other than that, all feeling was gone. He watched impassively as Cassidy clicked open his knife.

"Now, run!" There was amusement in Cassidy's voice.

Mark was looking at Cassidy, but it was Adam he was speaking to. "You'd enjoy seeing me run, wouldn't you? The hare and the hound. Then when you get bored with your game, you trip me and send me sprawling to the ground."

"I said run. It's your only chance."

Mark didn't move. He was tempted to laugh. His life had been a mockery and now so was his death. It was an irrelevant thought, but it seemed to burn more brightly than the fear or even the indifference. He saw Becky's face. Mark dropped his hands to his side, allowing the knife to slip from his fingers. "No. I won't do it. The only thing I've got left is not letting you enjoy my death."

Cassidy smiled knowingly. "You'll fight. In the end, you'll fight with everything in you." He paused, and when he continued, his voice was more human. "For all your whimpering and moaning, you were always a fighter. That's what I loved about you."

"Oh God, Cassidy!" Mark's voice was a lament.

But Cassidy had long ago gone beyond that. "The knife's right by your feet. Pick it up."

Mark was motionless; he didn't even bother to shake his head. Cassidy nodded, then slowly started walking toward Mark, the knife held out in front of him.

Mark watched him, his body tensed, crying out to fight but holding tightly to the ground, a statue in the quickly shifting night.

Cassidy continued forward. The knife blade caught the silver moon and reflected it. Mark saw the irony of Cassidy walking toward him like a gunfighter, just like his name. He laughed, but the laugh was ghastly. He wasn't going to enjoy dying. He hardly knew what it meant to live, but he knew he wasn't going to enjoy dying.

Still, Cassidy closed in. Mark could feel Adam watching. Maybe Cassidy was right. He was no longer in his brain. He was everywhere. Mark saw Cassidy's fingers grip the handle of his knife as he stopped only a foot from him. Then he watched as Cassidy's arm began to move back, gathering energy for the thrust.

Suddenly Mark's whole being rebelled and he was reaching to the ground, feeling for the hardness of the knife, grabbing at the damp ground desperately until his fingers touched the handle. In one swift motion, Mark began to thrust the blade up toward Cassidy's stomach.

Mark screamed. Ice pierced his heart. Waves of brilliant pain spread through his body. His knife was poised in midair, glittering in the moonlight, unused, just inches short of Cassidy's belly. It fell from his hands.

Mark heard laughter resounding through his head. It seemed to come from all around him, jeering, ridiculing, overlooking his existence. As he slipped to the ground, Cassidy's legs rose over him, and they too mocked him.

Again Cassidy struck downward with the knife. But Mark had become severed from himself, and he lay watching, detached and uncaring, as the blade slipped into what he assumed was his heart. There was no more pain, only the sensation of extreme cold and a dimming of light. The laughter was still there, but it too was fading.

Clouds slipped over the moon, and Mark could only see the outline of Cassidy as he plunged the knife into him once more. Mark felt himself floating off into a black, warm pool of nothingness, and almost at once, all light and laughter faded and was no more.

Cassidy wiped off the knife blade on his shirt, slid his hands under Mark's armpits, and began pulling him backward toward their land. It took him close to fifteen minutes to drag the heavy body across the rain-dampened ground and place it under a clump of brush. Every once in a while he'd stop, looking out at the road. But the cars truly were gone. He wondered vaguely what Adam had done with them. Cassidy gathered some tumbleweed and arranged it over Mark. No one would find him there, at least not until they were long gone.

Cassidy stood over Mark for a moment, but any feeling of connection had passed forever, and he quickly turned back to the factory.

Adam was sitting at Gilda playing chess, but his mind wasn't on the game. He was wearing pajamas and slippers; his hair was rumpled and there were pillow marks on his cheek. Down the hall, he could hear Lenny pounding on her door. He wished Cassidy would hurry back. Perhaps he'd be able to calm her. It wasn't good for her to be so upset.

Adam heard the steel door opening, then Cassidy's footsteps as he walked down the corridor. He stopped at Lenny's door, and Adam could hear him telling her that everything would be all right, that Mark had gotten away. This seemed to calm Lenny, and Cassidy retraced his steps back to Adam's room.

Cassidy stood in the doorway, hunched and rain-drenched. He was covered with blood, and clots of mud clung to his boots.

Adam made a face. "Ech!" Then, laughing, he held out his arms and made a flying leap into Cassidy's embrace, allowing himself to be lifted into the air.

"I love you." He clapped his hands together, delighted. "Adam loves Cassidy."

Mark's words about Adam went through Cassidy's head as he heard the childish lisping voice, but he shut them out.

Adam cuddled to Cassidy's chest. "Now it's just you and me," he said happily. "Of course we'll have to do something about Molly."

Cassidy looked at Adam surprised. "Do something?"

"Well, Cassidy, we don't exactly need her anymore."

Cassidy sighed. "All right, I'll call someone to get her in the morning."

"That's hardly a possibility now." Adam smiled ironically, then wriggled around in Cassidy's arm, the signal that he wanted to be put down. Cassidy lowered him to the ground reluctantly. Adam stood watching him with crossed arms, like an irritated dwarf.

"Well?" Adam said impatiently.

Cassidy looked at him in disbelief. "You want me to kill her?"

Adam's voice was businesslike. "We can't chance involving anyone else. It's that damn hand talking, Cassidy. A cute trick, but hardly one we'd like to see performed elsewhere."

A tremor went through Cassidy. "You love Molly."

Adam smiled slyly. "You loved Mark. Ironies, ironies. Mark was right. Life is full of them."

Cassidy shook his head. "I couldn't kill Molly, even if I wanted to. She's too strong. I wouldn't stand a chance against her."

Adam laughed. "I don't expect you to fight her, Cassidy. Just give her a shot of something or other. I'll be there. I'll tell her it's okay. She trusts me perfectly."

Adam walked to the door, and Cassidy noted that he'd grown over an inch in the past few weeks. Then Adam turned back and smiled for Cassidy to follow. It was the mirthless smile of an old man.

Molly shuffled around her cage room, agitated, cut off, tracing the walls in endless rounds. The thunder had frightened her and she'd swung on her bar and rattled at her cage, hoping that Adam would come to comfort her. No one came. Even after the storm had cleared, the feeling of agitation hadn't left. And the flashes of green leaves sparkling with moisture kept her up and moving around her cage.

Something was going on. She heard the banging of

doors, the hushed voices, and Lenny's pounding. At first she'd tried to break through the bars and rush to Adam. But the soft hum of Gilda and Adam's occasional piping voice reassured her. Still, the smell of blood seemed to cling to her nostrils, and she knew something was happening.

Molly heard footsteps and stopped. She recognized the steps as Adam's and rushed to the bars, pressing close to them, listening to every creak, trying to read in them what was happening. The footsteps were moving toward her cage, and she pushed even closer to the bars, waiting, hoping.

As Adam opened the door, Molly let out a happy howl, rattling the bars in anticipation. Adam smiled at her, then fumbled with the lock. Molly waited, too excited even to sign.

Finally Adam got the lock open and rushed to her. She lifted him carefully so that he could bury himself deep into her soft hairy chest.

But a moment later, Molly heard another set of footsteps, and she felt Adam tense in her arms, wanting to be let down. Adam moved from Molly to the door and Molly went deep into her cage, watching resentfully as Cassidy walked in and he and Adam spoke. She turned her head to the wall. The happiness of only a moment before faded, and she slumped to the ground, staring at the wall, hearing the buzz of a language she would never understand.

Suddenly she felt a hand on her shoulder. She whirled around and saw Adam's smiling face looking at her. Adam threw his small arms around her neck and kissed her on her leathery face. He nudged his way onto her lap and they sat together facing the wall.

Adam began to sign. Molly watched his little fingers as they formed, "Adam loves Molly."

She signed back excitedly, "Molly loves Adam."

Once again, Adam began signing. Molly looked at Adam, confused, and Adam repeated his signing. But it wasn't that Molly didn't understand the words, it was that she couldn't believe that she did.

Adam signed the words to her once more, then got up from her lap and pressed himself tightly to the wall. It was then that Molly noticed that Cassidy was walking toward her. There was a needle in his hands.

Molly hesitated, turning back to Adam. Again he signed, "Kill him. Kill Cassidy."

Molly pivoted back to Cassidy. He was walking toward her with a reassuring smile. The needle seemed to gleam at her. The pain and fear of childbirth, the smell of danger from Cassidy came rushing back at her. That's all Cassidy had been for a long time, the gleam of a needle and pain and separation from Adam. She stood to face him.

Cassidy stopped next to Molly, speaking softly, calmly, though he knew Molly couldn't understand.

Suddenly Molly howled, loud and angry, lifting her black arm high into the air. Cassidy fell back, trying to get away, but it was too late. Molly screamed brutally. Her huge hand crashed down on Cassidy's head. There was a terrible crack as Cassidy's skull snapped under her blow, followed by the smell of blood.

Cassidy crumpled to the ground, shock and horror contorting his face. Still half-conscious, he stared up at Molly with the remnants of understanding. But Molly was no longer aware of Cassidy, only of a bleeding creature lying beneath her.

Once again her great arm lifted into the air, poised to crash down. Cassidy's eyes turned to Adam. They shifted quickly from shock to understanding to unspeakable grief. They were the eyes of the betrayed.

Molly's arm remained in midair, poised over Cassidy, but he never turned his gaze from Adam, as if he were experiencing something far worse than death.

Molly shifted and looked at Adam sitting in the corner. He was signing impatiently, "Kill him."

But when Molly turned back to Cassidy, she could see his death: the blood that no longer pounded, the brain that had slowed into random impulses. The look of horror and betrayal was fixed on his face, his head turned toward Adam, as if for all eternity.

Molly's arm dropped to her side and she backed from the sight of Cassidy. Adam was smiling at her. "Good Molly," he signed. "Adam loves Molly. She is good."

"Adam loves Cassidy," Molly signed, repeating what she had seen so many times.

Adam merely smiled, opening his arms to let Molly know he wanted to be lifted up.

Again Molly signed, "Adam loves Cassidy," not knowing why, though in her dimly lit mind, the answer was already there.

Molly brought the little boy into her arms and pressed him to her. But revolving around in her brain was the smell of the damp waxy leaves mixed with blood, and as she pressed the little body tighter to her, feeling his tiny beating heart next to her, he felt foreign. He was not part of herself; herself lay in the damp, warm, earthy smell and the moist green leaves.

Suddenly Molly forgot how to sign, how to open doors, how to do anything she'd been taught, and she was once again roaming the jungle, alive with her instincts.

Adam wriggled in her arms and tried to get down. Molly still held tightly to him, feeling the return of smells that had once been a whole language to her, in many ways more varied and compex than the new one she'd learned and much more true.

"Down. I want to get down!" Adam tried to sign. But Molly was clasping him too tightly in her strong dark arms, and he was buried in her thick black hair.

"Let me go!" Adam screamed, suddenly fearful of the thick-necked animal that held him. "Let go!"

Molly heard his screams, but they too meant nothing to her. All she could smell was danger and evil; all she could feel was a great hollow emptiness, with molten anger burning in its center.

She pulled Adam from her chest and held him out in front of her. Adam kicked his legs and screamed as Molly lifted him parallel with her face and looked deep into his eyes. They were alien eyes, the eyes of the panther.

Instinct took over. There was a cracking under her fingers that grew louder as Adam's frail little body collapsed under her grasp. Adam's scream turned into a howl, then quickly into a hissing of breath. And then there was silence.

Molly looked down at her hands and the broken little body she held in them. The acrid odor of danger receded, and what she held was once again Adam. A great cry of pain and sorrow resounded through the cage as she clutched the tiny, fractured body to her breast. It was Adam, and she'd killed him. She clutched him tightly, revolving around the cage in frenzied horror.

Suddenly she stopped. Her wild eyes closed as a fiery pain shot from her chest into her arm. The pain grew, radiating outward with fiery licks, spreading throughout her body until she was filled with it. She clutched to Adam, trembling, then crumpled forward, still holding Adam tightly to her breast, a black inert shadow, next to the twisted form of Cassidy.

And that's how they were when Cason and twenty men broke through the steel door and entered the factory the next morning.

Lenny tilted her head to the sun, feeling the warmth touch her face lightly. Ahead was a nice grassy spot under the trees, and she walked to it, stretching her swollen body onto the cool ground, smelling the delicious odor as she crushed grass underneath her.

The sun broke through the leaves and reminded her of the sunlight slatting through the boards of the old factory. She shivered at the thought, but it didn't stay with her long. That was the thing about being pregnant. Bad thoughts didn't stay very long. The heaviness and tiredness took care of that.

She picked a blade of grass from the earth and munched on the end, then started to laugh. She really was exactly like a cow with her big rolling belly and her contented, half-formed thoughts. Now she was even eating grass.

Deep inside her, she felt the baby shift, and she smiled. With her luck, poor little what's-its-name would end up with her brains and Cassidy's looks.

Considering the alternative, it was a chance she was delighted to take.

Lenny promised herself that she'd never lie to the baby about Cassidy. She saw him before her as he'd appeared that one last time they were together, his curly black hair standing out like a halo all around him. He had been a man who risked everything for a dream; a man who died, betrayed and alone, his beautiful brain crushed by his own creation. But Cassidy had done what he felt was right, and that was all any of them had in the end.

Somewhere inside her came the question, what about Adam? Lenny shifted sleepily under the warm rays of the sun. She supposed that meant she would have to forgive even Adam. For if absolute good didn't exist, neither did absolute evil.

But it was all too complicated to hold her attention for very long, and soon Lenny had lapsed into sleep, her huge belly like a mound, heaving with breath, while deep inside the tiny weightless astronaut was becoming wedged even tighter in the dark red-blackness.

The child stretched his perfect little arms and legs, uncomfortable in his cramped cradle. Already it was easy to see his blond hair and blue eyes. Even his ironical expression betrayed by a burning power and desire was already coded within him. It was all written there, waiting to be expressed.

The child kicked violently. Though only a faint stirring in Adam's primitive memory explained what the world was, he was anxious to come out into it and fulfill his destiny.

Dell Bestsellers

- ☐ TO LOVE AGAIN by Danielle Steel $2.50 (18631-5)
- ☐ SECOND GENERATION by Howard Fast $2.75 (17892-4)
- ☐ EVERGREEN by Belva Plain $2.75 (13294-0)
- ☐ AMERICAN CAESAR by William Manchester . . . $3.50 (10413-0)
- ☐ THERE SHOULD HAVE BEEN CASTLES
  by Herman Raucher $2.75 (18500-9)
- ☐ THE FAR ARENA by Richard Ben Sapir $2.75 (12671-1)
- ☐ THE SAVIOR by Marvin Werlin and Mark Werlin . $2.75 (17748-0)
- ☐ SUMMER'S END by Danielle Steel $2.50 (18418-5)
- ☐ SHARKY'S MACHINE by William Diehl $2.50 (18292-1)
- ☐ DOWNRIVER by Peter Collier $2.75 (11830-1)
- ☐ CRY FOR THE STRANGERS by John Saul $2.50 (11869-7)
- ☐ BITTER EDEN by Sharon Salvato $2.75 (10771-7)
- ☐ WILD TIMES by Brian Garfield $2.50 (19457-1)
- ☐ 1407 BROADWAY by Joel Gross $2.50 (12819-6)
- ☐ A SPARROW FALLS by Wilbur Smith $2.75 (17707-3)
- ☐ FOR LOVE AND HONOR by Antonia Van-Loon . . $2.50 (12574-X)
- ☐ COLD IS THE SEA by Edward L. Beach $2.50 (11045-9)
- ☐ TROCADERO by Leslie Waller $2.50 (18613-7)
- ☐ THE BURNING LAND by Emma Drummond $2.50 (10274-X)
- ☐ HOUSE OF GOD by Samuel Shem, M.D. $2.50 (13371-8)
- ☐ SMALL TOWN by Sloan Wilson $2.50 (17474-0)

THE SAVIOR

He moved in celestial light and
lived in a nightmare of blood and evil

Marvin Werlin
and
Mark Werlin

Christopher McKenzie had youth, grace, beauty—
and the unearthly power to know the unknowable, to
heal, to command. But for every miracle, for every
saintly act, there was the mounting satanic frenzy,
the dark, unspeakable price—to be paid in blood by
the Savior.

"Telekinetic razzle-dazzle."—*Los Angeles Times*

"A marvelous engrossing story . I loved it."—Mary
Higgins Clark, author of *A Stranger is Watching*

"A winner—suspenseful, terrifying, and very, very
human. Bravo!"—Frank De Felitta, author of *Audrey
Rose*

A DELL BOOK $2.75   (17748-0)

THE SUPERCHILLER THAT GOES BEYOND THE SHOCKING, SHEER TERROR OF *THE BOYS FROM BRAZIL*

THE AXMANN AGENDA

MIKE PETTIT

1944: Lebensborn—a sinister scheme and a dread arm of the SS that stormed across Europe killing, raping, destroying and stealing the children.
NOW: Victory—a small, mysteriously wealthy organization of simple, hard-working Americans—is linked to a sudden rush of deaths.

Behind the grass-roots patriotism of Victory does the evil of Lebensborn live on? Is there a link between Victory and the Odessa fortune—the largest and most lethal economic weapon the world has ever known? *The Axmann Agenda*—it may be unstoppable!

A Dell Book   **$2.50   (10152-2)**

At your local bookstore or use this handy coupon for ordering: